Totally Bound Publishing books by Zoe Normandie

Unbreakable Heroes
Under Control
Under Pressure

I0524364

Unbreakable Heroes

UNDER PRESSURE

ZOE NORMANDIE

UNDER
PRESSURE

Dedication

To my parents for always believing in me,
even though they are forbidden from ever
reading my books.

Chapter One

Matteo 'Delta' Valente ran out of his Californian bungalow a little too damn early in the morning. Hell, he'd only been home for a few hours. After jamming his aching arm through his hunter green utility shirt, he buttoned it, trying to multi-task as he unlocked the dark truck which awaited him in his driveway. He was running behind—again.

For fuck's sake.

Damn, sleeping a couple of hours a night is bound to catch up with me sooner rather than later. He grumbled as he slipped on his dark sunglasses to protect his hurting eyes from the blistering sun. Even in January, the sun was still beating down on him stronger than a direct RPG blast. Or maybe it just seemed that way because he was so damn drained.

"Matteo!" An elderly lady's voice called out quietly from behind him, her Italian accent pouring through.

He whipped around, checking to make sure she was okay. The tiny old Italian lady stood at the edge of her bungalow's stoop, a worried look in her eye. Using his hand to flatten back his chaotic dark blond hair, he regrettably realized another thing. He was way past due for a shave.

"Mrs. Romano." Delta attempted a polite smile at his neighbor, hoping she wouldn't notice the gashes on his knuckles from the previous night.

Mrs. Romano fretted, wringing her yellow dotted handkerchief as she batted her eyelashes up at him. He gritted his teeth under her gaze, willfully rejecting any concern she had—or judgment.

"Lovely morning, Matteo." Her voice fluttered, darting her eyes down her empty driveway to the street.

Every other neighbor on the street had bins out. It was garbage day. Immediately, Delta realized that she needed help—but she didn't want to ask.

"Want me to take your bins to the street, Mrs. Romano?" He shot that same, self-assured smile, like he was the most relaxed man in the world. It was a mask he was used to wearing.

A wide, relieved smile crossed her lips. "Yes, son. Please."

Wasting no time, Delta moved around to the back of her home and shuffled out her garbage and recycling bins. It was the least he could do to try to keep up the ruse. He wasn't an idiot. People had been looking at him funny since he'd rotated back from Syria again, three weeks before. Maybe it was the bruises that didn't seem to heal or the fact that he always looked like he'd been ridden hard and put away wet the night before. Whatever it was, home had stopped feeling like home. He didn't belong there anymore.

As he finished, Mrs. Romano waited at the top of her bungalow stoop with a homemade pistachio biscotti for him. Her kind eyes and compassionate spirit reminded him of his late mother's—the last memories he had.

"Thanks," Delta grunted as he took the baked good from Mrs. Romano.

His stomach was rumbling from the lack of sustenance. He was used to pushing his body to extremes, neglecting his own needs for the sake of his platoon, but things were going too far now.

"You're a good man, Matteo…a very good man." Mrs. Romano's voice cut into his thoughts, a knowing twinkle in her eyes. "When are you going to find a Mrs. Valente?"

Delta let out a loud, sarcastic laugh, sloughing off the question. Shrugging, he coyly took a bite of the biscotti and moved toward his truck, waving goodbye. All she saw was his façade, like everyone else. *If she only knew.*

Mrs. Romano's gaze didn't relent as he leaped into the cab. He was in a rush—but it wasn't just because of where he had to be. It was because of what he needed to get away from. He was damn sure that Mrs. Romano wouldn't think so much of him if she knew what lingered underneath the surface.

I'm not a good guy. Not even close.

Slamming the gears of his truck into reverse, he pulled out of the driveway of his place, saluting Mrs. Romano on his way out. The fun and games were over. Now, he really had to focus. He was on a mission that morning—and things could get ugly.

Barreling down Oceanside Drive, Delta flipped on the radio—local LA news—and listened to the newscasters talking about a body discovered in South Central in one of the roughest blocks. It had been on the news all morning—tragedy porn for LA'ers. Delta listened for any pertinent intel as he set his GPS for the crime scene. He had questions that needed answers.

Gripping the steering wheel, Delta rolled his shirt sleeves up to let a little heat off, revealing his winding tattoos. It was far too hot for long sleeves, even by LA standards. They were in the middle of a bizarre mid-winter heat wave. But he didn't have a choice. He had to cover up. There were things he didn't want *anyone* to see — like the fresh laceration on his arm that was only going to add another scar.

As he stopped his truck at a red light, he pulled off his sunglasses and absently traced his fingers over the long scar that ran from his cheekbone up to his temple and eyebrow. A little less than two years old, it was a reminder that he should have died in the Syrian mountains. Hell, he should have died in a lot of operations, but *undeniably* that one.

Now, he was on borrowed time. He could feel it. He was never wrong about those things. He was playing with fire and some sort of fucked up luck that was about to run out.

The light turned green, and he hit the gas hard, not wanting to think about how he was spending that second chance at life. It sure as hell would make a priest cry. His mother had always said that he didn't need to be led into temptation because he already knew the way.

The drive from his bungalow up into South Central wasn't fast, but he drove aggressively. He knew how to scare the piss out of LA's richest, stalling out the fast lane in their luxury cars.

Revving his truck and nearly eating up some dinky coupe in front of him, he peeled off the highway. Rounding the streets in the impoverished neighborhood, he transitioned into a different type of vigilant and cautious. Those streets bled a type of desperation that he'd only seen in war.

Delta drove up to the vicinity of the taped-off scene and chose to park well off in the distance to keep a low profile. Before jumping out of his truck, he popped a black baseball hat on, pulling the brim down low for as much anonymity as possible. He adjusted his long sleeves across his muscled forearms so his unpolished appearance would help him not to stand out too much. He looked like any hungover blue-collar laborer who spent too much time at the gym. Then again, that pretty much described any SEAL.

He walked up to the periphery of a building that police were investigating—an abandoned commercial warehouse. Delta guessed that whoever owned the aging building had been hit hard in the economic crash, so they'd left it to rot. From the insecure doors and broken windows, he would bet that criminals and drifters had been trespassing for a long time.

Delta gripped the police tape surrounding the epicenter and glanced around to see if the cops off to the side had noticed him. They had their backs turned, just for a moment, so he took his chance. As he slipped past, he slunk around the building into the shadows, and he observed. He paused in an enclave, watching cops come and go from the building, listening to the broken conversations of the investigators.

In all his years in the special forces, he'd become skilled at going unseen when he needed to. He could be a goddamn ninja. A lot of it just had to do with confidence—and looking like he belonged. That had turned out to be damn useful the previous few weeks. He'd been on leave from work, but it hadn't been a fucking vacation. He'd been working on something else — something serious. And, in true Delta fashion, he'd been going it alone.

Crouching low and moving slow, Delta approached a broken window near the back of the building. He checked inside, seeing the room was empty. A ton of blood was splashed across the concrete floor, but there was no body in sight. *Fuck.* Had the cops already moved the corpse out? He reached into his pocket, readying his cell phone to snap pictures of anything that could aid him. Delta scanned the room for pertinent info. The graying building interior had the feel of an unrealized horror film, and a chill ran up his back as he wondered what the fuck had happened there.

Voices echoed from the front hall of the building, and Delta ducked down outside the window. He could hear the voice of someone entering the room, calling back details of the scene to the front of the building. His first instinct hadn't been wrong. The victim had been using. And, unfortunately, his second instinct had been right too. *She* was there.

His body stiffened and his skin prickled, awareness flushing over him. He'd never forget her voice, even though he hadn't heard it for a while. He'd bumped into her at Carrick's wedding, just weeks after they'd hooked up, but that hardly counted. Had it already been a year? Hearty, feminine, sincere — every word she said danced out of her mouth. As he tried to regain focus, he slowly looked up and into the open window, enough to fully take in her candid, clever words. Her voice alone ran a wave of sensation up his spine that surprised him, after all that time. But it was nothing in comparison to when he finally laid eyes on her.

Sergeant Kendra Larose's natural blonde hair bobbed into view. Delta adjusted his position, getting eyes on the interior of the crime scene and a better view of her—a woman he hadn't seen since he'd deployed, spending the year fighting enemies with half the resolve that she had. A woman who had grown to hate him—and rightfully so.

I can't let her see me.

After she tucked a stray lock behind her ear, Kendra was focused on the warehouse floor. Delta's cock twitched as he watched her shift on her feet, her hips swaying. Blood pumped through his shaft as he drank in her body—a form that drew him to arousal so quickly, without fail. Never had he met such a natural beauty as her. Some guys might find her ordinary or plain, but he found her simply intoxicating. There was always just something about her—something that really got to him.

Even at a distance, he admired the machinations of her clever mind. She was looking down at a cluster of blood where a body once had lain, her lips and nose twitching that certain way that showed when she was really deep in thought. She was on to something. How much did she already know? Delta tried to see what she was seeing. He flexed his jaw, wondering if maybe it wasn't fate that they'd met again. On his own, tracing the source of the drugs had proven to be an impossible task.

And just as a familiar man's voice echoed through the space, Delta realized he was biting the side of his cheek, breathing heavier than usual and gripping the edge of the window like he was going to snap.

"This city is falling to pieces." The man scoffed, coming into view.

Delta recognized him immediately as Staff Sergeant Hunter Greenwood. Delta had met the guy a year ago, around the same time that he had met Kendra. The

Navy had put on a one-week training course for partners in law enforcement, extending the invite to LAPD. At the time, Delta had shown Kendra the ropes—training her how to safely rappel, while realizing that he needed to train her on protecting herself from creeps. Something about the way that Hunter looked at Kendra...

"He's another military vet." Kendra shook her head and furiously scribbled in her notebook. "They've already identified him."

Prickles ran up the back of Delta's neck as he watched Hunter stalk Kendra in the middle of the crime scene. Everything in Delta's body screamed for violence as Hunter licked his bottom lip, carefully examining her. The scowl on his face deepened as she furthered her point.

"What do you bet his blood has traces of doxycycline?" Kendra turned to her boss.

"Come on." He shook his head dismissively, straightening his jacket. "It's a common antibiotic. Stop."

"This is real, Hunter. We've seen traces of it in the other two bodies." Kendra glared at her staff sergeant, standing her ground. "There's a pattern here. Are they being targeted?"

"For what purpose?" he asked, an underlying threat in his voice.

"I don't know yet."

Hunter stilled, clearly judging her. The man looked damn tired, like he hadn't slept for weeks.

"Let's not start jumping to conclusions," Hunter snapped back, his eye twitching. "Anything is possible, Kendra. Let's check with the gangs first."

"Hunter, please. The first two have been soldiers, not gangbangers," Kendra replied slowly, flipping through her notes. "But why? Who's after them—?"

A flash of rage visibly taking over, he cut her off. "We don't have any reason to believe there are links between cases. This is LA. Murders happen all the time."

"But there must be a connection." Kendra glanced between her notebook, the blood splatter and Hunter, apparently confused by his messaging. "It's this doxycycline. Isn't it known to be used by the military as an antimalaria drug?"

"You're asking the wrong questions." Hunter strode toward her, his face darkening.

"Yes, but doxycycline—"

"You don't get it."

"They were soldiers—" Kendra countered again but halted as Hunter's hand whipped up into the air, matched by a growl escaping his lips.

For a split second, Delta's protective instinct thrust him forward, ready to fuck the guy up. But Hunter had recovered, using his raised hand to smooth back his hair.

"Fuck," Hunter grumbled, shaking as he regained control.

Delta stiffened, his eyes wide open. *What the fuck is he going to do with that hand?* Kendra stumbled back in surprise, audibly sucking in breath. But before Delta could jump to her side, the enraged staff sergeant spun and marched toward the front of the building. Whatever he was up to, Delta saw a man who was losing control—a man who posed a threat. He was a ticking time-bomb. Didn't she realize it?

Stunned, Kendra stood there alone, tightly clutching her notebook. She bit her lip, trembling, as if trying to get back to work. Delta sat back, confused as fuck at what he'd just witnessed. Delta knew right then and there that he had little choice. Things had just gotten more complicated.

I have to protect her.

Pulling out black gloves from his pocket, he slipped them on, preparing to leave no trace of what he was about to do. The scene before him had validated everything he'd seen since he'd been back from deployment. The body count was climbing.

Moving around the building a little farther, he gained entry to the interior. As he stalked through the shadows, making note of everything he saw, he was careful not to disturb anything, not even caked-on grime from years of abandonment. In stealth-mode, he slid out of the hallway into the darkest corner of the large room, not too far from Kendra. For a split second, he found himself just staring at her, drinking her in — the way she poured over her notebook then sharply analyzed the room before her. He had no doubt that her cunning mind was finding every anomalous detail.

And, yet again, he was proven right.

"And why are *you* here?" Kendra's exasperated tone echoed over to where he stood, though she didn't flinch or glance up from scribbling in her notebook.

Delta sucked in his breath, wondering if she meant...

"Yes, *you*." She turned her chin slightly and shot a warning into the darkness, seeming to slice into his core. "Do you think I'm daft?"

Releasing the air in his lungs, he stepped forward — confident and relaxed, offering her a sly look as he crossed his arms. His charming ruse was too goddamn easy for him to make people see his way.

"Sergeant." Delta shrugged. He narrowed his focus on her, giving her that grin that women loved. "Here we are, crossing paths again."

"Crossing paths?" She balked.

"That's right." He kept his gaze intense, his body squared.

Turning away, she scoffed, "You're acting like we've stumbled across each other at the grocery store."

She shook her head in deep discontent, seemingly impervious to his charm. A chill ran up the back of his neck, her rejection biting. He hated it—but deserved it. Still, he stood there, watching.

"I'm too busy for *this* right now." She spun, crossing her arms tightly, as if shielding herself. Her body language screamed of a woman who would not be fooled again.

"Too busy for me?" Delta pushed.

"I'll go back to my original question." She raised her eyebrows accusingly. "Why are you here? This is a secure crime scene, so *you* don't belong here. I don't care what security clearances you *say* you have."

All the air got sucked out of the room, and he found himself momentarily searching for a response. Her bright, intelligent eyes left no stone unturned and demanded answers. She anxiously chewed her lip, giving him a rare glimpse of her girlish vulnerability— the type of vulnerability that made him voracious.

"We have a mutual purpose." Delta let his face become stone cold serious, imparting the intensity he felt.

"Which would be?" she asked.

"Keeping you safe."

Chapter Two

What a conceited, egotistical asshole, Sergeant Kendra Larose seethed, staring down the Navy SEAL who had once taken too much from her. Where did he get off? *Wait, no.* She didn't want to know the answer to that.

"Keeping me safe, huh?" She stared into his dark, haunting eyes. "It's so nice that you've started to care about my wellbeing."

Watching his jaw tense gave her all the confirmation she needed to continue. She still had the ability to get under his perfectly rough skin. *Good.*

"We need to talk," he ground out.

"Isn't that what we are doing?"

"In private," he clarified. "My truck's around the corner —"

"Not a chance," she said, cutting him off. All she could do was push him away, because anything less felt terrible. Without hesitation, she peeled her gaze off him and something inside her squirmed.

"You need to listen to me."

Turning away but quivering inside, she protectively shot at him, "To whom?"

"Look… I think we got off wrong."

"When? Today or *last* time?" she barked out.

He fell silent, his dark gaze following her.

She leaned forward, unable to believe his audacity. "You show up here—to my workplace—after not so much as trying to call. And what's the real reason? Did I miss your application to LAPD?" She'd transformed her tone to accusatory, insinuating the worst. "You know, it's not uncommon for predators to revisit their crime scenes and admire their own work…"

"Predators, huh?" Fire flashed in his dark eyes. "I think you are overlooking who the predator is here."

"Get the hell out of here. Isn't there some mortal combat you can sign up for?" She dismissed him. "I'm *busy*. Find someone else who's interested in your misplaced heroics."

Only infuriating her further, he didn't move one sculpted muscle, which she should have expected would be the case. She gritted her teeth together as anger flushed up her body, nearly turning her vision as black as his soul. Why the hell was he standing before her? The unconscionable arrogance that it would take to show up then and there was astounding. Turning and marching away from him, inhaling to catch her rattling breath, Kendra hated the agony she was in—all because of him.

She pleaded with God that he would just go away, stop existing, but her prayers were unanswered. Heavy footsteps edging around the blood splatters on the concrete told her what she didn't want to know.

He's not leaving.

"What happened here?" Delta pushed her, trying to take back control of the conversation. She recognized his tactic.

"What makes you think I'd answer that?" Kendra whipped her head back to sneer at him. She watched him carefully, reading every movement. "You think I trust you?"

"Why wouldn't you?"

A tougher woman wouldn't have responded, but she snapped up her head, taking his bait and narrowing her eyes on his stupidly sexy face. She replied, "For reasons you should know."

"Tell me," he continued, unrelenting.

"No," she replied, a little surprised. Was it just her, or was his approach lacking his typical charm?

Analyzing him, she had to avert her gaze quickly again. Unfortunately, his just-returned-from-war roughness only made her want to feel his impossibly muscular body on top of hers once again. That locked-away part of her mind wandered to the feel of his thick cock in her…

Breathless, she looked up and witnessed him staring right back at her. His mouth twisted into a sly grin, as if knowing she was just melting inside. No doubt that was exactly what he wanted. If there was one thing she knew about Delta—he always wanted something.

"Okay, hotshot, you didn't come here to spray luminol for me," she snapped at him. "So, what are you after?"

"You," Delta offered up fast. *Too fast.* "It's that fucking simple."

"Why? After all this time?" Kendra shook her head. "After you couldn't even be bothered to—"

Call. She finished the sentence silently, forcing her mouth shut. That hot feeling rising, she admitted to herself that she was letting him get under her skin. And now her words were slipping from sharp to vulnerable. Showing her true feelings wasn't something she was prepared to do. He didn't deserve to know how he'd left her.

She turned her full attention back to the warehouse floor, trying to ignore the wall of masculine heat that was stalking her. Wild, unwelcome thoughts flooded her mind as his presence loomed just out of reach. Instinctively, she flitted her gaze back up to his tall form, only to see him much closer than she expected, looking down his long, perfectly straight nose at her.

"Enough of the games." Delta drove it home, clear and authoritative. "I saw what Hunter almost did to you. We can't let that slide."

Absorbing his words, she took an unstable step backward, her thighs vibrating slightly from the intensity of his sharp gaze. Her heel clicked on the concrete floor as she stumbled, the sound echoing throughout the room.

"*We* can't let that slide?" Kendra whispered into the dusty air. "There's no 'we'."

"He's dangerous," Delta growled, that familiar fire in his eyes driving warning alarms in her. "Don't trust him."

"I don't know what you think you saw, but Hunter would never hurt me." As she slid backward, everything in her body screamed for help.

Without explanation, Delta trailed in her wake, his eyes locked on her. There was no getting away. It was one thing to be warned, another to be warned by a man who made her feel patently unsafe. She flashed her gaze to the entrance, hearing the distant voices of her colleagues outside the building. Any second, someone could come in. She begged for that to happen.

"It's you who I can't trust," she replied, keeping her eyes locked on Delta.

"Wrong."

"You need to leave."

With crossed arms, he planted his powerful legs like tree trunks, clearly unwilling to be moved, waiting for her submission.

"I swear to God, Matteo. I'll shoot you." A pained tone escaped her lips, like a cornered animal.

"You wouldn't—"

The voices that she'd heard outside suddenly grew louder, yelling to take cover. In a flash, Delta lunged toward her, grabbing her protectively, shielding her. Gunshots ricocheted outside, followed by unintelligible shrieking. Chills ran up and down her body while Delta squeezed her closer.

What the hell is going on?

Shaking, she glanced up and drank in his determined face. She realized he'd made himself into her human shield as he pulled her toward the side of the room. He'd switched into fight mode, and she observed his calculating eyes searching the room, likely looking for any detail that could make the difference between survival and death. She sucked in a breath, hearing sirens outside and continued shouting.

At the side of the room, they stopped. Delta assessed her, his grip tightening while she strained to listen, trying to comprehend what the situation was. His searching eyes reminded her of another time — of things she'd rather forget. It was the first time she'd had his body against hers in a long while. She wasn't ready to experience his effect. His darkened gaze, angry yet intent, drove a familiar deep need in her core, so intoxicating that she had no choice but to react one way or another. Choosing self-protection, she reflexively slammed on his chest to push him away.

A bullet crashed through one of the intact windows near the front of the building, sending shattered glass everywhere. Kendra shrieked, unwillingly stumbling into his warm body. Holding her to his chest, he swiftly moved them into an adjoining hallway, pulling her farther into the darkness, silently and without permission. Just like him, he didn't ask. He simply did what he wanted. She panted, detained in a bear-hug against his hard chest, as the war continued in front of the building, complimenting the war that raged within her.

Delta dropped his head, uttering into her ear, "Now's a good time to pull out your gun."

"I don't actually have it." She whispered her confession, knowing full well she rarely brought her service weapon anywhere anymore. Shooting him had been an empty threat.

"You lied to me?" his gravelly voice questioned, his forearms flexing as he tightened her back against him. Her breath shortened with his hold as he continued, "Do you know what happens to girls who lie to me?"

I know very well. The reminder sent tremors up her thighs as she sensed his touch rising up her chest toward her neck. The torture tactics he engaged in were unconscionable, both physical and psychological. Moving her as he wished, he spun her around slowly in his grasp, as though she were his ballerina, so that they came face to face. Her mind cried in revolt, but her body grew increasingly supple, willing, acquiescing to his silent demands, like she was wont to do.

Reluctantly, she tilted her chin up to him, inhaling that heady wood smell she distinctly remembered. He had always been so much taller than her, well into the six-foot-three range, but with heels she was tall enough that all he had to do was drop his head and find her mouth. That fact was both terrifying and thrilling. She couldn't believe that there she was, held in his arms once again.

"You never told me what you wanted." He stationed his mouth just inches above hers.

A *kiss*, she fantasized, but she tightened her lips. "I'm not doing this," she said, shaking her head slightly, affirming that she wouldn't fall victim to the man twice—a man who was certainly guilty of using her for his own gratification.

She pressed her eyes shut—not wanting to believe her own sensations, not wanting to acknowledge the burning desire she still carried for him. She was not going to go through that again.

"I wanted to call," Delta explained too easily, driving pain through her chest. "I wanted to see you again."

"No, you did not," she ground out, attesting her truth.

As the words rolled off her tongue, Delta snapped off one of his dark gloves and reached his bare hand up to her chin, angling her mouth upward. The motion was so smooth, so fast, that she was caught off guard, shocked and paralyzed as he held her face. Submitting to him was easy—and it was her expected state.

"You think you know what I wanted?" he challenged her, as his grip tightened on her jaw.

"I think we both know."

"No," he growled, his mouth too close to hers, "you have no idea."

She pouted, questioning if he would take her mouth. The anticipation was the same as his grasp—gripping and consuming, just the way she remembered it from that one fateful night so long ago when she'd lain under his body, taking every inch of him.

He slipped his hand down her throat, controlling, caressing and pushing her hair behind her ear, like he was assessing his prize. Whatever buzz he drove in her was threatening to pop. God, he made her so high. And the way that he was breathing down on her promised things that he still wanted to do.

"I know bad intentions when I see them," he admitted, dropping his head to brush her lips with his. "Don't let your guard down."

Reflexively, like touching a hot stove, Kendra snapped her head back. Simultaneously, the sounds of car tires squealed, clearly pulling away from the street.

Spinning in Delta's arms and pushing away, she cried out in finality, "Just leave me alone —" As she spoke, the glove that he'd taken off dropped onto her foot, and he sank back into the shadows, leaving her alone in the hallway.

"I want you out of my life," she called out to no one.

All she could see was a momentary crack of daylight as the back door opened and shut. A hollowing silence filled the space, and she felt an emptiness inside. The man she'd thought of too much for an entire year had disappeared once again. Yet this time, it was just as she'd asked.

"Kendra!" Hunter called from the front of the building, pulling her attention back to reality.

She turned to her boss' voice, disoriented, expecting to wake up from a dream.

"Kendra! Where are you? I told you this was fucking gang related."

Hunter's calls drove an undeniable feeling within her. She wished it were another man calling her name.

She turned to leave but remembered the lump at her foot. Reaching down in the shadows, she fumbled for Delta's forgotten glove — the only piece of evidence that proved it wasn't a dream at all. Walking back into the main room where there was light and she could get a better look, she ran her fingers over the rough black material of the glove. Surprised, she observed holes in it from overuse and detected a substance akin to dried blood on a few of the knuckles.

What the hell has he been up to?

Chapter Three

"The components are separated," the laboratorian called over to Kendra as she reviewed the centrifuge results across the counter. "Can you pass me my notebook?"

"Sure, just give me a second," Kendra mumbled back, glued to her own analysis.

Carefully, Kendra repositioned Delta's glove on her lab plate, getting a better angle of it under the microscope. The glove was black and tactical—like something the military would issue. She knew that type of gear well from her early policing days on the road, having been issued something similar. With reminders like those, she thanked her lucky stars that she'd gotten in with LAPD's forensics lab, leveraging her master's in science. She'd settled right into the behind-the-scenes role, trying to forget every bad call she'd made in uniform.

Delta's glove really told a story. The knuckles were well used, with rips and holes, like someone had been punching concrete walls—or concrete faces. Knowing him, anything was possible. Kendra was validated to see indicators of blood, just as she had supposed. It wasn't that fresh, but it wasn't too old either. His knuckles must have bled through at some point recently, leaving a trace on the stiff material. But why had his hand been bleeding? Surely, he couldn't *actually* be punching concrete. Idle curiosity flowed through her mind. What did that man get up to at night?

"Cooling sufficient." The feminine voice of her colleague carried back to Kendra. "May want to consider a deeper impression."

"Were we able to collect an appropriate sample?" Kendra tilted her head, looking up from Delta's glove, gazing around the small gray-and-white forensics lab.

"Depends on what you need this to tell you." Lily, the young laboratorian, glanced up and smiled at Kendra.

Kendra stilled. What *exactly* was she after? It was the first of many questions she hoped to answer. Aside from what type of substances were on the glove and where had he been, she was struggling with how to articulate what she was ultimately after without sounding like a psychopath.

Gazing over at her colleague, Kendra studied the young woman with a knotted black bun who was deep in thought, a line expanding between her barely-there eyebrows. Lily, a recent master's graduate, was a breath of fresh air in the lab, where they processed certain types of substances.

"You know, I really would like the department to invest in a more sensitive machine," she explained to Kendra. "You'd think the high-and-mighty LAPD would *actually* put money into its forensic lab."

"We aren't as fancy as your Harvard lab," Kendra countered. "But we sure as hell are lucky to have you."

Lily let out a low chuckle, tilting her head in knowing. Then she narrowed her eyes on Kendra, eyeing the glove. She tucked a loose lock of pin-straight black hair behind her ear, focusing on the seizure.

"So, have you found something?" Lily probed. "I know that look on your face."

Kendra shook her head. "All I've found is *doubt* that we have enough of a sample to tell us anything. The substance on the fabric is less than fresh."

"Well, which case is this related to?" Lily asked as she approached, her white lab coat swishing as she walked.

Kendra looked back up at her student, not really wanting to say it. It was the first and only time that she had ever brought something into the lab for personal reasons. She was guilty enough about it, let alone explaining to Lily what her intentions were. And that guilt was *powerful*.

"It's not related specifically…to a case," Kendra admitted, her poker face unpracticed. "But I think it's blood."

"I see," Lily said softly, understanding. She moved forward to scrutinize the glove and continued, "Hmm—the blood is all dried up, but we should be able to profile the DNA. We'll need the PCR for this one, of course."

"It was discarded, to be clear," Kendra iterated, in reference to the glove. She didn't want Lily to assume she was breaking any rules. She wasn't. A discarded possession was fair game in the eyes of the law.

Lily nodded.

"It's just something I want to check out," Kendra concluded.

"Ah, so this is a case study?" Lily offered. "An example, just to test on? That's good timing, since we have just received a brand-new PCR microchip and I've been itching to take it for a test drive on something not case-related. I've heard enough about this thing's high throughput and small footprint."

As Kendra nodded in approval, Lily moved to prepare her station and get a scraping of the dried blood into the PCR. Lily's slight frame—surprisingly thin given the amount of ramen noodles she consumed—rustled as she worked. Her enthusiasm for fluorescence-based quantitative polymerase chain reactions never failed, something Kendra truly admired. Their shared love of science had bridged the cop-civilian divide, bonding them over the years.

After a few minutes, Lily carefully took the plate holding the glove over to her work area. Kendra watched as Lily began zoning in on Delta's dried blood, humming along to the latest pop song that was quietly playing on the radio at the back of the lab.

"I might be able to get a little bit more here," Lily mumbled, her hands as deft as a surgeon's. "This shouldn't be an issue for the microchip. Thank God we convinced the inspector to fund us an updated version."

Though Lily's words were reassuring, Kendra leaned back against the bench, questioning the ethics of what she was doing. Lily worked quickly, preparing a strip of eight PCR tubes for the thermal cycler.

Despite the fact that Kendra had seized the glove in the morning, she'd taken the day to justify putting it on the lab plate, oscillating between the argument that she wasn't doing anything wrong and that she was in violation of every professional creed she claimed to adhere to. On top of that, then there was the issue of…what did she hope to do with the information she found?

"Weird," Lily interrupted as she reviewed the extraction.

"What?" Kendra grilled, lunging closer.

Lily continued mumbling to herself, shaking her head. "This can't be right. Oh, this can't be human blood."

"Not human blood?" Kendra said, leaning over Lily's shoulder to see for herself. "I didn't think that was—"

"Sorry... I should say—not *normal* human blood."

"I don't understand," Kendra jumped in, her brows snapping together in concern. "What do you mean?"

Lily shook her head slowly, backtracking. "Perhaps I spoke too soon. This is a brand-new machine. It's not calibrated correctly yet. How old did you say this evidence is?"

"I just seized it this morning."

"I see," Lily said. "I'd like to take a little more time to sequence this properly before I jump to conclusions. We've barely scratched the surface."

Kendra gripped the lab counter before her for balance. A rush ran through her head, and she bit her lip. *Not normal human blood? What's wrong with it?* Despite Lily's correction, the original comment stuck. Kendra reminded herself that Lily was right. It was a new machine, fresh out of the box.

But then again, something isn't sitting right, she thought as she eyed the extraction.

What the hell is on that glove?

Lily turned around, apparently sensing Kendra's unease. "Hey, are you okay? I just need a bit more time with this substance and I'll get you a full analysis."

The young woman's bright brown eyes opened empathetically as she assessed Kendra. They both knew something was wrong. Alarm bells were going off in Kendra's head. *I shouldn't be doing this.*

"Forget it." Kendra lunged forward and snapped up the glove, throwing it into a plastic evidence bag.

She urgently stuffed Delta's glove in her tote bag, nearly rushing to the lab's door. She turned back to Lily, explaining, "Please, do me a favor, and forget all about this. Dump the extraction. I have to go. It's getting late."

Lily shot a look at her in obvious confusion. She very clearly had questions she wasn't articulating. Kendra tried to give her some sort of explanation, but an interruption came.

A bell sounded at the lab door—and Kendra shot a guilty look back and forth from Lily to the door. Typically, they didn't receive visitors, and Kendra wasn't about to wait around and let Lily get in trouble. Hoisting her tote on her shoulder, Kendra rushed out of the lab door, finding Hunter standing in the hallway. Dread coiled up her throat as she stopped in front of him, letting the door lock behind her. Unwilling to showcase her anxiety, Kendra wasted no time, pushing onward down the long, quiet hallway.

"Staff." She cordially addressed her boss by his rank as she slipped past.

Hunter narrowed his eyes, smoothing back his brownish hair. Kendra wondered if he knew what she'd been up to, and for the umpteenth time that day, self-reproach flooded through her mind. Leveraging police resources for personal ends was deeply unethical, a fireable offense.

"Calling it a day?" Hunter grilled, following her as she distanced herself.

"Yes," Kendra replied, trying to keep it casual.

"We need to debrief," he remarked, "about this morning."

"I can't stay late. I have to get home," she replied, a soft 'no'.

The allusion to her personal life was met with a twitch in his eye. He took in a noticeable breath and moved the conversation on.

"The body… What are we seeing?" Hunter probed, bringing her back to what she was supposed to be investigating — the scene of the crime, not Delta.

"We'll have a report to you by tomorrow." Kendra nodded, tightening her hand around her tote as she reached the end of the hallway where the exit was to the parking structure. When she reached the far wing of the building, she grabbed the exit's doorhandle. She glanced back up to Hunter, chewing her lip.

"Why do I feel like you are running from me?" He gave her a look, as if trying to read her mind.

"I'm — I-I just —" she stammered, but rolled up her tongue immediately.

Shaking her head at her own inability to keep it together, Kendra pushed out into the parking structure to find her car. Unfortunately, Hunter followed close behind. He was only the second man to trail in her wake that day, driving something up her throat. She was *losing* it — ever since she'd seen Delta. He'd rattled her.

"You… just?" Hunter didn't relent, calling after her as she marched. "Go ahead, finish your thought."

In a row of cars, Kendra stopped in her tracks to face him, realizing that he'd stopped as well — too close to her body for comfort. She caught an unwelcome whiff of him. Unlike Delta, when Hunter's scent filled her nose, it was downright disagreeable. Not that he had a bad odor, but she couldn't deny that she disliked the way he smelled and had felt that way for the entire year.

"Listen, Kendra. You're acting *different*. I know there's something wrong." Her boss cocked his head, staring at her, as if knowing. "Talk to me. You can trust me."

Trust. That awkward thing. She bit her lip and felt overwhelmed by guilt as she stared into Hunter's face. *I should be trusting him. Isn't he on my side?* She repeated the question again and again in her head, trying to convince herself to come back to the light.

Finally, her true nature overcame her, and she confessed. "Look... I found something on the ground at the crime scene and I brought it back to the lab to test it."

Hunter nodded, appreciative. "Perfect. What is it?"

She gnashed her teeth harder against her lip as she chastised herself for the admission. Shifting on her feet, she shook her head. "No, you don't understand. It doesn't really belong to the case. And the reason why I'm telling you this—"

Hunter cut her off. "If it was at the crime scene, it belongs to the case. Simple."

"No, it doesn't, and the reason why I'm telling you this is—" Kendra again tried to articulate, but found herself stumbling over her words, trying to stop the runaway train. She strained her neck back, finally just reiterating, "It doesn't belong to the case."

Hunter wouldn't let her continue. "You aren't making sense. What the fuck are you talking about?"

"I saw this glove fall off someone, so all I'm doing is running DNA elimination tests—"

"Fall off?" Hunter's head tilted, his eyes narrowing. "Who?"

Kendra let out a slow breath, her conscience getting the best of her. "You aren't going to like it."

"Trust me," Hunter restated. "I'm not the bad guy."

Kendra tried to breathe in as much air as she could, releasing it slowly to calm herself. She was such a prudish do-gooder, unable to handle this type of pressure. She locked eyes with her boss, wishing for compassion that wouldn't come — not when it had to do with his nemesis. Kendra knew mentioning Delta was going to be a terrible mistake. Last year, the two men had birthed a very strong hatred for each other.

She looked deeper into Hunter's eyes as he waited, blinking back at her expectantly. He shrugged, as if telling her to get on with it. She knew she just needed to come clean, especially if she wanted to save her ass.

He probed her again. "Whose glove is it?"

"Delta —" She closed her eyes, feeling the immediate tension. "It was Delta's."

"Don't you fucking say it."

Kendra nodded uncomfortably, the air thickening around her. "He was there, at the scene."

"How the hell — ?" Hunter snapped into a sudden rage, his heated voice lashing through the parking structure.

She stumbled back, her hands raised, trying to calm him. "I don't know. I have no idea. But there he was, warning me —"

"Warning you? What the fuck does that mean?" Hunter's voice grew more incredulous, as if she'd personally betrayed him. The anger boomed off him even worse than she'd seen before.

She instinctively backed up again, hitting a car, wishing to God she'd brought her pistol that day.

"I don't know."

Hunter stopped a few feet in front of her, trapping her against the car. "Tell me what the fuck he said to you."

"To be careful," she said, biting her lip, holding her tote to her chest. "To not let my guard down."

"Was that before or after he dropped his glove?"

Kendra opened her mouth to respond, as she considered his question.

Hunter's furious tone grew suspicious. "I want to know everything that asshole said to you. He's up to something—and you've played right into his hands, contaminating our lab."

"What was I supposed to do? Leave his glove there?" Kendra stepped back farther into the parking structure, tightening her hand on her bag. "There was blood on it. I had to eliminate his DNA."

Blood. Hunter's eyes drilled into her. She watched his jaw twitch, his neck pulse. Clearly, the mention of Delta's blood was a bridge too far.

"Where is it? Give it to me," Hunter demanded, lunging forward to search. He grabbed at her tote, trying to get into it. "Give it to me!"

"No," she cried, pulling to the side. She had to get to her own car as fast as fucking possible and get the hell away. The situation was moving from bad to worse.

This is all a big mistake.

"Hand it over!"

"I'm sorry— I should have never brought it here. I'll give it back," she apologized to her boss, quickly looking over her shoulder to where her blue sedan was parked.

Hunter grabbed her hands. "No!"

It was in that split second that Kendra saw what she should have seen before—a desperation in his eyes.

"Stay the fuck away from him," he snarled, his grasp tightening on her. "Do *not* go to him. I swear to God."

"Hunter, *please*." She tried to tug her hands away.

He seethed, his panicked eyes flitting back and forth over her face. "He's trying to manipulate you. He wants you to go back to him, Kendra. Don't you fucking do it."

She blinked back, trying to withhold tears. "He wants nothing from me. He never has."

As the words filled the space between them, a perplexed expression crossed Hunter's face, stilling his attack. Using the moment's pause, Kendra slipped out from under him. She sped off to her car, her heart pounding through her chest. She felt short of breath, spiraling into a deep panic.

Without hesitation, she peeled out of the lot, as far away as she could get from Hunter. His unbelievable, uncontrollable desperation had been so shocking. She knew he hated Delta, but this? What was she missing? Her trembling hands white-knuckle-gripping the steering wheel, she pulled out of the parking structure into the open air of the mounting evening. A thousand thoughts should have been at the forefront of her mind, but one important question took over.

What am I going to do with this glove?

Like a bad omen, she sensed it burning a hole in her bag—and into the shell she'd formed.

Chapter Four

On her way home, Kendra's nerves were still running high, in shock from what had just happened. She had no words for Hunter's behavior and didn't know what the hell to do. Her mind spun at a thousand miles per hour, and she was beating herself up for her continued inaction. She'd always been certain that she'd be the woman who wouldn't put up with bullshit. She was strong. She'd stand up for herself. But there she was — shaking in her seat, doing nothing about it.

I just have to get home.

Chewing at her quivering mouth, she blitzed around a steep corner in the heart of the Malibu hills on autopilot. LA traffic out of the basin had been predictably terrible. As she climbed from the oceanside up the side of the rocky hill, the sunset finally fell below the horizon. Dusk was upon her, making the drive a little less relaxed and a little more perilous. Drunken celebrities and millionaires sometimes sped around the unguarded hills, and crashes down the encampment occurred all-too-often.

It had taken hours of sitting in LA traffic and listening to her mindfulness app to finally get her to breathe properly. Was she crazy or had Hunter attacked her? She had to report Hunter for his belligerence and abuse. She paused, thinking. Then again, she didn't want anyone looking into what she was doing with Delta's glove. If she complained about Hunter, they'd find her out.

She didn't know what to think, nor did she want to. Her judgment was growing impaired, more and more so. It was too damn hard to be on her game when her whole day had been thrown off since that morning. A reprieve would be nice to process, as opposed to drinking from a firehose.

It seemed like every man professing to 'protect her' was prepared to hurt her. Her head was pounding. Seeing Delta again was the worst thing that could have happened. It had drummed up all the emotions she'd gone through the past year, trying to get over that damn fling. She'd never forget that guilty look on his face when she'd seen him at the hospital when his friend Carrick had been shot then caught him at Carrick's wedding, weeks after they'd hooked up. She'd finally accepted he was never going to call. She was never going to see him again.

But he'd just reappeared.

Why? What did he want? As the street darkened, she ran one hand up her face in embarrassment. She was being manipulated by him, yet again. She wasn't quite sure how exactly, or why — but it was clear he had an endgame.

And that was when she decided to pull her car over onto the side of the road in a small shoulder in the rocky hill. Her car idling, she reached over to her bag and pulled the glove out, feeling the stiff fabric through the plastic evidence bag. She could throw it out of the window and be done with it. Or she could take it back to Delta and confront him, tell him off once and for all. *What should I do?* Biting her lip, she had to decide.

It took a minute or two, but emotion overcame her. She pulled a big U-turn and started heading back down the hill, driving away from her neighborhood. She grabbed her phone and scrolled through her contacts to find Delta's old cell number. *Does he still use that one?* One hand on the wheel, one hand hitting the button to call Delta's cell, she spun around a hairpin corner.

But just at the same time, another car rocketed up the turn—straight toward her, like it wasn't going to turn at all. Her eyes widened and she screamed, whipping the steering wheel all the way to the right and accelerating to avoid collision. The other car's tires squealed as it missed her only slightly, but it was too late. Her car had already driven into brush on the hilly side of the road. She smacked her head against the steering wheel as she impacted against a tree, sending a ripping pain through her forehead and into her skull.

Damn, she thought, as things got fuzzy. Blood trickled down her forehead and her view of the blinking lights of LA down the slope grew blurrier.

The other car peeled off, and her heart beat faster and faster, realizing that all that was saving her and her car from plummeting straight down the hillside was a sturdy little cactus tree that appeared to be partially lodged under the front of her car. Snapping noises permeated the air, sending a clear message. It wasn't going to hold long, and she was going to crash down the steep, unforgiving hill into the rocks below

"Shit!" she shrieked, jamming her door open to jump out.

But the injury to her head was slowing her movements. She was fumbling, her aim inaccurate. Anything she'd learned in the police academy about vehicle extraction got lost in her aching skull, her roadside instincts dulled by too many years behind the microscope. Her car slowly crunched over the cactus, not offering apology as it consumed it. As she was edging down the fulcrum of the hillside, death calling for her, tears streamed down her cheek as she fumbled desperately at the door, searching for escape. Her distorted vision rendered her helpless, somewhere between lucid and not. The sound of a baby crying in the distance rang through her ears.

Then her car stopped edging forward.

And began to reverse.

Nausea darted through her throat as the ground shifted below her. Suddenly, the horizon was not where she thought it was. The LA lights were no longer in direct sight, but farther and farther away, as if her car was moving back up the hillside. Sitting cockeyed in the driver's seat, she was going to throw up. Either she was already dying or her car was magically moving back and over the fulcrum of its own accord. *Funny, I don't believe in magic.*

Her car came to a full stop back on the roadside, unmoving. Her driver's door then whipped open, and a masculine form with a black mask covering his face and a black hood up reached in to grab her. Like she weighed nothing, he heaved her out, then threw her over his shoulder.

Then she blacked out.

When she woke up, after God knew how long, she was still in the arms of the masked man, being carried somewhere. In the darkness, she had no idea where she was. All she knew was that she wasn't far from the crash, and he was moving her to a second location.

"No," she slurred, her head still disconnected and pounding. *Never go to the second location.* Survival words flashed through her mind, but she had little recourse to offer.

Her captor slid her off his back and tried to stand her up against the side of what felt like a pickup truck, taking her shoulders in his hands to stabilize her. Still incapacitated and worsening, she tried to step away from him but lost her balance and collapsed into his warm, strong body. Holding her close, he grumbled words, though she couldn't make out what. The sudden change to being back on her feet seemed to drive all the blood out of her head. As if realizing that, he quickly grabbed the back of her neck and held on to her while she fell, passing out again. The last thing she remembered was trying to catch her breath against his masculine, hard chest, inhaling a woody scent that was too good to be true.

Kendra didn't know how long she was out or what happened to her, but when she woke up, she was in the darkness of her small backyard in the Malibu hills, seated comfortably upright on her favorite chaise.

She wasn't alone.

Slowly blinking open her eyes, she sensed someone holding a wet cloth on her forehead. Through the dim moonlight, she could see a concerned masculine gaze looking down on her behind a black mask. Her captor. So, he hadn't killed her...*yet.* Her back stiffening and alarmed as all hell, she tried to rise — but he pushed her back down, firm and commanding.

"Keep your head down," he ordered, keeping his voice low. "The bleeding has stopped, but you still need to chill." He touched above her brow with the cloth, retracting it to assess the amount of blood it had collected.

She felt deep soreness as she raised her eyebrows, trying to get a better look. Her head pounding, she struggled to rub two thoughts together.

"Who are you?" she coughed out. "How did you find me?"

He didn't answer as he held her wrist with his fingers, counting the beats in her pulse. He ran his rough hands up her arm, likely inspecting for further damage. The way he moved them over her body, it was like he knew his way. She clenched her teeth as he ran his hand up her neck to her face, where the bruising was sure to be starting. She had no ability to push back, since she was still recovering from the blow on the steering wheel. Had she been concussed?

Perched on the edge of the chaise, studying her intently, his voice, his eyes — there was something too familiar to deny, but she didn't want to concede it. She sucked in breath, tension tightening its hold on her throat. When was she going to wake up?

"Why are you doing this?" she demanded in a weak voice.

He locked his widened eyes with hers, exposing just how livid he was. Staring down into her aching face, he shot back with a question. "Why the hell would someone do this to you?"

"I don't know. It was an accident. Someone was speeding — " she started to rationalize.

"No," the masked man revised, very matter-of-factly. "Someone tried to *force* you off the road. This wasn't an accident."

She sucked in breath as he touched a sore spot on her head, wincing beneath his rough, thick fingers. *Drive me off the road? It was intentional?* That didn't make sense.

But...where did he come from? She leaned back, her senses still hurting. She batted his hand away — or tried to — but he caught it, sending her a dogged look. He was in control, not her. And that was a reminder she didn't need.

"You need more help than I can give," he stated, removing the cloth from her forehead. "I'm taking you to a hospital."

"I'm fine." She struggled to push herself up into a sitting position, trying to prove it.

"You're not fine" — his gaze changed as he watched her sit up, never breaking eye contact — "and I'm not a doctor."

"Then, who *are* you?"

Now sitting before him, she could see how much longer his limbs were. He was tall, very tall. Strapping, even. As she leaned forward, blinking him into focus, she could sense him breathing in harder the closer she got. Something about his scent was familiar and mouth-watering. His reaction to her was telling, and the air between them grew heavy.

A little punch drunk, she reached over, delicately trailing her hands up his neck. Seeming to allow her, he ran his hands down her forearms, supporting her, embracing her, as she inched forward, like she was touching an animal in the wild for the first time. She kept pushing her luck as he seemed to allow her to run her fingers over his black mask and its soft, stretchy fabric. She slowly pulled it up, inch by inch, revealing a strong jaw that needed a shave followed by a beautiful, wide mouth. She'd never forget that mouth — how it tasted and what it had once done to her.

"Why are you here?" she whispered, meaning something much more complex.

There was a pause between them before he replied.

"You don't know?"

Her heart beat faster and faster, and she couldn't stop herself. There were things she needed to know, answers that he owed her. As she pulled the mask up, revealing the face of her protector, she traced a long scar on his cheek that shot upward underneath the mask toward his brow — one that she'd always wanted to understand, but that he would never explain. Drawing in breath as she touched it, he retracted, leaving her hand hovering in thin air. Her body involuntarily tensed in response, as if waking up, and suddenly, the dynamic shifted.

Now that there was a clear separation between them, he watched her as she came to her senses and realized that she'd known all along exactly who he was. It was just that…she hadn't wanted to believe it. He wasn't supposed to be her bodyguard. He was the enemy.

"He must have been following you," Delta pushed on, steering the conversation back to where he wanted it. "I don't know if he's trying to scare you or kill you, but this is what — "

"No," Kendra cut him off, crossing her arms tightly. "It was an accident. There's no way Hunter would have done this. He's on my side."

"Like hell."

"At least he's been here. Where have *you* been?"

She bit her lip after the words came out. He studied her in response, letting the conversation lapse, refusing to acknowledge her question. His mouth twisted in a way she hadn't seen before — wild anger clearly lingering just one level under the surface.

"You can't stay here" — he nodded to her house — "not without protection."

"Back to this, are we?"

"I'm warning you. Don't take it lightly," he growled at her, his frustration apparently mounting. "I've seen enough."

"And why should I trust you?" she pushed back, unwilling to yield. "Why should I trust you over him?"

Delta broke, seizing her wrists and yanking her hard into his body. His voice deepened, dark and intimidating, as he glared at her. "You can and you *will* trust me."

"Give me one good reason to," she snapped.

"I knew I was going to regret this."

Abruptly dropping his head, he took her mouth his own, his kiss as rough as it was unapologetic.

Chapter Five

Delta held the back of Kendra's head as he consumed her, relishing in the sweetness of her lips. He shouldn't, but he couldn't *not*. Her feminine, fuck-me pout felt like it belonged with his, and he didn't hesitate to command the kiss to his liking. Her eyes were hazy, the needy sigh escaping her mouth only encouraging him. Damn, he'd felt her surrender to him like that before—and he wanted it again and again. She was the obsession he'd tried to excise.

A hot rush of pure desire ripped up his chest as he dropped his hand from the back of her head. He toyed with her tongue, remembering what it felt like to kiss her. He traced her curves, holding her against him, needing more.

As he deepened the kiss, things he tried to forget crashed to the front of his thoughts—memories he'd pushed away. He replayed that one night last year when her body had been under his as he'd fucked her to within an inch of her life, drawing every goddamn orgasm possible out of her. Now his cock hardened as he held her tight once again. He grinned, never letting up, seizing a moment they would likely both regret. And that was when it hit him. It was all a dream, turning fast into a nightmare.

He didn't want to be there. He didn't want to be back. He didn't want any of it.

But he had to be.

He retreated slightly, but the way she moaned his name onto his lips again drew him back in. He allowed himself one last chance to taste her, taste the 'one that got away'. Feeling her tight waist matched by soft hips, he needed to squeeze her harder and harder until he made her scream. He knew he should stop before he lost it and he did just that.

"Please," she pleaded, just as he liked. "Please... Matteo."

Then he realized she was pushing him *away*. And using his Christian name was a sure-fire way to bring him to his senses. He gazed into her eyes and his assessment wasn't good. She was still as pissed off as she'd ever been. In fact, it was worse. He'd stepped over the line.

"What the hell are you doing?" Kendra gasped, clearly at a loss. She blinked her big, blue eyes rapidly at him, likely in shock.

His mouth dropped as she pushed herself back on the chaise, clearly trying to process what he'd done. It was goddamn strange, but he couldn't ignore how something in him felt stretched as she moved away and formed a chasm between them. He ran his gaze up and down the raw, natural beauty he'd thought about every day for a fucking year, wondering what the hell had just come over him and where he'd lost control.

"Well?" Kendra pressed, folding her arms protectively once again as she sat in front of him, pert and stubborn.

"Well, what?"

She narrowed her eyes on him, waiting for his response. It was clear that she wasn't willing to play games anymore. He bit into the inside his cheek, self-punishing. How the fuck had he ever landed her? She was so damn analytical, so damn smart.

And I'm just a fucking idiot.

"I didn't plan that." Delta straightened his back, compartmentalizing.

"Yeah, sure—I wasn't born yesterday. How the fuck do I know it wasn't you who ran me off the road, just to have a chance to play the hero role?"

Fury flushed to the tip of his tongue, but he held back. He flexed every muscle in his body, controlling his response, and chose to pivot the conversation. He threw out the olive branch, deciding he had to do something.

"Let's cut a deal."

Taken aback, she darted her eyes back and forth across his face, a wrinkle appearing between her brows.

"A deal?"

"I'll watch out for you until we can figure out what the hell happened tonight with the car," he offered, knowing full well who was going to benefit more from the situation.

"And in return?" she reacted, searching him for the second shoe to drop. "You'll stay the fuck away?"

Christ. That was a damn good question. He clenched his teeth so hard they hurt, reeling in her contempt. He tried to answer in the affirmative that she'd requested but couldn't. Staying away was no longer an option, at least for the short term.

With his silence, she then tilted her head, adding, "So, what do you want in return?"

"To teach you a lesson."

"Always so selfless, Matteo. A veritable knight in shining armor."

Dismissing him, she snapped her eyebrows together disapprovingly. She then simply shook her head, obviously bitter as hell. His muscles involuntarily flinched with her slight, driving a blaze of pain up his scar.

Without thinking, he grabbed her arm, yanking her into him and threatening to kiss her again if she kept it up. He welcomed the seeming fear spreading across her face — the fear that he'd do something neither of them could stop. It was a barbaric tactic, but the way she made him feel caused him to do those kinds of things.

It drove him wild to know that he could turn her on just as much as she could him. When he gripped her harder, she blinked rapidly, her eyelashes flickering and biting her lip. He let himself breathe her in. She was so much *more* than she ever gave herself credit for, he thought, as he absorbed every last freckle on her sun-kissed nose.

"You can't do this alone," he concluded. "You know you can't."

"I can" — she pulled back, snarling — "and you'd better get it straight. I don't want your lecture. I don't like you. And you are *not* welcome in my life."

She made to stand, wobbling and struggling to catch her balance on her feet. He lunged, reflexively reaching, gripping her waist to prevent her from falling face first onto her patio stones.

"For fuck's sake, Kendra."

Of course, she irritably pushed him away, a fraught cry escaping her throat. She was clearly desperate to be on her own two feet—to be alone. He heard that as he watched her stumble toward her back door. His mind running at a thousand miles per second, he accepted that he couldn't let her handle things alone. He'd seen enough in one day to trigger deep concern.

He crept farther back in her yard, closer to the fence, watching her sway in the darkness. Hurt. Vulnerable. She exhaled in frustration in the distance, saying nothing, but meaning everything. He felt it too. He'd shown up with one plan and was leaving with another.

One final time, she turned her face back to him, watching his shadow in the darkness. Putting his mask and hood back on, he listened to her final request.

"Stay away from me."

A few ungentlemanly thoughts crossed his mind as he watched her disappear. It wasn't like him to allow things to end like this—not on his terms—but he had to be somewhere else. Readying himself to hop her fence, he pulled the second glove out of his pocket, matching it up with the first—the second most important thing he'd recovered from Kendra's car.

Chapter Six

Out of the Malibu hills and back into the LA basin, it didn't take Delta more than an hour before he found himself at his target destination. Willow Avenue had found itself home to a number of commercial and industrial spaces, including a non-descript five-story red brick building on the edge of the city. It was a building that wanted no attention and advertised nothing.

Delta considered himself an open-minded kind of guy, but there was one thing he didn't do — visitor's passes. And that was partially why he found himself taking the shadowy side entrance to the building he'd once visited legitimately in the sober light of day. Plus, he didn't doubt building security would have questions about why he was carrying a pistol and a bunch of gear that could only be described as break-in tools.

Ninja shit.

In dusty black jeans—ripped in the thigh from hopping a barbed fence the past week—and a thick black long-sleeve shirt with enough pockets to carry gear, he pulled out an instrument used to pick the lock on the delivery receiving door. By that time of night, it was closed off and secured. It was a good thing he was an expert at that shit. He could do it in his sleep. He had his black hood up, his black mask on and the barrel of his pistol dug into his tailbone, held by a pancake holster in the back of his jeans. He didn't expect trouble—but he intended to create it.

Delta was comforted by the cold steel of the gun's barrel chilling his skin as he crouched low to assess a light he saw on the bottom part of the door frame. It flickered, and he flinched before taking a deep breath to calm his mind. It wasn't a camera. Just a light reflection, he realized, before returning to his task.

Seeing Kendra was a mindfuck and had left him feeling all shades of messed up—even more messed up than a guy who spent all night, every night, doing anything but sleeping. Hell, every goddamn night, being alone reminded him of what he'd lost. Though, he wasn't sure if he'd really lost something he'd never gained. It had only been one night.

Unfortunately, the memory of her pouting, sexy mouth pressed against his was just fucking distracting—so much so that he nearly dropped his instrument on the concrete. Fumbling to catch it, he felt the lock crack. *Shit.* He froze, holding the door handle tightly, praying to fucking God that he hadn't wrecked the damn mission.

Damn, memories of Kendra were wildly disruptive. It had been a year since their one-night stand, but he'd never gotten over it. His mind stirred, unable to shake the sensory details — her long, lean back arching as he held her wrists down, on top of her, giving her everything he had. She liked it hard and rough, liked it when he owned her. She wanted to be claimed, and he had been more than happy to do it. That aging memory had served him more times than he'd like to count that year, deployed in another hellhole with nothing but a helmet to serve as a pillow.

Delta sucked in air, dazed. It was time to raid. He braced himself against the door, exhaling slowly, trying to refocus his mind and urging the blood back out of his cock. He didn't have enough in his system to supply both his dick and his brain at the same time. And once he breached the door, it was fucking time. He had to get his game face on. He had to be in and out — and be smart about it, too — get what he needed and get out before getting caught.

Turning the handle to test, he gazed down at his glove, the one he'd recovered, and noticed a small hole in the knuckle. Letting out a breath of relief, he counted his blessings when the door popped and opened. He shook his head. Luck was always on his side. A cold rush rippled up his arms, like an icy storm brewing.

Within seconds, Delta was stalking silently up the stairs, honing in on the lab stationed on the top floor. He'd been there before, so he knew where he was going. Out of the stairwell, the hallway was as quiet as the night, and he needed it to stay that way. He slunk low and quick, making his path to the secure entry to the lab, where he knew guards were stationed. He'd have to fight his way in.

Delta had fought for his country for years — fighting for what was right, fighting for the innocent in the worst, most insane war zones. Now, he should be like his best friend — retired with a girl on his arm and a kid on the way. But that wasn't him. He was a hunter, and he was hunting…because he didn't have a choice.

Why the fuck are they doing it? Delta thought, gripping his pistol outside the secure entry, listening to the voices inside. He didn't fear the fight into the lab, but he feared what he would find inside. They'd been progressing faster than planned, faster than Delta could keep up with. Innocent people were getting caught up in a game they didn't understand.

Pulling his pistol out of the back of his jeans, he leaned against the wall beside the secure entry, out of sight of the camera that hung in the corner as well as the peephole on the office door. Delta knew the angles. He'd been trained to know. They'd trained him to be the best, and he'd trained himself to be better than that.

With a curt rap on the door, he waited patiently as surprised voices scuffled about within. The guards were checking security cameras. Cameras, he knew, were everywhere in the building. But that was exactly what was on his side. There were too many cameras for them to adequately watch them all. Delta relied on his inhuman speed and stealth for the element of surprise.

So, he remained out of sight, which allowed the familiar sound of shock and fear to be heard from the interior. Those were sounds he recognized well — ones that energized him and ran through his veins like a tonic. Sounds that gave him the feeling that shit was about to go down.

The security door opened a crack, but before he let the staff get a good look, he hurtled his heavy foot against the door, crashing it open and aiming his gun at the guards.

"Get the fuck down!" he ordered.

Chapter Seven

One year before

"Why are we training with the SEALs?" Kendra balked as she tied her running shoe that was propped against her car.

Beside her, adjusting his workout shorts, Hunter snickered. "Don't worry, kid. They won't bite."

Kid? Kendra stood, giving her staff sergeant the side-eye. Fiddling with her outfit—black athletic tights and slack-fit light gray T-shirt—she silently fumed. Hunter's words surprisingly failed to comfort her.

Hunter kicked off, marching through the SEAL base toward the training course, forcing Kendra to catch up behind him. Since she'd been jogging, the heat rose at the back of her neck. For the middle of an LA winter, it was unseasonably warm. Up in the mountain traverses, she gazed down to the valley where the afternoon's sweltering heat was rising. She tugged again at her T-shirt, wondering if it was too tight. Or was it too loose?

Or maybe it was too warm for the weather? Whatever it was, it wasn't good enough.

She was freaking out.

"Jesus." She brushed a bead of sweat off her forehead, observing the obstacle course set up by the Navy to train special operators in urban warfare.

She was more nervous than her time at the police academy—the young, female academic who hadn't quite belonged then or even now. And the guys sure as hell hadn't let her forget it. She was a scientist, first and foremost—a bookish nerd. Forensics was the only place she felt at ease.

Certainly not at military facilities, she thought as she gazed in horror over the scene in front of her. The only thing more intimidating than the rope climbs and tower jumps was the array of SEALs lined up in the distance, confident and assured, casually chatting with the cops from her group. There were about thirty of them in total, and they'd formed a small crowd around the first obstacle—where their 'team building' session was supposed to start. It reminded her of everything she'd done at the police academy—and everything she sucked at.

She trailed behind Hunter, hiding in his wake, as they made their way to the larger group of cops waiting for further instruction. Most of the cops were eager to get on with it, eager to train alongside the infamous rough-and-ready SEALs. Adding to her dread, she was one of the few women there. And the way her blonde hair caught the sun like a beacon, she knew she'd be a target. It wasn't easy being a woman in a man's world.

Let's just get this over with. Kendra breathed in shakily as she secretly watched the military operators leaning against the rappelling tower not far from her.

Everything in her body screamed for her to get back to her car and drive away. The whole experience, which promised to be fun for the guys, represented the maximum in discomfort to her.

She didn't miss the sly looks she was getting from the SEALs, who were sniffing her out. Crossing her arms tightly, like a self-hug, she found herself trying to appear unapproachable, serious.

"Heads up, people," gray-haired Inspector Hall called over the crowd from the front, checking to make sure everyone was there. *The big boss from LAPD.*

As the group silenced, he continued, "Thanks for showing up today — and thanks to Paul for giving us the opportunity for a different type of training."

Hall nodded to a veteran SEAL beside him who was literally shaped like an upside-down triangle. With a shaved head and aerodynamic sunglasses, the man stood as still as a statue, seemingly scanning the group for weakness. Once he got to Kendra, she felt like she'd been X-rayed and diagnosed as 'soft'.

After Hall continued with safety protocols and instructions, the mass of cops and operators were split up into teams to run the obstacle course. Hall made it clear that after the tower climbs, rope jumps and holding bars, they were expected to rappel off a three-story metal structure. Kendra literally shook at the thought, already knowing the truth.

I can't do this, a little voice inside her head shrieked. Embarrassed already, she watched the first wave of teams attack the course with ferocity — leaping, jumping and barreling over obstacles.

Doesn't anyone else have any fear? Her question was quickly answered as teams started breaking off onto the course. Her team was the last scheduled to go — *even worse*. They'd all have time to sit back and watch her fail.

"Nervous?" a deep voice came from behind her.

She whipped around, searching.

And there *he* stood — a towering, muscled SEAL with a boyish grin, perfect teeth and flowing dark blond hair. His brown eyes poured into her, his mouth widening in understanding, assessing her.

"It's okay if you are," he added, keeping his voice down.

"I'm not," she rebuffed quickly, unwilling to get vulnerable.

"Are you Kendra?"

Her eyebrow raised, she nodded quickly, feeling a little shellshocked under his alluring gaze.

"Delta." He reached out, offering her his hand. "You're on my team."

She took it, feeling his rough, calloused powerful handshake. She pumped back as hard as possible, promising herself that she wouldn't be weak — that she could be tough.

"I'll walk you through this," Delta assured her, nodding to the course.

But someone else cut in.

"I've got her. Don't worry." A less-than-amused voice belonging to Hunter appeared on the other side of her.

Kendra's head spun, observing Hunter to her right and Delta to her left. She didn't want to say it, but Delta was everything Hunter was not. The SEAL was a dominant, bold presence — Alpha. Hunter clearly felt that, felt threatened, and pushed forward to stand closer to Kendra, as if being closer meant that they were a tight duo.

Someone at the starting line called for their team, letting them know they were on deck. Hunter sped off, leaving the SEAL in his dust. Kendra didn't mistake the competitiveness rising in the air.

Watching the last teams break out onto the course, she let out a breath she hadn't known she was holding as she caught up to the starting line. The first obstacle was like a net made of rope that one had to climb up to the top. It was probably close to two stories high. In her usual habit, she ran her teeth along her bottom lip, feeling nervousness creep up. She had to climb... *that* in front of everyone?

"I just can't."

"Sure, you can"—Delta's head dropped beside her—"mind over matter."

She turned up to him, realizing how close he was standing. *Where'd he come from?*

"I'll go with you," he added.

"With me?" she repeated.

"Sure, and you don't have to crest the top." His eyes glimmered as he checked her out, his gaze trailing up and down. "You've got this."

She took in a deep breath, following behind him as he positioned them at the starting line. She surprised herself as she breathed him in, relishing the masculine scent of his body. Something mounted inside her, like an awakening.

"I won't let you fall," he added, seeming to understand. His golden hair glinted in the raging sunlight as he gazed down, continually assessing her.

She only could guess what he was thinking.

"Thanks," she squeaked out before trying to appear more relaxed.

"Do you want me to stay behind you?" he asked, exposing the fact that he was the only man in the entire group who gave a fuck.

She bit her lip again, glancing back up at the ridiculous obstacle, then at him.

"I don't want to put you out," she replied, feeling guilty for being fucking dead weight. "I'm sure you want to do your best. You don't have to follow me around."

Delta laughed, dismissing her. "Nah, I do this one all the time. I'd rather get you through it. Come on."

She blinked back at him, lost for words. His casual confidence was more than reassuring. In the sea of chaos and male grunting in the background, no one seemed to notice what was happening between them — no one except Hunter, who stood off to the side, giving the SEAL a fierce side-eye.

It didn't take long for all the other teams to get through the obstacles, and the timekeeper yelled at them to go. Right away, a huffing Hunter made for the ropes, likely attempting to prove his masculinity was equal to that of the SEALs.

"So, what do you say?" Delta focused on her, watching Hunter race off.

She gazed at him, realizing he was the only guy left standing beside her. She bit her lip and nodded.

"Okay. Sure."

Sprinting with him to the first obstacle, she realized that he made her feel like she could do it. Absorbing the energy off his body as he ran behind her, she realized he was staying close. Not weirdly close, but close enough to be promising. He was there.

He had her back.

Abruptly halting before the first obstacle — the rope structure — she glanced up, watching Hunter climb to what seemed like impossible heights.

"You can do this." Delta's voice was quiet but firm as he motioned for her to come beside him, stepping on the first rope. "Come on."

Kendra sucked in a bottomless breath and jumped up onto the first rope beside Delta to start her climb. For the first time, she felt like it was going to be okay. She began to feel relief washing over her, knowing that she wasn't going to have to do it alone.

The ropes swayed in the wind. It was damn hard, testing her physically and mentally. She climbed up and up, feeling Delta beside her, watching her. He stayed right there, close enough to grab her if she fell. On the other side, Hunter was already climbing down and glaring at her through the ropes.

Seeing that she wasn't far from the top, her next question was — *how the hell am I supposed to flip myself over the top and climb back down the other side?* Her body shook when she understood her problem.

"Please, legs, don't fail me now," she begged.

"Just don't look down," Delta ordered, and she realized he was reaching out to hold her.

His warm touch assured her just a little — just enough to get her nodding her understanding.

He continued, unrelenting, "Just pretend you're hopping a fence. Crest the top, and crawl down the other side."

"Oh my God," she whispered again as she grabbed the top, trying to heave herself up and over. "Like I'm hopping a fence? Who do you think I am?"

He laughed, working to get her to the top. She tensed, unsure if it was the fear of heights or just the feeling of his hands on her.

White-knuckled and gripping the top rope, she grumbled to him, "This isn't my thing. I like thinking and books and stuff."

Delta's thick paw was on her waist, stabilizing her, and he quipped back, "Thinking is cool and all, but have you ever rappelled off a building?"

"I'll be lucky if I never do," she countered, swinging her leg over the top.

"Well, have I got a surprise for you." He chuckled as he heaved her over the fulcrum. His support and encouragement were all that kept her moving, thawing her frozen limbs.

"Oh God." Her grip tightening in abject fear, she wanted to scream as she observed all the people below. They were like ants.

"You're almost there," Delta assured her. "Just get the other leg over. I told you that I won't let you fall. I've got you, so just *trust* me." His words hit her hard, and they locked eyes. She let out a tense breath, taking in his stunning brown gaze that was caught in sunlight as their bodies swayed on the ropes.

Trust him?

"Okay," she replied, her voice shaking. "Okay."

She followed his commands as he directed her, and next thing she knew, she was on the other side. She let out a little yelp of joy, followed by Delta chuckling to himself. Once he was over the top and on the other side, he began climbing down next to her.

"Nice guy," Delta grumbled sarcastically, his eyes narrowing on her staff sergeant before turning back to her. She tightened her hands on the rope, watching

Hunter moving fast through the next obstacle, like he'd forgotten she existed.

"And people ask me what it's like being a woman in a male-dominated job." Kendra exhaled as she shakily lowered herself down onto the next rope, moving slowly down the structure. "You're always on your own, at least by my experience."

Feeling Delta's presence beside her, he said, "On my team, you're never alone."

She froze, but this time for a different reason. If only she'd had someone whispering those supportive words to her at police academy and throughout her career. Connecting with him, she couldn't deny that he lit something in her that she couldn't explain—a confidence to push forward, to push herself.

More determined and more focused, she moved methodically down the ropes, watching Delta climb down beside her and mirroring his movements. He was much, much better at it than her, obviously. She was unstable, to say the least. But she was trying and, surprisingly, she was still alive.

She was overjoyed when her feet landed on the grassy ground. Delta jumped off the ropes, thumping down onto the ground beside her. He held up his palms for a double high-five, beaming at her.

"Good fucking job, tiger," Delta chuckled as she enthusiastically smacked his hands. "You aren't so bad at this. I don't know what you were all worried about."

She grinned in return, feeling a high. Shooting him a look, she replied, "Thanks." Her gaze flitted around, realizing they were the only two people left on the course.

"This is why they put me at the end," she sighed as they jogged toward the next obstacle. "They knew I would suck."

"Nah, it's just saving the best for last." He reached over, squeezing her shoulder into him, literally melting her against his rock-solid body. *I'm the best?* A little smile tugged at her lips, and for the first time, she felt like less of an outsider and more like she belonged.

With that newfound sense of confidence, she leaped at the next obstacle, letting Delta help her again. He pumped her up, lifting her at her waist so she could grab the metal bars at the top, swinging herself across the structure like playground monkey bars that crossed over a swampy mess below. She stopped caring that everyone was watching them and seeing how much fun they were having together.

As he kept her pushing through the rest of the course, Delta laughed behind her as she slipped and fell off the last bar, but at least managed to jump to the side into the sand.

"It's a tough one," he said, pulling her up and dusting her off. "Let's keep at it."

He hoisted her back up to grab the last bar again so she could complete it without fail, making her feel like it didn't matter how long she was taking. He was going to see her finish it. He didn't seem to give a fuck what anyone else thought, either, showing that he was clearly a confident leader in the group.

"I can do this," she told herself as she leaped off the last bar, completing another obstacle.

"Damn straight," he called behind her, "with a goddamn vengeance."

As they finished up the course, having crushed one obstacle after another, her heart was beating faster and faster. Her muscles were growing exhausted, but she didn't care — something about being next to Delta made her feel things she hadn't felt in a long time. Everyone else had expected her to quit, to flunk it — but she wasn't. She was doing it.

With his final encouragement, they sprinted toward a tall tower. She nearly stopped before it, but he grabbed her hand and pulled her with him. He apparently wasn't going to let her fail now, and he wasn't going to leave her behind. Taking the narrow, winding staircase upward, Kendra gathered that the entire group at the training facility had crowded around the bottom of the rappelling tower — some cheering her on, some not.

As she and Delta made it to the top of the tower, she lost her breath, collapsing and taking a knee on the metal. Three stories high on an open structure was pretty fucking scary. If the rope climb had seemed high, this was practically a skyscraper. Even though she logically knew that wasn't the case, her fear of heights spiraled out of control. Delta put his arm around her, pulling her in. He beamed down on her, having way too much fun with what he was putting her through.

"Holy fuck," she squeaked, feeling that unadulterated vertigo.

"Don't worry. I'll go down with you."

"I'm freaking out." She blinked back at him, trying to not look around at the danger right before her. "I think I'm going to pass."

"You've come all this way. You've got this."

Delta's voice was reassuring beside her, and once again he reached for her hand to lead her over the edge. However pliant they'd been before, her limbs had returned quickly to being tense and reluctant. She couldn't even move. Her heart rate was through the roof. All eyes were on her. *Am I going to do it?* She stood stiffly, trying not to pass out.

She bit her lip, deeply regretting that she'd ever signed that consent waiver. That seemed like an oversight. Trying to ignore the fact that there were no guard rails, she perched on the narrow platform, wishing she'd given her sister a copy of her will.

Delta knelt and slipped a rappel belt up her thighs, harnessing it in place across her waist. He flicked the snaps and tightened it to fit her properly. His deft hands, working too close to her core, made her ache for his touch all over, making her even more uncomfortable.

"I don't know what to do," she murmured.

"I'll let you down slow. Hold on to the rope," he said calmly as he was explaining the process to her. "Just swing your foot over the edge, and I'll do the rest. All you have to do is hold the rope and climb down."

"Okay, okay," she replied, her voice cracking.

As he made his final adjustments, heaving at the rappel system to ensure stability, she confessed, "They think I'm going to eat it. I'm a joke to them."

He turned her toward him, speaking so low that no one else could hear. "Does it matter what they think? Fuck those guys." His dark, determined focus poured that last little bit of needed confidence into her.

"I'm not cut out for this. I'm just not good at —" Her anxious voice trailed off.

"I bet you are damn good at a lot of things, Kendra." Delta's gaze hardened as he drove his words into her. "That's very clear to me."

As his assertion washed over her, she grew even more breathless gazing into his striking face, giving herself permission to feel what she'd been repressing all afternoon.

"Just listen to me. Trust me—and I promise you won't be eatin' nothing but dinner tonight," he again assured her, straightening his spine as he stared down the tower. "So, you better tell me where I'm taking you."

When he held the rope where it was bound to the handrail, his muscles flexed as he gripped her only lifeline. Biting her lip, she flashed her eyes over the side. It was happening. It was going to happen.

"I've got you," he once again reminded her, encouraging her on. "Let's go."

So, she listened—and she trusted. For the first time in a long time, she did—blindly trusting Delta with her life. Swinging her foot over the edge, gripping the rope for dear life, she allowed her body to rappel down the wood planks bolted onto the side of the structure. Delta was the only thing between her and falling several stories down. Lowering herself one step at a time, she softened her grip on the rope slowly and surely.

"Oh my God," she said to herself, "I'm doing this!"

She was one third of the way down—*not bad*. When she gazed up at Delta, he beamed down on her, shouting words of encouragement. Something warm hit Kendra in her chest—in her heart.

But...then her rope got stuck.

"Shit," she said, tugging at it. "*Shit*."

"Wait," Delta ordered. "Stop."

But she was too damn nervous to stop as she pulled at the rope again and again to release it. Then she realized it had lost its tautness. The mechanism at the top had faltered. She looked up, grasping the urgency splashed across Delta's face.

"*Fuck.*"

"Oh God!" she cried out, while shouting commenced below her.

Delta immediately jumped down, grabbing the rope in one hand and sliding down the side of the tower — with no rappel belt. Just as he flung his body next to hers, the rope attached to her belt finally broke away from the mechanism and began dropping her in free fall. But, before she could plummet to her doom, Delta grabbed her to him just in time, and expertly kicked off the side of the building — rappelling fast and hard, bringing them both safely to the ground.

"Oh my God, oh my God." She tried to catch her breath, feeling a crowd rush around her.

He'd *saved* her.

Delta leaned into her, grinning. "I told you it was fun."

Inspector Hall tapped on her other shoulder, drawing her attention and asking her if she was okay. He eyed the head SEAL to the side as they both examined her. It was clear that they'd just dodged a nasty bullet.

Trying to smile like she was fine, she couldn't ignore the hot knife stabbing into her back when she overheard some guy making a snide comment about why they shouldn't bring women to this type of training. Leaning back against the wooden side of the tower, she struggled to stabilize herself as she fielded questions from onlookers. Everyone was trying to figure out what the hell had happened. She felt dizzy, but now not just because of the near accident.

"What the fuck did you do?" Hunter's voice hit her from the side. "You could have gotten hurt or worse, Kendra."

She turned to him, struggling for words. He was shooting looks between her and Delta, who was momentarily distracted, fielding questions from his boss.

"I-I didn't do anything," she stammered to Hunter in disbelief.

Delta spun, apparently realizing she was getting grilled. His shoulders tensed as he shot Hunter a fierce look.

"Is there a problem here?"

Hunter stepped in between her and Delta, snarling. "Yeah, there's a fucking problem. You almost killed her."

"I did, did I?" Delta remained cool, studying his opponent.

"I'm taking her home." Hunter grabbed at her arm.

"Sit the fuck down." Delta took one intimidating step closer.

"Fucking SEALs." Hunter fell back, grumbling as he released her. "She's my fucking sergeant. Who is she to you?"

"She ain't yours like that." Delta squared himself, planting his body firmly in between them.

Before Hunter could counter, Inspector Hall spun back around, looking between the three of them. Kendra wondered if he saw what she saw — a protective SEAL and a retreating staff sergeant.

As she cast a side glance at Delta, he shot her a mysterious grin, like he had something up his sleeve. There was something glinting in his eyes. Then, he stood to his full height, confident and solid, calling out over the crowd.

"First round's on me, boys," Delta boomed, and his announcement was met by cheers.

She slipped the rappel belt off her shaking thighs, wanting to disappear.

"You need to refuel. Dinner?" Delta said down to her, pressuring her to accept. "Come on."

"I—" Kendra started, searching for words. "I shouldn't—"

He crossed his arms, scowling down his nose at her in his 'don't fuck with me' way—both intimidating and stirring. He was simply undeniable.

She bit her lip as she grew the courage to ask him, "Why did you help me?" She nodded back to the obstacle course. "You were the only one—and I just want to know *why* you did it?"

"You don't know?"

A little grin tugged one side of his mouth up, exposing his row of straight white teeth. Dipping his head and locking eyes with her, he demanded, "Just *come*."

Her lips parted at the words, a hot pink flush running up her face. *Did he mean to say it that way?* She stirred, nearly jumping out of her skin. He curled his lips at her reaction, and Kendra knew then exactly what his game was. It was just that under his gaze, something inside her felt electrified. It was the something inside that had been alone, lost in her books for too long.

He wanted her to trust him.

And so, she cautiously accepted his invitation.

Chapter Eight

Present day

"I'm starting to get the feeling you really wanted to know what was in that blood." Lily leaned against the lab counter, fiddling with test tubes while side-assessing Kendra.

Kendra exhaled slowly, knowing it was true. "But it's not possible now, is it? We didn't get enough of a sample, and I've lost the glove now. It's gone."

She bit her lip, hating how the glove had suspiciously disappeared in the car accident days before. She'd had the repair shop search her car for anything left inside, but its absence only led her to one conclusion. Delta had taken it back.

Lily grinned, looking down into the microcentrifuge between them. "Well, you may not have the glove, but we still have that small sample."

Kendra lunged forward. "But it's not enough? We barely scraped it for the PCR."

"Sure, it is. I trimmed a piece of material off the glove's knuckle, right where the dried blood was — very small, barely noticeable," Lily said as they watched the machine work. "I hope it's enough to give you the answers you seek."

Kendra blinked as she observed the machine working, running aspects of the sample inside it. The answers she was looking for were just hours away.

"God, I hope so, too," Kendra whispered to herself.

She couldn't admit out loud just how important it had become to her — how much she wanted to understand the irregularities in Delta's blood. Lily watched her, checking out the bruising that lingered on her temple from the car accident. Pensively, she reached up to touch her aching face. Kendra wasn't the type of woman to engage in games with trust.

"Are you okay, Kendra?" Lily asked in a lower voice, concerned and compassionate. "Have you gone to see a doctor yet?"

Kendra let out a low breath, shaking her head. "No, I'm fine. I don't need to see a doctor."

"Don't need to — or don't want to?" Lily challenged her.

Kendra's focus shot to her junior colleague. The truth hurt. Don't *want* to was a far better description of how she felt. She did not want to go into the hospital or the clinic — or wherever. She did not want to see a doctor, just to hear them reiterate everything that she knew was wrong with her.

"You've got to take care of yourself, Kendra." Lily spoke gently, as if knowing she was overstepping.

"I am doing just fine," Kendra answered as she smoothed the outside of her brow where her head had hit the steering wheel, feeling the pain that lingered. "It's going to heal. It was just an accident."

Her final words came out like someone trying to convince themself, so she stopped. Lily raised her eyebrows but said nothing else, seeming to know more than she let on. It was no secret that Kendra was ultra-independent—to the point of pure stubbornness.

Kendra relented. "I don't feel great right now. My head hurts, and it's all been a bit much lately."

Lily agreed, a sympathetic glimmer in her eyes. "The transition back to work is never easy. You've only been back at the lab for, what—a month now?"

Kendra gave a quick nod but didn't reply. She hadn't ever confided in Lily about all that had happened to her when she had been off work the past year—and she didn't want to. She didn't want to see those compassionate eyes flashing at her. She just wanted to feel normal, feel like she was good enough.

She just wanted to start over.

Taking in a deep breath secretly so Lily wouldn't hear, Kendra watched the young laboratorian jotting down analyses in her lab report book, diligently working through the list of standard checks.

"It may help your report to know that the owner of the glove was in the military," Kendra explained slowly, trying to get the conversation back on track. "The SEALs, to be exact."

Lily's lips formed an understanding circle as she nodded, her analytical eyes darting toward the test tubes and back to Kendra.

"I don't know what you expect to see," Lily began assuring her, "but I'm sure it's all normal."

"I just— I just need to see what's in his genes."

After a moment, the machine clicked, alerting them that it had an error. Lily immediately started working the console, trying to understand what the error code was telling her. She pulled out the instructions of the brand-new machine that were still hanging on the side.

"Error 72— Okay, now it's telling us that it needs the optimizer add-on to complete the analysis," Lily sighed, reading the material from the company. "The microchip optimizer assists in low-material situations—"

"The optimizer?"

Lily flipped through the pages of the manual.

"Ah, yes. It's an added cost to buy it, of course. And that makes sense—another way to make money." She sighed, slamming the manual down in frustration. "They don't give things away for free anymore."

Kendra darted her gaze back and forth, trying to figure out a solution. *Are we the only lab that has the new machine?*

"What about our sister lab up north—in Bakersfield?" Kendra pressed, wondering what options they had. "They always get the best equipment."

"Actually, I think they did buy the optimizer. Smaller police department, bigger lab budget—go figure," Lily scoffed in disbelief. "Field trip?"

Kendra reached forward and released the lock on the machine, pulling out the sample. Lily gave her a bright, questioning expression.

Kendra explained, "I'll take it to Bakersfield myself. I need you here to finish the real cases. Keep your eye out for plasma levels of doxycycline in those bodies. Don't tell Hunter anything, if he asks."

"So, you're skipping town?"

"Just for the night."

"You really need answers on this glove, don't you?" Lily let out a low laugh. "Okay, I won't say anything, and I'll get Hunter his report."

"God, I owe you. Thank you."

Palming the sample from the glove, Kendra moved to the exit. It was a long enough drive to Bakersfield that she needed to go home first and make arrangements. She hadn't gone away overnight for a long time, but this was something she needed to do, even if it meant being away from her baby for one night.

She had to understand her son's genetic inheritance. She had no choice.

Then it happened — the thing she really, really didn't want. A creeping sensation of guilt rushed through her mind, alerting her conscience to something she was failing to do. It was a question of morality at that point, something that Delta might be bereft of, but she wasn't. She had to tell him — eventually. She had to tell him that he had a son.

Clenching her teeth, she stuffed that feeling of guilt away in a locked corner of her mind. Until he proved worthy of trust, she had no obligation to tell Delta anything. But she did have an obligation to protect her son, and she would do anything to do that.

Chapter Nine

Delta moved through a shadowy bar not far from Venice Beach, finding his way to the back patio that looked out over the Pacific Ocean, the sun setting before him. It had been days since he'd been in Kendra's back yard, but it felt like months. He'd been damn busy. Each limb had its own level of pain and exhaustion—and no amount of lying in bed that afternoon had helped. He pushed through, determined not to show weakness.

A tall man with dark hair, graying at the temples, stood from a table in the corner of the patio as Delta approached. A wild smile crossed his mouth as he greeted his old friend.

"Don't you sleep anymore?" Carrick Byrne said as he shot out his hand to slap with Delta's. "I'd have thought time away from the platoon would do you some good."

"It hasn't been much of a vacation," Delta replied and nodded to the third man there. "Chief."

A serious man with reddish hair and bright blue eyes nodded back curtly. The platoon's boss, Leading Chief Petty Officer Warren Cameron, raised his drink — a stout, already half-drank.

"Finally, the man of honor, our own military hero, graces our presence."

"Give it a rest," Delta groaned, signing to the waitress to bring another round. "Don't give me that bullshit — not from you guys."

Carrick chuckled, taking a gulp of his brew. Something in his face seemed lighter, happier than Delta had ever seen him.

"Enjoying marital bliss?" Delta grunted at his best friend, raising his eyebrow.

"Hell yeah," Carrick grinned, leaning back on his chair, glancing out over the crashing waves of the ocean. "Wife and a kid — I'm living the dream. You should try it sometime."

"I think I have enough problems on the go." Delta shook his head, flexing his jaw and dismissing the possibility altogether.

Just few months earlier, Carrick's son had been born — nine months after Carrick had gotten married in a beachside affair. A part of Delta tweaked with jealousy, knowing he'd never have that for himself.

"I wouldn't think a man receiving the Medal of Honor would have problems," Warren said, his cunning eyes watchful. He saw right through Delta — always had. "Care to share?"

Delta opened his mouth to make something up, but the waitress appeared with a tray of freshly poured stouts, plunking down the dark pints in front of each man. Delta licked his lips, feeling thirstier than he'd thought. He brought the stout to his mouth, savoring the roasted caramel flavor, ingesting the only vitamins he was getting these days.

But Warren wouldn't let up.

"You are still going to the ceremony, right?" the chief pressed, pushing up his shirt sleeves as he studied Delta, who sat across the table from him. "Not every day this medal is handed out."

A frosted beer glass in his hand, Delta turned it in contemplation. A warning tone escaped his mouth. "It shouldn't be me getting it. It's not right, man."

Both Carrick and Warren raised their eyebrows, leaning in. It was clear that drinks with the guys had a purpose that night. They were there to pressure him.

"I knew you weren't planning on showing up," Carrick said, his elbows on the table. "Ever since we got back, you've been twisted. This isn't you."

"You can't just *not* go to a goddamn White House ceremony that is specifically for *you*, you fucking cocksucker," Warren lambasted, as if Delta had totally lost it. "The damn President is taking time out of his day to award you this medal. Tell me, buddy. Have you reached such heights of narcissism that you are *really* going to snub our commander-in-chief?"

Pushing the brutal words away, forcing them to roll off his back like bath water, Delta shook his head, taking a swig of his heavy pint. Neither of his friends understood. Neither of them knew who he had become, what he'd done. He wasn't about to tarnish the values he'd fought so hard for.

"Just stop," Delta growled, averting his eyes.

"You fucking saved an American hostage, man," Warren argued. "You brought down an entire compound and took fucking bullets to get that guy out alive. Come on."

"You don't know everything." Delta shrugged the words off, reaching up to touch the scar on his temple that was goddamn throbbing.

"Don't forget that I was there," Warren reminded, nodding to Delta's scar. "That hostage wasn't the only life you saved that day. What am I missing?"

A silence filled the space where the three men sat, and Delta felt their intense eyes on him. They wanted him to accept the medal on behalf of all of them, but he couldn't. It wouldn't be right. Warren stood, grunting about how he didn't have time for bullshit and was off to find the pisser. As he moved away from the table, he left Carrick and Delta alone, staring at each other.

"You don't look right, man," Carrick assessed, eyeing his friend, probably for material damage. "What have you been up to?"

"Working." Delta shrugged but kept it very vague.

Carrick narrowed his eyes. "Working on what? You are on vacation, last time I checked."

Delta opened his mouth to argue but decided to leave it at that. He didn't need any more questions.

Before Carrick could challenge further, his cell phone rang in his pocket, and he flipped it out. Taking the call, he motioned 'one minute' to Delta and moved to the side of the patio where there were no tables. Delta watched his friend—a determined professional, a retired SEAL—who was trying damn hard to make his private security business work. It wasn't easy transitioning from special operator, from SEAL, to real life. Carrick had made it look easy.

Delta was struggling.

Needing a distraction, Delta flipped out his phone and fingered through his notifications. Nothing new. *Well, nothing interesting.* Alone, sifted through an old text conversation…one that he hadn't replied to. It was Kendra. It was the last message she'd sent him, almost a year ago…

Coffee? the old message read.

He'd typed a thousand replies but hadn't sent any of them. It was never clear to him what she wanted and what she meant. The only thing that was clear was that he was unfit to be with anyone. Things at work had gotten more intense and the battle rhythm was untenable, making him into someone he didn't recognize.

He'd deployed again to Syria not long after he'd seen her last, believing he'd be returning home in a casket. So, he'd never responded to her, figuring she was better off without him. Selfishly, he knew he was better off without her in his life, too. From the moment he'd met her, he'd known. She'd captured his attention like no other. He was drawn to her, and that was why he couldn't.

Shouldn't.

Wouldn't.

But, damn—his thoughts trailed, as he remembered what her ass felt like, gripping her cheeks, slamming his cock into her…but Warren's voice coming up behind him broke him out of his head.

"You know, I used to have a saying." Warren grunted as he sat down at the table again.

"And what was that?" Delta asked, dropping his forearms on the table, trying to appear more relaxed than he was.

Warren leaned in. "When you see someone with a medal, look to the guy beside him. That's the guy who probably deserved it more." And his eyes flitted to Carrick, who was joining them again.

Delta stared at Carrick, who shot him a grin.

"Damn right—I nominate Carrick," Delta agreed, wincing from the pulsing deep under the scar on his temple.

Delta could still feel the burning knife from that day—and how it had hurt when the enemy sentry had cut open his face as he'd taken him down. The doctors called it ghost pain, but it was real to him.

"You really don't want it, huh?" Carrick shook his head, grinning. "Why don't they just give it to Timber? Your dog's the real hero out of this."

"Fuck yes," Delta grinned, taking another gulp of beer.

"She's seen more action than half the SEALs out there."

Delta laughed with his two friends, chugging back pints and turning the conversation from serious to casual.

"What are you driving these days?" Carrick nodded to Warren, the man with a Hellcat addiction. The two of them dove into a conversation on pickup trucks— and who had a bigger hemi. Warren won on that—but he always did.

Delta tried to pay attention, but his mind was elsewhere, enjoying the lingering taste of his trailing memories. As if to reward him, his phone vibrated in his pocket, and his muscles unconsciously flexed. He couldn't get his phone out fast enough. *Kendra?*

Pulling it out, he saw it wasn't her. Of course, it wasn't her. She'd made it damn clear where they stood. Nowhere. He'd never hear from her again, not if she could help it, which of course only drove him harder. He was nothing if not competitive.

Checking the display on his phone, there was an unread message from a training contact he had saved as 'Sky'.

Target is leaving town. Headed up north.

He wrote back instantly, leaning forward and alert as hell.

How far is she?

Sky responded immediately.

Thirty-minute lead. I would have gone after her, but I've got eyes on your staff sergeant.

Wasting no time, Delta jumped up from his chair, nearly knocking over the empty pint glass in front of him. Both guys at the table snapped toward him, likely trying to figure out what the hell he was doing.

"I've got to go." Delta threw cash down on the table. "Sorry, gents."

The tracking beacon he'd put on Kendra's rental car had a tendency to go dark when he needed it most. He needed better equipment.

"Where's the fire?" Warren asked suspiciously, standing with him.

Carrick stood as well. "Buddy, you don't seem good."

"Don't worry about it," Delta dismissed his friends.

He casually saluted them both, unwilling to say anything. He spun and marched off the patio, taking a rear staircase that led farther down into the marina beside them—into the shadows of the night. Reaching into the back of his jeans, he adjusted the pistol he always carried concealed, comforted by the steel's presence.

"Hey," Warren called after him in the dark alley between buildings, "wait up."

Delta rotated, seeing his friend and boss appear in the shadows. He remained silent, feeling his phone vibrating again in his pocket.

"What are you up to?" Warren asked in a low, serious tone. "I know you, man. Something isn't right."

"I'm fine," Delta lied. "Seriously, I've just got stuff to take care of."

"Stuff?" Warren probed.

"Stuff."

"I need you to deploy in two weeks. I'm questioning if I need to get you assessed first."

Delta raised his eyebrows, knowing what that meant. "I'm good. I'll be there."

Warren crossed his arms, a threatening tone taking over. "What aren't you telling me?"

The challenge was clear. Delta squared his shoulders, flexing his fists. The guy was like his brother, and that meant they'd fought...a lot.

"Are you seeing her again?" Warren quizzed. "Is that what this is?"

"Who?"

"Your lady cop." Warren's gaze intensified. "She gets under your skin, huh?"

"My business is my own," Delta growled, making his boundaries understood.

Warren clicked his tongue, shaking his head. "Stubborn, as always. Like a mule."

"Like a *bull*," Delta corrected his friend and turned to leave. "I'll see you in two weeks."

"I'll find out," Warren called after him as Delta made his way away down the alley. "I always do."

Delta cocked his head over his shoulder and casually grinned. "Be my guest."

Exiting the dark space, Delta rattled his keys in his fingers, coming into the bar's parking lot. Today, he hadn't taken the truck. Jumping on the back of his Harley, he inserted the keys and revved.

Warren was onto him and wasn't going to let up. That wasn't his style. Delta admitted to himself that he had a choice. Show Warren what he'd taken when he'd broken into the lab — or hide it, fall on his sword or wait to be found out.

Chapter Ten

Spinning through Bakersfield, Kendra listened to the directions blasting through her car's console. She'd just finished doing what she needed to do, but dusk was setting in. She was vibrating with anxiety. It was much later than she'd wanted to be out, but the stopover at home had taken longer than she'd planned. Though that was par for the course these days.

Kendra's life had significantly changed over the past year, between pregnancy and delivering her son. Before she'd come back to work about a month before, she had hardly left the house except for hospital appointments and groceries. She didn't know if it was in her head, but she swore that people had seemed to look at her funny when she'd had that big pregnant belly and no wedding ring.

It's like they'd known — and she'd felt that shame, that guilt. She'd let it happen to her.

She rolled down the road in the unfamiliar city, wondering what she'd do if the DNA results weren't the ones she was hoping for? She had left the sample with her trusted colleague at the Bakersfield lab — someone she knew would keep things discreet. It was a good thing they had the equipment to finalize what her lab had started.

Letting out a deep, forced breath, hands gripping the steering wheel, she reminded herself that she just had to be patient. They'd regrow the DNA string via the optimizer and assess. Were there irregularities or not?

She found her way into the downtown core, finally parking in the hotel lot. Gazing into the drab lobby, her stomach sank. It was one of those last-minute discount hotels, but now, she found herself questioning if she should even bother. Sure, it was late, but shouldn't she just drive home? God, she wanted to just be with her son. She felt so stretched being away from him. But home was hours away, and text messages from her sister reassured her that her baby was happy as a clam.

The memory of being spun off the road and nearly crashing down the Malibu hillside flashed to the front of her mind, causing her hands to tremble. Her tired brain grew dizzy momentarily, making up her mind for her. As much as she'd rather be home, it would be safer to spend the night. She wasn't fully recovered from the crash, emotionally or otherwise. Traversing back through the rocky ridges between Bakersfield and Malibu seemed like a bad idea. She had to think about more than one life now.

Kendra got out of the rental, throwing her overnight bag over her shoulder as she marched on the darkened pavement toward the hotel entrance. In strappy sandals, girlfriend jeans and a relaxed, white-knit top, she blended in with the up-tempo young people moving around the sidewalks as they found their way to whatever nightly entertainment they had planned.

At the side of the hotel, she paused, suddenly getting that weird feeling that someone was watching her. An eerie sensation climbed up her body, and instinctively she whipped out her cell phone. Covertly glancing around, her heart pounding, she prayed it wasn't real.

Kendra swiveled her head around, analyzing her surroundings. There was no one, and nothing suspicious presented. She was alone on the edge of the small hotel parking lot, which was framed by other downtown buildings. Still, she couldn't deny the prickles running up her back. Someone was watching her.

Am I imagining things? She tried to calm herself, taking in a deep breath. Bitterly, she recalled Delta's warnings and his suggested deal.

"He's just playing games," she muttered, trying to reassure herself. "Selfish prick."

Accidents happened all the time in the Malibu hills, she told herself again and again. No one was trying to drive her off the road. She couldn't play into Delta's hands. There was nothing to be scared of. Delta hadn't shown her any evidence that she should be worried, but he had shown her evidence that he was willing to use her. Who knew what his agenda was?

Kendra forced the chilling feeling to pass as she observed a young couple stopping in front of the hotel, not far from where she stood, to kiss passionately. It was the type of moment that would be sweet to anyone in love and agonizing for anyone in heartbreak. The man playfully tucked the woman's hair behind her ear, adoring her and loving her. The moment the woman's engagement ring glinted in the light of the streetlamp, Kendra flinched.

She fell against the concrete side of the building, instinctively deploying her Lamaze breathing. Her ring finger felt as lonesome as she'd been, going through pregnancy and childbirth alone. The doctor had been so confused. What did she mean, her husband wouldn't be attending? She wasn't married. Did she even know the father?

The couple on the street released from their kiss, whispering privately. It both sickened Kendra and drove a need deep inside her. It was in that split second that she finally admitted that she had to let go. Delta, like an addiction, got her so high and made her so low. All year long she just couldn't stop thinking about him and feeling so damn angry.

She watched the couple continue walking up the street, nearly craning her neck to see them go. Distant tropical music slipped into her senses from the very direction they walked, and her focus drifted to a lively tiki bar. Maybe she should trade one addiction for another? Maybe she should get drunk, call him and tell him everything. Or maybe she should just say 'fuck it' and grab a pina colada. It really had been a *day*.

And so that was exactly what she decided to do.

Within ten minutes, Kendra found herself letting her ponytail out and releasing her blonde locks over her tan shoulders as she leaned over a tiny, sticky bar, sipping on a delicious, fresh pina colada. She loved a bar that used real coconut, and that hipster joint was all over it. The sweet taste of the beachy drink lingered in her mouth as she flipped through her phone, muting every friend on social media who was showing off engagement pictures. She had to take care of her own mental health.

"Rough week?" the bartender laughed as he approached her, his green eyes twinkling. She leaned back, wondering for a second if he was flirting.

"You could say that."

Then he slung two shots of tequila on the bar top. "On the house."

She sucked in her breath, shaking her head. She didn't want to be rude—but she hadn't had shots of tequila in a long, long time. That wasn't her speed. He leaned over the bar, waiting for her to drink. Picking her shot up, she clinked her glass to his and sucked it back for no other reason than to not be so damn stiff for just one night.

"From around here?" the bartender followed up, wiping down the bar top.

"LA," Kendra replied, tracing a crack in the wood with her finger.

"Ah, what brings you up here?"

"I'm trying to make a decision," she confessed, surprising herself.

"This will help with that." The bartender nodded at her drink before spinning to go check on other patrons.

He left Kendra alone with her thoughts, absently staring at whatever was on the TV positioned over the bar. It was one of those instant wedding reality shows—where the couple barely knew each other. She tightened her hand around her glass as she watched, feeling that deep resentment burning.

The bartender returned to pour a stout at her end of the bar, nodding to the TV. "I think they missed my application."

"Don't go on one of those shows"—Kendra rolled her eyes—"please."

"Why not?" he asked. "It's an easy solution to a big problem."

"This isn't how love and marriage are supposed to work," she pointed out, "and what is so wrong with being traditional about it? A proper courtship and engagement."

"Ah," he grinned, picking up the full beers, "you're one of those conservative types."

"So what?" She sipped her drink, her back stiffening. *If he only knew.*

He cocked his head back, offering her a casual laugh, drawing a smile out of her, too. As he moved away, Kendra realized her phone was vibrating. It was a call...from a blocked number. She bit her lip, not wanting to pick it up. So, the call kept going...and going. It was just about to go to voicemail, so she let it, exhaling deeply.

The bartender came back, eyeing her up and down. "A conservative woman like you should be at home, in bed—not having another shot, right?"

He grabbed two shot glasses, and poured tequila into them, seeming to wait for her response.

She checked the time. It was getting late. But, then again, she found her lips curling into a conspiratorial smile, meeting his grin. Reluctantly, she nodded at the bartender, taking the burning liquid down her throat within seconds. Elbows on the bar, she held her last empty shot glass in her hand, feeling a little less stiff than she had all week.

"Tell me... Why do men make it so hard?" she demanded, a little slur in her words.

"Ah, is this the decision you have to make?" He cocked his head, chuckling. "What's going on?"

"I'm stuck between a man I can't have and a man I don't want," Kendra admitted, thinking about Delta and Hunter. "I don't have faith in either of them."

"I think you should forget about the man you don't want," he said, putting both hands on the bar and leaning toward her. His kind green eyes twinkled as he watched her, something knowing in his face.

"And the guy I can't have?" she probed, gazing up at him with wonder, like he was the oracle she'd always needed. "We have a past... and he really hurt me last time I let him in."

"Why didn't it work out?"

She bit her lip. "I wasn't good enough for him — wasn't good enough to be with him in a real way."

"Did he say that?"

"He could have any woman he wants — gorgeous women, successful women — "

The bartender cut in with, "*You* are a gorgeous woman."

She flipped her blonde hair over her shoulder, shaking her head. It was nice to be complimented by a stranger — but he just didn't understand. Women threw themselves at SEALs. She would barely measure up to any of them. There was no doubt that she wasn't good enough to be with him.

Why had she gone and slept with a fucking Navy SEAL? What was she thinking? It was never going to be a thing — nothing more than a 'one and done'. He was always just going to toy with her, play games to gratify himself.

"Well, I'd date you," the bartender said in earnest, bringing the conversation back into a lighter place as he dried glasses from the washer. "You're a catch."

She opened her mouth a little but there was nothing to say. She was a little shy. *Is he flirting with me?*

"That's funny." She waved her hand dismissively, but deep down appreciating the comment all the same.

As she pushed back on her stool, making to get up, the bartender's words lingered. *"I'd date you."* She shrugged, dropping cash on the bar, hating how she couldn't have it all.

The bartender picked up the cash, putting it away. Then, with all seriousness, he added, "Just talk to him. Tell him what you want. Have you tried that?"

"Not exactly," she replied, picking up her bag. "It's not that easy."

He locked eyes with her, knowing.

She sighed. "I just can't."

"Then he's not the right guy for you."

The advice hit her like a bag of bricks — or maybe it was the very good tequila. Either way, she found herself nearly faltering over the stool as she nodded a goodbye at the bartender.

I just can't. The words ricocheted through her mind. There was another time, another day, when she'd said those exact same words.

As she moved out of the bar, back onto the street, her phone vibrated in her bag yet again. She pulled it out and found she was getting a call from a blocked number — again. She bit her lip, dipping into the alleyway connecting to the hotel parking lot. Maybe she was a little tipsy, maybe her judgment was just compromised — but what if it was really Delta? What did *he* want?

She crumbled, answering the call.

"Hello?" she demanded in a very serious tone, cutting through the alleyway on her way back to her hotel.

There was a pause, and Delta's familiar voice questioned, "Where are you?"

"That doesn't concern you," she snapped, looking side to side as she hit a darker spot in the alley.

Holding her phone to her ear, which impaired her vision, made chills run up her spine as she realized how vulnerable she'd just become. The tequila really had contributed to some bad decisions. Delta chuckled darkly into the line, seemingly amused by her defiance. His rich, warm voice rushed over her body, like he was there in person. Like she could reach out and strangle him.

"You have no idea what concerns me." His tone turned intimidating, as usual. She was used to it— though it still stirred her to her core.

"I'm not doing this," she countered, but just as she said it, she heard shuffling to her right.

Her gaze flashed in that direction, and a beefy man taking a piss in the alleyway spun toward her. She brought the phone down from her ear, moving quickly to get through the alley. *Shit.*

"Where are you going?" The man's slurred voice followed her as she walked. All she could smell was booze. "Wait."

"Oh shit," she exhaled as she leapt forth like a drunken gazelle, hearing the man's footsteps quicken behind her.

Not soon enough, she reached the end of the alley, learning that she wasn't alone anymore. Another man dressed in black—with a familiar mask—appeared, waiting for her, clicking his tongue with disappointment. Through the dark, she spun around, and the drunken man swayed, feet away from her.

"What's your name?" the drunk garbled, motioning at Kendra.

"She's mine. Move along." Delta extended his long arm, pushing her behind his tall, solid form. Commanding and imposing, he made his territory damn clear.

The orders loud and clear, the drunk didn't hesitate, quickly vanishing back down the alley, leaving Delta with Kendra. Once they were alone again, Delta stood back, waiting smugly.

"I'm getting tired of you feeling the need to save me," she snapped, pushing his hands off her and straightening her spine. "I had that completely under control."

"Did you?" He smirked, lifting his black mask to reveal his gorgeous face. "And I'm getting tired of you not listening to me."

"I don't need to listen to you, if you haven't realized. You're not my father."

"But I have been your *daddy*," Delta toyed, pushing his own agenda, taking a step into her space.

She sucked in her breath, feeling the warmth of his close body, inhaling his scent.

His deep growl continued, "Do you think I've fabricated this whole thing?"

"Without a doubt, you have," she argued, trying to push away, a little drunk and really guarded. Her body still in fight or flight, she took a step back.

"I have?" he rebuffed in a deep drawl, taking a step forward. "What a way to appreciate someone. And I'd think you'd be thanking me."

"Why would I thank you?" she snapped, irritated at his casual tone. "You are stalking me! For what reason? Look at what you are doing to me. Hell, look at what you've done to me!"

A few tears threatened to escape her eyes, though she bit her lip to contain the eruption. She held it back, reminding herself that he didn't deserve to see her like that.

After a brief pause, he replied coolly, "And what exactly have I done to you — except for saving your tight little ass?"

"Why don't you save me from yourself?" She slammed against his chest, trying to send the unmovable mass of muscle backward. "Save me from what you are *doing* to me."

But his body didn't budge, continuing to loom over her.

"Pray tell... What am I doing to you?" He rolled his tongue along his bottom lip, seeming to savor every moment of her agony.

"God, Delta — isn't it obvious?" She waved her hands, livid. She didn't want to spell it out for him, but a tear betrayed her, trickling down her heated cheek.

"Tell me — I want to know what I'm doing to you."

Kendra was resolved to remain silent, unwilling to give him what he sought, but passion flushed up her neck. He drilled his dark gaze into her. It was damn clear that he knew exactly what he was doing and wanted gratification. He wanted her to break. Even in that shadowy parking lot, she could see his jaw flexing and his shoulders tightening in that same way she remembered when he once was on top of her, ravaging her.

"As stubborn as always" — he gripped her arms, yanking her up into him — "with a resolve that I'd love nothing more than to break."

"You'll never break me," she cried, wriggling to break free. "Get that into your fucked-up head."

"A little discipline would go a long way in smartening you up."

He let out a low, dark laugh — less amused, more threatening — holding her tighter against his chest. Digging in, he roughly traced down to the small of her back, driving sensation through her body.

"I'm sure you'd love to discipline me." Her lips parted as her tone grew mocking. "Wouldn't you, *Daddy*?"

"I would."

His tone didn't waver as he trailed his eyes up and down her body. He edged his teeth over his bottom lip, machinations clearly roiling in his mind.

"Don't even try," she countered, trying to push away. "You have no authority here."

"Don't challenge me," he growled, tightening his grip to keep her where he wanted. "You know I'm competitive, and you know I like to win."

"I know something else, too. I'll never be yours."

Her lips pursed as she tried to prevent her voice from cracking, not wanting to show him the agony he caused her. Her words seemed to echo through the space, processing what she said. She was struck by a sudden silence, locking eyes with him when it hit Kendra — the strange aching in his gaze.

"Matteo…" she quickly whispered, a rawness escaping from her throat. "I—"

"Don't—" he snapped back.

Eyes on fire, Delta dropped his head to take her mouth for his own once more — without permission, without apologies. And she remembered he didn't take orders. He *gave* them, which only made her thighs shake. He kissed her well, just how she liked it — opening her mouth with his, passionately compelling her to play. Her blood pumped harder and harder as she surrendered to him, tasting his tongue. Her chest continued to lurch as she fell harder into his sculpted arms, letting him hold her, feeling her emotions boiling over.

Something about that kiss must have been different — less controlled, wilder, like he was sending a clear message. The dominance that always turned her on intensified, frightening her just enough. One thing was for sure. Delta never had to try to dominate her. He just did. She hated it, but it was true. And like she was his to enjoy, he roughly ran his hands up and down her body, gripping and grabbing as he wanted, stirring that crazy response in her. Lingering, burning desire and wetness tingled at the entrance to her pussy, pleading once again for his masterful touch.

He's winning, a bitter voice screamed in the back of her mind. *Don't let him.*

"Enough!" She pushed back like she'd touched open flame.

Spinning on her heels, unwilling to catch his gaze lest she falter, she sped into the hotel. If there was one thing she heard as she left, it was a hungry growl escaping his likely enraged mouth. Sure enough, there was one thing she could depend on with Delta. He never ceased to keep things exciting.

Chapter Eleven

The mattress in this hotel is a little too hard and lumpy for someone coming off the type of day I've had, Kendra thought as she ran her fingers over the starchy white sheets, closing her eyes. If she hadn't had so much to drink, she'd be driving home and getting the hell out of Dodge — and the room wouldn't be spinning.

Knowing Delta wasn't far and knew exactly where she was — she was in the last place she wanted to be. As it was, she couldn't get behind the wheel in her state, and the idea of gallivanting down the sidewalk for another hotel room seemed sketchy.

Kendra's internal conflict revved on, and she found herself holding her chest, on guard. Alone with her scars, with nothing but moonlight for company, her aching body grew heavy. Her walls sturdy, she resolved to just be alone.

Delta... What a joke it all was. What was he after? Why did he keep showing up? No doubt, just to prove he could have her if he wanted to. Selfish, always. He didn't want much else than to torture her for his own ego. *The conceited asshole...* Any chance they had to be something had all but dried up, like that blood on his glove.

Too tired to cry, too alone to care, she drifted into hard sleep, much harder than she'd wanted it to be. She didn't know what time it was when she woke up but was shocked awake realizing that someone was on top of her, holding a warm, rough hand over her mouth. She tried to scream and kick and punch—but he was just too damn strong.

Inhumanly strong.

"What the hell!" She tried to scream through the hand over her mouth, trying to bite it.

From the moonlight cascading in through the window, all she could see was that the man on top of her had a dark hood up and a familiar wide smirk on his lips.

"You've been causing me enough trouble," Delta rumbled, pressing his calloused hand to her mouth. "Look at how careless you are—how vulnerable you are. You think I have time to watch your ass night and day?"

She shook and squirmed, trying to push him off, helpless under his gripping power. Muffled by his hand, she begged, "What are you doing?"

"Teaching you a lesson."

He pressed his mouth onto her throat, tasting her sensitive flesh. He wasn't gentle, just as rough as he wanted to be. Using his teeth to rake upward to her jaw, he hit the bruising on her face from the night of the car accident and she winced. Through her muffled cries, he furthered his lecture.

"This is what happens to girls who don't listen. A big bad wolf will come in here and eat you alive."

She reeled under his hot breath as he found his way to her ear with his tongue, gnawing until it hurt, driving her to need him desperately. What was he going to do to her? Her hips jolted under the weight of his body as he slid his mouth down, biting at her throbbing neck like she was his game.

"You want this, don't you?" Delta challenged her.

"Yes," she whispered.

"I can't hear you."

"Yes!"

Her pussy ached as she felt his raw authority, that dominance she craved. She was his for the taking—no matter what her better judgment told her. Hovering over her, he gripped her jaw, locking eyes.

"Moving forward, you *will* obey me."

Releasing his hand, he drew out a rope from his pocket, pushed her arms above her head and tied them tightly to the headboard without mercy. She let out a cry as he did so, which was met by his punishing amusement.

"Is that clear?" Delta demanded as he tested the integrity of his knot, causing her to wince in pain.

She didn't answer right away, so he grabbed her jaw again, just as harsh as before, staring her down.

"Is that fucking clear?"

Biting her lip, she replied, "Yes, Daddy."

Then he kissed her…hard.

And in that kiss, he whispered a promise. He was going to protect her, whether she liked it or not. Lowering his body onto hers, he glided his tongue into her watering mouth. The weight of his big, strong form pressed into her, and a moan escaped her throat. She didn't want to want it as much as she did. They entangled, his scruffy beard against her soft skin, and she inhaled the intoxicating smell of his pure masculinity.

The kiss was devolving into a messy make-out, and she arched her back as she found herself needing and wanting his touch everywhere, just like he'd promised once upon a time. Hearing her moans, it seemed like he had the playbook to her fantasies. He moved his hands down her chest, feeling her peaked nipples. She was completely at his mercy. He wasn't gentle, kind or loving. He was an assailant, a hungry predator, showing her that her only chance at survival was to give in. It was the scenario she'd fantasized about all year. Demanding her surrender, he kept his hard mouth on top of hers, tightening his hands at her neck, proving he could do more than just dominate the fuck out of her.

Finally, he drew back, biting at her lower lip as he did, as if that were all just a taste of what was to come. Leaning away, he seemed to visibly calculate, savoring. She trembled, reeling in the hurt he caused. That frightening amusement lingered on his mouth — the only part of his face showing underneath his dark hood.

"So, you'll never be mine?" he challenged, running his hands down to the zipper on her jeans.

"No."

She lurched, trying to wrestle out of her wrist binds, knowing the effort was futile. A Navy SEAL didn't fail at knots.

"I think you will," he said, his amusement persisting as he toyed with her fly. "Let's see."

"You're wrong," she shot back, rocking her head from left to right.

He let out another laugh and ripped open the fly to her jeans. They'd been here before and he'd done exactly that. Through her cries, her hips stayed firmly square, even lifting to him — clearly out of sync with her words. Betrayed by her reactions, the truth she didn't want to admit was — hell yeah, she wanted him. She wanted every *inch* of him.

And he fucking knew that.

"What am I going to feel?" he demanded, toying with her white, lacy panties.

She clamped her knees together, half-heartedly fighting him off.

He tore the loose-fitting jeans down her hips, uncaring, throwing them across the room. A ruthless sound emerged from his throat as he took in the sight of her naked thighs as he trailed his hands down her hips.

"Let's play a game. You know I love games." He slammed his hand down on the side of the bed, trapping her underneath him once again. That memorable wily smile lingered on his lips.

He dropped his head to her core, teasing and kissing her as he moved down her body, inch by inch under his wet tongue and with hot breath unrelenting against her skin. She tilted her head back, spinning. He was going to take whatever he wanted, get whatever he wanted — and that was *her*. That he wouldn't take no for an answer made her ache for him like never before.

Hovering over the edge of her panties, he gazed back up to her, plotting. He slid his fingers up, tracing the exterior of her undergarments, making her so needy.

"If you don't want me, I'll leave you alone… forever."

She moaned as his mouth got closer to her pussy and ground her hips up to him. He seemed to enjoy teasing her and watching her get hotter and hotter. God, he knew how to get a reaction. Her body was more than willing to reveal what she couldn't.

"Now, if I feel what I think I'm going to feel" — he slid his finger underneath the edge of the delicate white lace — "then you're fucking mine."

She bit her lip, spinning between the desire to protect her heart and the need to feel his touch.

"Tell me… Do you want me?" he growled, running his finger just an inch underneath the lace, provoking her.

While her hips bucked at his touch, so close but not quite where she needed, he expertly paused, waiting for her reply. She said nothing, exhaling deeply to keep her cool.

He pulled back suddenly, making her feel an emptiness she couldn't describe. Staring her down, he asked for the last time.

"Do you?"

"Yes."

He lunged forward, ripping off the white lace and running his hand down her wet clit. She moaned as he felt the sopping wet mess of arousal at the opening of her pussy. There was no mistaking what was happening.

"Fucking right," he groaned.

He leaned back, whipping off his black hoodie, leaving him in his dark T-shirt and jeans. She bit her tongue, wanting him to take it all off, wanting to see him without *anything* on once more. She knew just what sort of masculinity was under those threads. His shredded abs and rippling muscle... It was enough to make her mouth water. But he kept it all on, turning his attention back to her.

"You're so fucking hot," he grunted, pressing her thighs down to better expose her pussy to him.

Right then, under him, was the first time in a long time that vulnerability had felt good. Her body throbbed, pleading with him to make her feel something. Without hesitation, he drew his tongue up her thigh, heading for the main event. Vibrating with arousal, she couldn't control her moans, giving him the feedback he obviously loved. He ran his hands up the inside of her thigh toward her wet pussy and locked his eyes with hers.

"Don't you ever fucking disobey me again—or you'll be choking on my cock in apology."

The memory of his rock-hard manhood sliding down her throat made her raise her hips to him, and she found herself praying for him to give it to her. Obliging, he pushed his thick fingers to the opening of her pussy, sliding easily inside her. He made short work of pleasing her aching core, dropping to taste her clit, circling and swirling it in his mouth. Her rocking hips only screamed how bad she needed an orgasm and how much she needed him to be drawing it out.

Gasping for breath as she neared the edge, she cried out his name, the ties cutting into her wrists as she writhed.

"Delta, please just fuck me."

"You haven't learned your lesson yet," came his dark reply.

Aching, she rolled her eyes back as he fingered her harder and harder, drawing every ounce of wetness out of her. His cock was hard as fuck, pressing on her leg through his jeans, and he was getting hotter and rougher with her. Pressure built to the surface, driving her to call out his name again and again as her first wave of ecstasy crested.

"Delta, please," she cried at his relentless touch, wishing she could reach out to him.

"Whether you fucking like it or not, I'm not afraid to hurt you."

"*Please*," she cried as she came, her orgasm flowing all over his fingers, "do it."

Seemingly satisfied with his work, he appeared to savor what liquid remained on his hand, enjoying every bit of her. Then he pulled back, seemingly admiring her nude body, issuing a warning.

"Don't tempt me."

"I want you to," she reiterated, loving the pain of the ropes cutting into her wrists, needing him to hurt her to make her feel better.

Something in his eyes flashed at her words and he pushed off the bed. Wasting no time, he kicked off his jeans and threw off his T-shirt. Only his boxers remained, which she was very happy to see drop immediately, giving her a prime view of that bouncing, hard cock she so worshipped.

He approached the side of the bed where she lay, untying her hands from the headboard. Reaching down, he dragged her body to his liking, angling her just right. He pumped his engorged cock with his talented hands and stood directly in front of her face. Her knees were digging into the scratchy hotel carpet, but she opened her mouth to welcome him.

Caveman-like, he grabbed at her hair, infusing his fingers into her blonde locks, pulling hard to guide her exactly how he wanted her. She nearly choked as he slid his throbbing cock into her mouth, quickly hitting the back of her throat without pause. The way he handled her hair and jaw started to hurt, but it was a damn good thing that he knew she fucking loved it. Her eyes rolled back as she relished the moment. She could never deny how weak she was for this heated, grizzly man who had more muscle and cock than sensitivity, his dick longer than his emotional bandwidth.

Rhythmically sliding in and out of her mouth, he grunted in pleasure, clearly taking his pleasure. As he was getting closer to his peak, he snarled down at her.

"You little slut, you like this cock in your mouth."

Tears fell out of her eyes as he pulled at her hair — pain that made her feel so damn good. His words were perfect. The sensation was perfect. She moaned, feeling her pussy ache more. He obviously *loved* what he was doing to her, knowing she could only give a muffled response.

He launched his cock farther down her throat until she gagged relentlessly. Laughing to himself, he kept rocking forward until she felt every delicious vein on his cock pulsing. There was no doubt he wasn't far from the edge himself, and the thought of his hot liquid exploding down her throat nearly sent her into a second orgasm.

Finally, Delta drew back, using his hands to pump his twitching cock toward her mouth. She licked up the drops of pre-cum that had snuck out of his round tip. Pursing her lips, she played lavishly with it, taking too much time. He groaned, dropping his head back, and looked down on her again.

"You're *my* slut. Get that?"

He ordered like he was issuing the ten commandments. The man never ceased to amaze her. His dirty bedroom talk was exactly what she'd expect of a sailor with too much time at sea.

"And after tonight — when I say jump, I want you to ask how high." His commands were unrelenting. "Whatever I say, whatever I want —"

"Yes," she submitted, too deep in the moment to care, as he picked her up in his arms and carried her toward the hotel wall.

She knew — as he surely did — what was going to happen next.

"I'm not letting you put yourself in danger," he said, getting real, his face hard and cold.

It was clear. His mindset was that he was damn ready to fuck the shit out of her, and she trembled, knowing what was to come. Holding her entire body up, he pushed her against the wall of the hotel room. His warm, rough hands felt her up and down, squeezing and claiming her.

"You're softer than before," he grunted as he gripped her expanded waistline. But, before she could respond, he added, "I like that."

Finally, he lifted her into a straddling position over his dick. His muscles pulsing and his cock twitching, he hovered her above his thick cockhead.

"Matteo —"

"You're mine now," Delta reiterated, pressing against her hot slit. "Don't fucking forget that."

As the words poured out of his mouth, they hit her hard. He'd never said anything like that to her ever before. Without a shadow of a doubt, something had changed in Delta since he'd been back. That was good, though, since something had changed in her, too.

She breathed out as he leaned in to take her mouth once more, feeling his heavy cock underneath her, teasing her opening. She hadn't had sex in a long time—not since everything she'd been through. A moment's anxiety shot through her as she worried about her scarring and if it would hurt. That wasn't the type of pain she wanted. That was a *different* type of pain.

Then, he pushed his cockhead up an inch into her aching pussy and hovered her body over him. She winced as his cock passed by her childbirth scars and he froze.

"Are you okay?"

"*Yes*," she whispered back, pushing herself down on him.

Groaning, he bit her neck and slid her down his long shaft. She gasped as she sensed him enter her, taking up way more space inside her than she ever remembered. Kissing her more deeply, he grinned at her reaction and gave her a second to recover. She locked eyes with him, softer than before, with one hand gripping his muscular shoulder for dear life, while her other hand rested on the long scar on his perfect cheekbone and temple. There were so many secrets between them.

"If you own me, that means you own me all the time," she said, as he moved his mouth down her throat to suck at her sensitive neck skin.

He grunted in reply, vigorously moving her body up and down his cock. Goddamn, she instantly melted with the sensation. He was her sexual kryptonite. He groaned in agreement as he bit her throat hard, pushing deeper into her.

"I want you *all* the time," Delta admitted.

She exhaled, inviting him to fuck her senseless. Rocking her body on his shaft the exact way he wanted to, he drove her to see stars as he fucked her to another orgasm. Holding her against the wall like she weighed nothing, his power was overwhelming, only intensifying her attraction to the SEAL. He was all-consuming, bringing her to a place she'd never been, promising things she'd never had.

Never before—not even the first time they'd messed around—had she felt what she felt then. She cried out with every thrust at the raw intensity he brought. It was delicious. It was terrible. It was amazing. She couldn't take it anymore. But she needed it to never stop. She wanted to have more and more and more.

"Baby," she cried and pleaded as explosions of pleasure ran up her core as he rocked her pussy, dripping her cum down his shaft to the base, "don't ever stop."

His only response was raw grunting alongside his teeth meeting the edge of her jaw and neck, like he needed her to fucking know just how he owned her. She was never, ever going to take another cock other than his for as long as she lived. He fucked her intensely, clearly enjoying every second that she gasped for breath. The closer he grew to the edge, the more savage he seemingly became—apparently caring even less about being tender, not that he ever was. He roughed her up like it might be the last fuck he was ever going to have.

"Ruin me for anyone else," she groaned, breathless as she came.

Tears streamed from the corners of her eyes as she got the words out, telling him more than he probably wanted to know.

"Fucking right."

He lapped her emotions up through a pained voice as he finally exploded inside her, holding her against the wall as his cum dripped down his cock and out of her. With his heart thudding hard and him breathing heavily, he rested his forehead against her. Everything about his sweaty, hot build and warm, manly scent filled her nose. She was open and relaxed — and *falling*.

And that was when her eyes flicked open, like a light switch turned on.

Falling.

That was exactly the feeling she'd had last time.

She bit her lip, not wanting to say anything when he drew her down onto the bed with him, holding her closer. It was clear that he had no words left to say. Kissing her hair and drawing the sheets over their bodies, he refused to let her go. Her head on his chest, his arms around her, she hadn't ever felt so blissful.

"I'm sorry," he confessed.

"For what?" she whispered.

"For being an asshole," he rumbled a sleepy reply. "For not being there."

"You're here now," she reminded him, wanting it all to be real, wanting to share everything with him. The longer he held her, the safer she felt. It was everything she'd ever wanted from the man she could never have.

"You need someone to be there for you."

"Is that going to be you?"

"I want it to be," he grumbled. "I'm trying."

His rhythmic breathing was deepening, and it was clear to her that he was passing out.

As she also slid into sleep, she found herself just as alone and confused. He couldn't be turning a corner... could he? She held tepidly on to the hope that things had changed, and she let her eyes flutter closed as he held her in his arms. Her dreams that night were not as calming as she'd wanted, however, given the remarkable release Delta had given her. His non-committal words tugged at the seams in her mind, threatening to unravel it all.

And when she woke in the first rays of morning, she realized that there was no one else in the hotel room.

He was gone.

Springing out of bed for no reason other than disbelief, she looked left and right, not even sure what she was looking for. Some evidence that it hadn't all been a dream? The only thing that told her it wasn't was her aching pussy and the bite marks across her neck, as she looked in the hotel mirror hanging on the wall.

He'd come, he'd seen, he'd conquered — and he'd left. All she heard was screaming ricocheting in her mind, the sound of her brain reminding her heart, 'I told you so'.

Her own vulnerability crushed her, and she came to regret everything. Looking at her face, her hair…disheveled, unkempt. Was it her? What was she doing? Kendra took in a heavy breath, shaking her head as tears welled in her eyes. How could anything be so important that he'd needed to run? How could he ghost her again?

Blinking into her reflection, seeing her blue eyes, only bluer from the tears pouring out, she realized something. Little had she known that when he'd apologized, it was for the past and for the *future*.

Because he wasn't going to stop being an asshole.

He *was* an asshole.

And she was, once again, in too deep.

Chapter Twelve

"So, who is she?"

Sky flicked back her long brown ponytail as she pulled at the collar of her tight-fitting leather jacket. Her face dead serious, she had obviously been waiting patiently for an explanation, ever since she'd helped track Kendra all the way to Bakersfield.

But he wasn't planning on explaining himself. Sky didn't need to know, so he just let out a low breath, trying to focus on the task at hand. He cocked his pistol, checking it for readiness, ignoring her questions. The cool steel in the night reminded him of a tour he wanted to forget. A chill ran up his back, flushing a shiver over his limbs as he gazed into the darkness on the wrong side of LA.

"Are you into her?" Sky pressed again for details as he tried to ignore her.

Delta shook his head, unwilling to give his trainee what she sought. And he damn well knew that she was seeking more than what she let on.

She continued, "Cough it up."

"Fuck off," he dismissed, and holstered his pistol.

Pushing off his Harley, he adjusted his dark jacket. He had shit to do and didn't have time for her whining. Walking down the alley behind the building, heading toward their destination, his irritation rose as he heard her trailing behind him.

"You know, I looked into her after you had me track her car, and I've gotta tell you that she wasn't what I expected."

"How's that?" Delta sneered, focused on his mission.

Sky jumped forward, thumping her hand into his chest, pushing him back. Her eyes were fixated on him.

"She's stunning. She's on the right side of the law. If I wanted to bet, she looks like someone you have history with."

"Like hell..." Delta pushed the spry brunette aside, moving forward without her. "You don't know what you're talking about."

"This whole time we've worked together," Sky called after him, "I've never seen you get in deep with a woman. I always wondered why."

Delta didn't reply, ignoring his half-trained apprentice who was lingering behind him. He didn't mistake the jealous huff that she let out and felt the proverbial daggers hitting his back. Things had been changing between him and Sky the past few weeks, since Kendra had come back into his life, but he was just ignoring it.

"I've got a job to do."

"Delta" — she moved in front of him again, stopping his body — "don't ignore me."

"I need to focus," he grunted, reminding her why they were there. "Just go home."

"You know I don't have one."

"They set you up pretty nice, last time I checked."

Visibly taken aback, she crossed her lean, strong arms, watching him closely. "It's base housing, Delta. Hardly a home."

"Didn't expect a soldier like you to want the warm and fuzzies," Delta said.

"Everyone needs—"

He shot a warning look down at her. "Enough. I have shit to do."

Whatever she had been about to say, he didn't want to go there.

She pouted, perhaps involuntarily. "Should I be offended that you're only ever *business* with me?"

"I wasn't looking for a buddy when I took you under my wing," he said.

"Then why'd you do it? Why did you take me on?"

He knew where she was headed and, once again, where she'd been driving their dynamic. She was pretty enough, in her own way—but he didn't want that. Never had.

"If I don't help you control what those hacks did to you, who the fuck will? The world doesn't need any more evil," he said.

"You're not that."

Sloughing her off, he paced around her and locked his focus on the destination. They were almost there. He couldn't waste any time.

She called after him, "You need to let yourself live."

"But I'm not alive," he grumbled back, meaning something she would never understand. "Not anymore."

Delta moved to the rear of the building, knocking on the large metal door that was rusted and chipped. The back entrance. He knew it well. It was an underground hangout for a certain type. Loud music emanated from behind the door—the typical thumping bass of nightclubs. The door quickly opened and a heavy-set man looked out on him, snarling. But then he recognized Delta's face and nodded.

"Brother," the doorman rumbled, opening the door wider to see Delta's apprentice tagging behind. "Bringing a friend today?"

"You could say that," Delta replied, stepping over the threshold and into the dark hallway where the music grew even louder.

Following the dim lighting down the hall, he moved into the open area in the club. Blacklights hanging off the ceilings illuminated the neon lingerie worn by dancing women all around. An audience of mostly men cheered and jeered as they watched the exotic dancers and threw cash on stage. Delta barely caught notice of them, moving deeper to the back, feeling Sky bringing up his tail.

He found a bench at the back wall of the club and slugged himself down to observe the room. He wasn't there to mess around. He was fucking serious. He was there to get answers from the horse's mouth.

He didn't know how pervasive the problem was, but so far, he'd gotten enough leads to point him there. The leads they had all said the same thing. Someone was scouting test dummies, getting them hooked in and throwing them to the scientists. There was no out for them after that.

"You think your guy's going to be here tonight?" Sky asked as she grabbed a seat beside him, overlooking the room. "The scout?"

"He better fucking be," Delta grunted, feeling the barrel of his pistol pressing into his lower back. "No more soldiers are going to turn up dead—not on my watch."

"What do you want me to do?" Sky started, staring him down again, placing her hand on his arm to pull him in, but she retracted as a dancer clad in electric green lingerie moved in on them.

"Hello there." The seductive woman pushed into him as she sat beside him on the bench, flickering her glittery eyes at him. "Drinking anything tonight?"

"Nah, I'm off the sauce." He shrugged casually, looking away and keeping his eyes on the crowd.

The dancer laughed hard, as if it was the funniest thing she'd ever heard, touching his arm flirtatiously. He inadvertently flexed at her touch, which seemed to only encourage her further. She flipped back her long black hair, which had a weird fake texture to it.

She gently pushed into him again. "And what's your name?" Her long, fake eyelashes didn't stop flickering, sending glitter dust onto his sleeve.

"Matt," Delta replied, obfuscating and withholding his true reaction. But he found himself wondering what type of man went after all that fake shit.

"Hi, Matt, I'm Jade," the dancer said, keeping the conversation going. "And are you two together?" She pointed back and forth between him and Sky, sussing out the details.

"I don't know. Are we?" Sky said slowly, watching him, waiting for him to answer.

He shot Sky a warning look, seeing her scheming face. She was always up to something, which was good when he needed an ally — not an enemy.

Jade laughed again, taking that as her leave to flirt harder with Delta. He clenched his jaw, flexing more. Sandwiched between the two of them, he was getting sick of all the fakery.

"Look, Jade," he began, trying to level with her. "You seem nice, but you might find a better customer over there." He nodded toward the pit of energetic, drunken men in an obvious attempt to offload her.

Jade didn't seem to get the memo and dropped her mouth in a fake-shocked way. "Am I going to have to convince you now to let me stay?" She lightly tapped him again and pulled a twenty out of the back of her thong.

Delta raised his eyebrow at her.

"I found this on the floor. Care for a dance in the champagne room?" She breathed on him, trying damn hard to get him hooked. "You seem like you need a little warming up."

He stared at her coolly, offering no response. He knew exactly what she was after, what almost every woman that approached him in *that* way was after. But he couldn't give it to her — not her, not even the woman he wanted to give it to. His emotional unavailability wasn't a ruse. It was damn real.

Jade pressed in farther, gunning for an entry point, distracting him. Everything from her hair to her face to her nails to her personality was a sales pitch — a big goddamn fake sales pitch. Delta hid his shudder, preferring his women far more natural — natural hair, natural face, natural vibe. He liked to *see* them...feel them. He was driven to realness, and damn, that was in short supply these days.

Hell, there was only one woman he'd ever met who had an unwavering realness—an authenticity that challenged him, forced him to look at himself, forced him to wonder if maybe things could be different for him. She was the type of woman... *Damn*, he thought, stopping himself. As he came back to the moment, feeling the dancer brushing up against him, he realized, *Fuck, I've got it bad.* He was fucking hooked on Kendra. But he was never, ever going to be able to give her what she needed.

He was a goddamn monster—and he had to find out why.

After realizing he wasn't giving in, Jade just flicked her long hair and cocked her head back in a hearty laugh, pushing her cleavage together and into him.

"Come on. You're acting like a cop," she said.

He shrugged. "See many of them in here?"

"Sure, just the other night."

He locked his eyes with hers, now focused as hell. "Get his name?"

She licked her lips, realizing she had something. Leaning in, she flickered her lashes again. He glared down his nose at her, unrelenting.

She conceded, "Hunter or something equally douche-y."

He wanted to freeze, but he pushed through, keeping it casual. Shrugging, he acted like it was no big deal that she'd just linked Kendra's boss to the fucking supply point.

Before Jade could press her tits on him any more, a familiar face appeared at the back of the club, sending chills up his spine. The scout—their target. He kneed

Sky and she casually observed what he saw. It was time to make their move. He waited until the man moved back into the dim hallway before standing.

Delta glanced down at Jade, her mouth still agape, giving her a curt nod. She had no idea how much of a lead she'd given him. Hunter was linked somehow to the scout — but for what purpose? All Delta could think about was the possibility that they'd done something to Hunter — and the danger that would pose to Kendra.

Delta, with no words left, ignored his companion tugging at his sleeve. His demeanor started changing, transforming. He could feel it. It was the emotion, the protectiveness that Kendra drove in him. He hadn't had that much purpose since saving hostages on deployment. Now, it was like Kendra was a hostage — a hostage under Hunter's thumb. He clenched his jaw, visions of Hunter hurting her flashing before his eyes.

With killer instincts, he moved through the back of the club, but before he got to the door into the hall, he spun, looking down on Sky to issue his final orders.

"Stay here — and keep an eye out."

She shook her head, defying him and pushing forward, obviously wanting to be with him. He grabbed her shoulder, immobilizing her. That wasn't what the deal was. Her eyes widened as he grew fiercer, causing heat to rise up his neck.

"Listen." His voice grew into a dark snarl, drawing immediate obedience from her. "Stay the fuck here."

He released her shoulder and spun into the hall, removing his pistol from the back of his jeans. He gripped it, his pulsing strength threatening to bend the steel. His focus was unbreakable as he deepened into the zone.

Dogged, he approached a closed door at the end of the hall, every muscle snapping in his body—that feeling he got when he was at the apex of a raid. Power surged through his veins, blazing both hot and icy cold. Thundering blood rushed to his extremities, and he felt like he could tear down the entire fucking building with one hand. He was so goddamn strong. *Too* strong.

One night with Kendra had reinvigorated him to the point that he feared. His self-control was on a hair trigger. It wouldn't take much...

"Delivery." Delta thumped on the door, demanding entrance. It whipped open, revealing the scout standing in the frame, shocked to see an angry motherfucker aiming a pistol at his face.

"Shit," the scout stumbled, trying to draw his own gun.

But Delta rushed him, lunging forward with precision. He wasn't worried about losing. He was worried about kicking the guy's ass *too* damn hard before he got any answers. Clutching the scout's neck, feeling life escape the man's body, Delta's lucidity faltered as all he could think of was what he had to do to protect Kendra from all of it.

Chapter Thirteen

It had been four days since Kendra had gotten home from Bakersfield. *Four.*

And there'd been complete radio silence from Delta.

Sitting over her breakfast bar, scrolling through her phone while sipping on her morning coffee, Kendra didn't know how to feel. Coming down off the Delta high was harder than she remembered, leaving her squarely depressed, and it wasn't just because she was exhausted. She'd thought about his words more times than she could count. She'd fought every urge to send him messages, begging him to care. And she'd found distractions to keep her heart from sinking.

The same narrative played through her head again. It was all a game. She meant nothing to him. The whole ridiculous story about a lurking, shadowy danger was cooked up to make her fall into him when he wanted her—when it was convenient for him. It was unconscionable that he wasted so much energy trying to get her to believe she was in danger and that he wanted to protect her. One minute, he was all in. The next minute, he was gone. It was a complete and utter rollercoaster. Her mind was made up. He was not allowed near her anymore.

She had never been good enough for him...not in a *real* way. Never good enough for a hot, ripped Navy SEAL who could have any woman he wanted. And who was she? Some boring forensic scientist with dry skin and thick thighs.

Sitting up straight in her chair, she tucked her cream blouse into her gray slacks. She had to be on the road shortly to get to the lab and get to work. It was a welcome distraction from her unending singledom, which she was not looking forward to explaining to her son one day.

A barrage of noise came from her front door as someone opened it and moved inside. Kendra turned in her chair to see her sister, Sienna, coming in. Flipping her much longer blonde hair over her shoulder, Sienna heaved the stroller into the front entrance landing. Kendra immediately jumped up, lunging forward to help.

"Good morning!" Kendra beamed as she greeted her older sister. "How was your walk?"

She smiled as she looked down into the stroller and saw a perfectly sleeping angel — her beautiful little boy.

"Little Leo can't seem to stay awake much past breakfast," Sienna whispered as she smiled down on the baby.

"Ah, well—he's barely grown out of his newborn days." Kendra leaned over, aching to pick him up. She really needed a hug.

"I'll just keep him in here for now, so we don't wake him up," Sienna said, gently rocking the stroller back and forth in the entranceway. "Are you heading to work?"

"Yes, I am—but I can stay back if you need me," Kendra said quickly, reassuring her sister that she wasn't trying to run out on her.

"No, no—it's okay. I know it's been crazy busy since you've been back at work."

"I'm asking a lot of you." Kendra looked down slightly, reflecting on how the past few weeks had gone.

"Not at all." Sienna offered a compassionate smile. "That's why I'm here."

Kendra stirred under the warmth of her gaze. *God*, she was so lucky to have her sister living with her. It added company and help was *so* appreciated. Sienna's husband, who in the Marine Corps, was overseas, so Kendra had invited her to shack up there temporarily so they could help each other out. It had been a hard year for them both.

She bit her lip, pushing memories out, not wanting to feel the pain.

"You know, I'm worried about you," Sienna whispered, her voice fraught with concern. "You've been distant, disconnected—ever since the car accident."

Kendra let out a deep breath, knowing she couldn't lie to her sister. They were too close for that to fly.

"Well, you're right. My head hurts," Kendra disclosed.

"And you aren't seeing a doctor—why?"

"Because I don't think it's from the accident." Her gaze flashed to her sister.

A brief moment of silence took over the front hall, and Sienna's compassionate eyes were too much for Kendra.

She turned, looking into the mirror hanging on the wall to inspect her temple. The bruising was almost healed by that point, but whatever hurt inside her head hadn't.

"Someone... Someone has come back into my life," Kendra said slowly, her voice cracking. "Someone I didn't expect."

"No...it's not *him*. He's not back, *is* he?" Sienna pushed, deep concern in her voice. "Why didn't you tell me?"

Kendra closed her eyes, her pain rising. "It all happened so fast. I should have said something."

"What happened? Is he trying to get back in?"

Kendra pursed her lips, not knowing how to answer that. She wished she hadn't brought it up at all.

"I don't know what his game is or why he's back," Kendra admitted, turning to her sister. "I can't trust a word the man says."

And yet I gave myself to him.

Sienna pressed on, venting, "This guy has been nothing but bad news, Kendra. You need to stay away from him."

"I'm trying to," Kendra grumbled.

"Like hell you are," Sienna sighed, knowing. "Just talk to me. What's been going on?"

Kendra found herself falling back against the wall, thinking about the past week. "He just showed up at a scene to warn me that I was in danger."

"A scene?"

"Yes—the military vet."

"Is that why he was there?"

"Either that—or me. I don't know anymore."

"He's got an angle. I know it," Sienna declared, shaking her head in disdain and looking down at the baby. "Be careful what you share with him."

"Don't you think I should tell him?"

Sienna took in a deep breath, finally replying, "Yes—eventually. But you need to be okay first, and you are not okay right now."

Kendra locked eyes with her sister, and things got too real. She pushed off the wall, searching for her exit.

"You know what? I should get to work. Let's catch up later."

Sienna took a step forward, looking down on her. "You have to ask yourself some serious questions first. What do you want?"

What I can't have—the thought ran through Kendra's mind. She bit her lip, hating it all the same. She could never admit those words to her sister. Tears welled in her eyes and a ball formed in her throat, which she should have expected.

"Look... I've got to go." Kendra grabbed her tote and leaned over the stroller to kiss her baby goodbye.

His face was so calm and peaceful, unaware of the turmoil between his parents. She didn't want to disturb him, though all she wanted to do was hold him. A tear rolled down her cheek, which she carefully wiped away. It was time to go. She had a lot to do—and strength to regain. She had to push through.

Her hand on the doorknob, pulling it open, she became aware of her sister's encouragement behind her.

"Remember that you are amazing. I'm here for you, Leo's here for you—and we are not leaving."

"Love you, sis." Kendra shot a forced smile over her shoulder, trying to let the kind words sink in.

She launched out of her house to find her rental car—a reminder she didn't need. The deal Delta had tried to cut with her was nothing more than an avenue

Zoe Normandie

to play more mind games. She didn't need any fucking lessons from him.

The long drive down into LA to the lab gave Kendra enough time to think things through and reflect on her sister's words. One day, she was going to have to have an honest conversation with Delta. It wasn't a matter of giving him a chance. It was a matter of what was right. There were things he needed to know. Things he didn't know right now.

Her fingers twitched on the steering wheel, drawing her attention once again to her naked ring finger. She was unwed. She wasn't even with the father. He wasn't there. That had been so hard to admit during her pregnancy.

"I wouldn't ever marry him anyway," she attested, dead sure. "It doesn't matter."

Shrugging it off and telling herself she really didn't care, Kendra finally pulled into the parking lot of her gray and white-bricked lab, which was situated in the busy core of the city. She turned off the car and pulled her cell phone off the charger. But before stepping out, she stared at the screen. Afraid that she was obsessed, she fought the urge to send a chaser message to Delta.

I need to talk to you.

Then she deleted it before once again retyping it.

Chewing her mouth, staring at the unsent message on her screen, she knew it would be wrong. She wasn't ready to have that talk. She wasn't okay yet. He hadn't known about the pregnancy, about his son. And even if she'd lain awake at night, thinking about how to tell him, she had no idea what she wanted out of it, aside from the fairy tale she'd never get.

But that familiar guilt rose up, pointing to the values she held dear. Her finger hovered over the 'send' button, and she bit her lip a little too hard, making herself flinch.

What am I doing?

She exhaled, finally deleting the words and never sending the message at all.

"Why can't I get him off my mind? I'm just wasting my time," she growled at herself, grabbing her building pass out of her tote.

Reaching for the door, she lifted her feet to swivel out as her cell phone pinged, notifying her that she'd received a message. Her heart practically thumped out of her chest as she stared as the lit screen in her hand, slowly raising it. But her stomach sank so hard that she fell back into her seat as she read it. It was from Hunter.

Available tonight?

Irritated, Kendra snapped back a message.

No, I'm not.

It's for work. If I text you a time and a place later, can you be there?

Goddamn. Kendra twisted in her seat, wishing she could break the stupid phone. Hunter, whether she liked it or not, was her boss. This was for work. He'd made clear. He could write her up.

I need back-up on this.

Can you get someone else?

No, I need you.

Kendra closed her eyes, caught in a bad spot. She hovered her fingers over the phone's keyboard, at a loss. She just couldn't go. Delta's words crashed through her mind. Hunter was dangerous. She needed to stay safe, stay away. For once, she agreed with him.

But Delta's other words sliced through her memories — *"All mine."* He wanted her to feel like she belonged to him, to wait for him — so no one else could have her. Kendra looked around the car, gazing at nothing particular but letting the truth sink in. There was not going to be a fairy tale for her. She had to get back to her real life, and that meant raising a child and making a living. She had to write back to her boss.

Is it urgent?

Yes.

Send me the details.

Chapter Fourteen

Kendra's black stilettos clicked down the sidewalk in West Hollywood as she approached a nightclub she'd never been to. In a black strappy tank top and a leather bomber jacket on top of dark jeans, she thought she cut the look of a good undercover operator. Protecting her identity, she'd even left her car at a quiet lot several blocks from her destination.

It wasn't often that she did this type of work, but apparently, she needed to this time, according to her boss. Moving through a small club-going crowd in front of a row of buildings, she tightened her jaw, feeling a little out of place, to say the least. Party people were younger than she remembered and wearing things she didn't quite understand. It took everything in her not to just turn around and bolt home. Home was the only place she wanted to be, the only place that felt right, cozy and safe.

But here she was — meeting Hunter.

Pulling out a twenty as she approached the bouncer at the entrance to a dark club, she observed the name — *Holywood*. A gothic, edgy design adorned the black doorway leading into a space down a shadowy hallway. As she strode into the bar, she spotted Hunter leaning up against the bar top, just where he had said he'd be.

"You came." Hunter licked his lips, possibly inebriated.

She grumbled to herself as he ushered her into a tight space next to him. The room, peppered with dim lamps, featured a long antique-looking wooden bar. Loud music echoed throughout, a type of dance-rock, enticing people to move. If vampires drank anywhere, Kendra didn't doubt they'd show up there, based on the crowd.

"This better be worth it," she noted, cold and unsociable, which didn't seem to dissuade Hunter from pawing up her back.

"You won't regret this." He slammed down on the bar beside her, leaning in to speak over the music. "What can I get you?"

Something in his gaze made her skin crawl, but it was a little unlike before. Something was different. The calculating look in his eye was unnerving, and she covertly inched away, creating space.

"Let's get to it," she prompted. "This is business."

Hunter grinned, tracing the rim on his cup, looking her up and down. "Why can't this be personal?"

"Why am I here, Hunter?" She grew incensed, looking around the bar. "What are we looking for?"

Hunter laughed, motioning to the bartender, ostensibly ordering her something. He always thought he knew what she wanted, she realized — and he always got it wrong. Now, both hands leaning on the bar, she couldn't miss how he was flexing his muscles and looking at her through the side of his eyes. He seemed *different*. A little wilder.

Leaning into her, he exhaled as a strange, self-satisfied look crossed his face.

"Your boy, Delta... He thinks he's pretty smooth, huh?"

Kendra's interest was piqued. "Okay?"

"But he's not as clever as he thinks."

"What does that mean?"

Hunter grinned and continued, "The thing about SEALs is that they chew through women – and were you any exception? I've been the only person looking out for you. I've been here when he wasn't."

The way his words came out was like a justification. She raised her eyebrow again, feeling that there was a deeper story behind what Hunter was up to.

"Has something happened you would like to share?"

She slowly probed Hunter, waiting for him to make sense, but the man just shrugged, holding firm in his space as the bartender slung a clear drink down in front of her with a lime on top. She went to reach into her jacket for cash, but Hunter aggressively flung down bills to cover her. The bartender snapped them up before she could protest, which she very much wanted to.

Fuck, she thought as she paced back.

"Are we sharing now?" Hunter quizzed, advancing toward her. "Have we decided to be honest with each other?"

She watched him, silently, waiting for him to play his cards. He continued, letting her in on his point.

"When are you going to recognize that he's a monster?"

"What the hell are you talking about?" Kendra said, confused as hell. *What does Hunter know?*

"He's dangerous, Kendra. I've been telling you that since the beginning. What more do you need?"

His focus followed her lips, on down her throat and resting there for a moment. Taking a swig of his pint, Hunter recovered, pausing the conversation. He then put the cold glass down and narrowed his eyes on her.

"As it is, I knew you wouldn't take my word. I know you've been hanging on to hopes for him. Well, Delta is going to just hurt you...again and again, like he already has. And I want you to see it for yourself."

As his words dripped out, she couldn't hide the surprise on her face. He was about to show her something that she didn't want to see. She *knew* it. He motioned to a dark wall on the edge of the room that clearly had line of sight to the antique bar in the middle of the room. It was, however, blocking the view of the back of the bar.

He continued, "I want you to walk to that wall, in the shadow, and look behind the bar. You'll see someone sitting there. You'll know what I mean."

Kendra raised her eyebrow, her nerves growing inside her. She couldn't explain why. It just didn't feel right. But she moved toward the wall, like he said, needing to see for herself. Hiding herself in the shadow, she turned to look behind the bar.

That was when her heart stopped.

It's Delta.

The man who made her feel too much, the man that never was available, sat there in his usual black hooded sweater, his hand on the bar, drinking whiskey. It wasn't so much that he was there, but that his head was dropped and he was conspiring with someone.

A woman.

The gorgeous, slim brunette with an athletic build leaned into him, taking in every word. *Is this a fucking date?* Kendra stumbled back against the wall, gripping it for stability. He'd never taken her out on a date. Feeling sick, she stood on the sidelines like an invader. That woman was so much closer to Delta than she'd ever be, whispering intimately and smiling.

To say that Kendra's heart died a little would be an understatement. Something inside her blackened just then. She was damn glad she was in the shadow, unseen—because she wanted to cry. Frenzy filled her as she watched Delta shoot his casual smile at the woman. It couldn't be any clearer what was going on. Furious with herself, she wished she would have just listened to her own good sense.

A familiar, crawling voice came up behind her in the shadow, cold hands gripping her shoulders.

"He never gave a fuck about you," Hunter grunted into her ear. "But I do."

She turned her head, taking in the self-congratulatory look that was emanating from his very being. He spun her in his arms, far more aggressive than he'd ever been. It was like the Hunter she'd known had mutated. With fiery eyes, he gazed down his nose at her, like a tiger ready to eat.

"He's not capable."

Her lips parted with his words, realizing what he was getting at—and where it was going.

"Why are you saying this?"

"He can never be a father. You know it."

Kendra felt herself breaking down, unwilling to lie to herself anymore. Hunter tightened his arms around her, pulling her into him. That unpleasant scent filled her nose and she tried to push away, her gaze drifting back to where Delta sat at the bar.

Except he was gone.

Stuck in Hunter's grip, Kendra pressed her eyes shut, feeling tears well. Searing tension ripped up her throat and she gasped for breath. She gave that man too much power over her.

"I'm the one who will *protect* you." Hunter wouldn't relent. "I'll marry you, Kendra."

She looked up at him, her eyes wet. "And what do you want in return?"

He lifted his hand and touched her, like she was the prize he finally was ready to claim for his own. Every muscle in her body screamed as she realized how close he was getting. As he ran his gaze up and down her face, Kendra suddenly felt nauseous. There was no doubt what Hunter wanted in return—and she'd known it all along. She just wanted him to be a man and finally say it.

"What do I want in return?" he asked, his breath sour. "Isn't it obvious?"

"Hunter," she pleaded through the loud music in the bar, shaking her head. She couldn't believe it—couldn't believe the position she was in.

Hunter tightened his grip on her chin, and he had that same vicious, entitled look shining in his eyes. He wasn't going to let her go. She flinched, but he grabbed her wrists, smacking her whole body against the wall, causing her to scream out, though it was dulled because of the loud music. She saw that same something in his eyes. He was losing control. Hunter's eyes twitched with an anger she'd never seen before. Even in the darkness, she could see his neck pulse, like he was becoming someone else.

"Think about it, Kendra. I'll take care of you."

"I don't need that." She exhaled sharply. "I have to go."

"You can't leave. I'm not letting him win."

Then Hunter's head dropped lower, and he was readying to take her mouth. Writhing underneath his cold grip, she screamed out for help, screaming for Delta, but no one heard her. She shook her head, fighting back against Hunter. A lone tear sprung from her eyes as she desperately tried to free herself.

But she couldn't.

Just before he could land his mouth on hers, a thick hand thumped on Hunter's shoulder, yanking him off her. Letting out a sharp shriek, she collapsed back against the wall in shock, watching a surprised expression whipping across Hunter's face. In the blink of an eye, the profile of a familiar tall man with a hood up and a black mask on pummeled Hunter to the ground.

She slid away, stumbling into the crowd. Through the loud music and the dark of the bar, all she could see was Hunter on the floor, bloodied and gasping. But, searching between the bobbing heads of the party people, she realized that Hunter was once again alone.

Delta was already gone…like a ghost.

Trying to process what the hell had just happened, she quickly slipped away and ran out of the bar, tears streaming down her face. It had all been a terrible mistake. Why the hell had she gone there? Trembling, Kendra launched herself back onto the street, her heels clicking noisily on the sidewalk as she paced back toward the lot where she'd left her car. Fear boiling over, she kept glancing over her shoulder, unsure who she was more afraid to see.

She sped off the main street into the connecting alleyway to the lot. She ran through the dark space, wishing she'd worn better shoes. The heels were new — and digging into her, making her hobble toward safety. Her car wasn't far. She just had to get there — and get out. Get home.

Then she could think.

Halfway down the alley, she passed a fire ladder, creaking in the night's breeze on the side of the building. A loud thud crashed behind her — like someone had jumped from the ladder onto the ground. She didn't have time to turn around.

Hands wrapped around her in an aggressive bear hug, pulling her body into his. She tried to scream, but a gloved hand on her mouth stifled her. She immediately used her police training to destabilize her assaulter, kicking back and trying to bite the glove. She was good at it — but he was better, easily fending her off. He was strong as hell.

Tightening his hold on her, he held her back against his chest in the alley. It caused her to flinch and fight all the more, though his familiar scent was calming her at the same time.

"Why did you come to meet him — when I specifically told you to stay away?" His low voice challenged, as fierce as she'd ever heard him.

Unable to answer, as his hand still covered her mouth, she turned her head more toward him. He continued his questioning, which was nearly a lecture.

"Why can't I get you to listen to me?"

Silent, she struggled to breathe as he held her mouth, wriggling and fighting his grasp. All she wanted to do was get away — get away from everything.

He yanked her harder into him, sending a clear message as he continued, "This is what happens when you don't listen to me."

His velvety growl was as intoxicating as ever. He just did something to her. Then he released his hand from her mouth, spinning her to face him for the first time, apparently satisfied that he'd scared her enough.

"You!" she cried out, thumping hard on his chest. "You are *worse* than him."

"I know I am," he growled low, holding her tight. He ran his gloves up the side of her face, caressing her cheek as he stared down into her eyes. "But I still need you to trust me."

"No. I'll never trust you."

The words seemed to hit him hard, and he widened his eyes with surprise as he released his grasp on her, allowing her take a step back from him...then another.

"Just how many girls are you fucking?" Kendra howled, incensed at his emotionless face.

"It's not what it looks like."

"Then why the hell were you there — with her?"

"Does it matter?" His angry boom carried in the alley, and Kendra took a step back, stunned.

A silence found the space between them, and he stared back without explaining who the woman was. The absence of explanation was all Kendra needed.

And that was when Kendra spun on her heels to find her way to her car. She didn't dare look back over her shoulder at him, unwilling to fall victim once more to his burning gaze.

Chapter Fifteen

One year before

"Cheers." Warren clinked Delta's pint, leaning against the bar.

A younger, less-broken Delta nodded in agreement, studying the LAPD officers mixing at the bar, enjoying the round he'd bought for everyone after the obstacle course. It was the least he could do for their guests.

"We should invite them back." Delta shrugged, keeping his gaze fixed on the crowd.

"Looking for something?" Warren pressed, spinning his pint thoughtfully on the bar. "Or someone?"

"No."

Delta replied a little too fast, likely stirring his best friend's suspicion. He couldn't hide that he was waiting for a memorable blonde and her bouncy ponytail to show up for drinks. He'd made it damn clear he wanted her there. Would she show? He slung back the rest of his stout, mulling on the big question of the day. The night would be a bust if she didn't. There was something about her, something he wanted to know better.

Warren cracked, "I didn't think she was going to survive the course."

"She was trying her best, man." Delta flashed fast, correcting him. "Don't start with that shit."

Warren snorted. "Don't you think it was a little out of her league? It seemed fucking careless as hell to let her run the damn thing."

"Dude, are you expecting her to sit it out just because she's a chick?"

Delta fired back at his friend, feeling heat rising in his throat, but he slowed his roll. He'd always been good at being the calm one. Attentive, the bartender dropped a fresh beer in front of him, giving him a second to recover.

"I'm not trying to be an asshole, but look around." Warren motioned to the rest of the crowd. "These guys know what they are doing. She didn't. It was dangerous."

"I was there with her. I wasn't going to let anything happen to her."

"I saw. We all saw."

Delta slammed his pint on the bar, staring down his friend. The ocean breeze floated through the open patio doors, blowing a tuft of his hair over his brow. He reached up, smoothing it back, narrowing his eyes on a certain voice carrying through the crowd. *The staff sergeant.* The fucking asshat had disappeared right as they'd jumped into the course. He'd deserted Kendra right when she'd needed help the most, and for that reason, Delta knew everything he needed to know about him.

"Be careful with him," Warren warned from the side, keeping his voice down.

"I'm not worried about that guy," Delta scoffed, his eyes fixated on Hunter's weak shoulders.

He didn't like him. Not at all.

"You've stepped on his territory, for sure."

"Fuck—I don't give a shit. He can come at me if he's got a problem," Delta snapped, watching and waiting.

Feeling his chest muscles tighten and flex, his protective instinct pulsed up his spine, driving him to plot and scheme, until that familiar blonde ponytail bobbed through the bar's entrance and interrupted his thoughts. As Kendra strode in, the muscles in his body relaxed momentarily, shifting gears. From the corner of his eye, he could see Warren watching him, a sly grin on his mouth. There was no mistaking what was happening, so Delta didn't bother trying to hide it.

Kendra slowly gazed around the crowd, over the clusters of cops and operators drinking in the sunset at the oceanside bar. Other patrons, local women, were trying to mingle with the guys, laughing and flirting. Delta knew where that was going. There wasn't much mystery to how the night would be ending for some of them. If he'd only be as lucky.

He shot a grin and a nod to Kendra, and her face lit up in return, beaming ear to ear. As she pushed through the crowd, her hips swaying, his cock hardened and he stifled a groan. Carefully adjusting his wood, he drank in all that was Kendra, a sight he had come to enjoy. Her light, natural look was what turned him on—her loose-fitting jeans, ripped in the knee, her white shirt, relaxed but revealing her mouth-watering cleavage with that golden tan. She looked fucking hot.

"Relax, man," Warren grumbled, drawing Delta's attention to the fact that his grip was literally about to snap his pint glass in half.

Delta sucked in a breath, chugged the rest of the beer and released the glass back to the bar top. He ran his teeth over his lip, averting his gaze and trying not to stare.

Warren added, "What is with you and this girl?"

From his peripheral vision, Delta observed Hunter striding to greet Kendra as she was halfway into the bar, causing Delta to tense up again. *Who the fuck does he think he is?* Something primal flooded Delta's senses, a hot rush running up his neck.

Warren grunted a final warning. "Don't get in the middle of that."

"Fuck off," Delta snapped at his friend as Kendra pulled away from Hunter and closed the gap between her and Delta.

Finally.

Delta adjusted, pushing Warren away and opening up space for Kendra to join him. With the sun dropping below the horizon, Delta enjoyed how the last rays of light lit up her blonde hair. It was like she was on fire.

"You're late," Delta joked as Kendra moved in beside him. Everything in his body grew hotter as she leaned against the bar, her shiny lips flashing up at him.

"I'm never late." She grinned and engaged with the bartender to order a drink.

Leaning back casually, he observed this new woman in his life. He appreciated how natural she kept it. If she was wearing any makeup, he didn't see it, not like the other women hanging around the bar. Those women, who'd layered on way too much war paint and were snapping posed selfies for their followers, were the type of woman who usually threw themselves at him, thinking he'd be all in. Kendra was a far cry from that type. She was clearly a woman who was just unapologetically herself — natural, *so take it or leave it.*

Turning back to him, she nodded. "Thanks for supporting me today. I'm used to having to do everything alone."

"It was nothing." He shrugged. "You were on my team."

Kendra picked up her pint as it was served, raising it to Delta.

"No, you don't understand. They said I was going to eat it on the course. I know they wanted me to screw it up."

"Why?"

Raising her brow, she slowly sipped on the glass, her mouth consuming the frothy liquid, before explaining, "To prove their theory — that I'm not cut out to be a cop. I belong behind a desk or a lab counter."

She brought the pint back to her mouth, dancing her lips on the edge of the glass. It was the most goddamn erotic thing Delta had ever seen. Stifling his reaction, he drilled his attention into her words, needing to stay focused.

"Dudes are fucking dumb sometimes," he assured her, trying to find the right words. "Don't worry about them."

"I guess. I couldn't have done it without you," Kendra confessed, her eyes big and thankful. "And, aside from keeping me alive, you actually made it fun."

He couldn't accept the compliment. "But you did it on your own. I just stood behind you."

"Yes, you did." She grinned, insinuating everything.

The sudden change from serious to playful was perfect, drawing a smile across Delta's mouth.

He leaned in. "Tell me you didn't like it."

She laughed, keeping her tone low. "Would it be wrong if I did?"

"Not at all." He gripped the bar top, assessing every inch of her body. In a deeper voice, he continued, "What else do you like?"

"Nerdy stuff."

"Like what?"

"Chemistry, experiments, bioethics," she began listing, her clear blue eyes flashing at him again as she abruptly halted.

"Damn." He gave a low laugh, looking around. "You're too smart for this group of idiots, and I include myself in that."

She let out a hearty laugh in response, shaking her head. He let the conversation lapse while she took another drink, enjoying himself thoroughly as he watched her. Like him, she obviously hated taking compliments. That much was clear. And the more he exchanged with her, the more intoxicated by her he felt.

"You and I—I'm sure we are exact opposites." She flickered her gaze up and down his body, and he knew what she saw.

"Opposites, huh?" He raised his eyebrow, wondering if this was her attempt at pushing him away. It surprised him. By that point, most women he met were inventing things they had in common, pretending to like everything he liked, including the back seat of his pickup truck.

He continued, "Let me guess... Your perfect Saturday involves a book and silence."

Cocking her head back and letting out a laugh, Kendra grumbled, "Guilty, and what the hell do you get up to?"

Taking his time, he sipped his beer again, thinking about how to phrase it.

She cut into his thoughts, calling him out, "Stop trying to massage the truth and just spit it."

Surprised at her quick tongue, he stiffened.

"You want to know the truth? I never tell girls this because I don't want to fucking scare them. My perfect Saturday involves the firing range, prepping for my next deployment and running survival scenarios in the mountains." Then he added, sarcastically, "So, yeah — I'm a pretty well-rounded guy."

"Wow," she said with a very unimpressed face. "Eat and sleep all things military, much?"

"I'm marriage material. What can I say?" He tilted his head, playacting as conceited.

Laughing at him, she said, "Seems like it. You should get a non-military hobby."

"Like what...basket weaving?" he teased. "Knitting?"

"Yeah, you'd be cute doing some arts and crafts," she baited right back, not missing a beat. "Make me a Hufflepuff scarf, please."

"Fuck, I'm not going to tell you what my real extra-curricular hobby is." He groaned under his breath as he downed the rest of his glass, the mere thought tensing his shoulders.

"Come on," she flirted in a gasping tone. "Tell me."

Toying, he brushed her off. "You couldn't handle it."

"You are too much." She shook her head, grinning back at the bartender for another pint.

"You saying you aren't interested?" Delta leaned back in, looking down his nose at her, calculating.

"Of course not — what did you think this was?" she countered, a little too much seriousness in her tone.

He shrugged, keeping it light, watching her every move.

"I'm not that easy," she added, changing the dynamic.

He shot her a cold glare. "I never said you were."

She doubled down, carving out boundaries. "Don't even try it with me. It's a waste of your time. I've got a chastity belt on."

"I don't see it." He dropped his gaze to her waist, challenging her.

"I'm more conservative than you think," she continued, holding her hand up to stop him. "I've been holding out for something a little more traditional."

As she said it, he grew hungrier.

"When you say stuff like that, it only makes me more determined." He watched the realization cross her face, and he added, "I'm a competitive guy. Really competitive."

A hunter, he just couldn't help himself, assessing her for weakness, like she was both his opponent and his prey. Stiffening her spine, she narrowed her eyes at him. Her demeanor had transformed to full-blown protective, which he regretted.

She warned, "It's not a competition, and I'm not looking for a quick and casual thing."

It's not a competition? He raised his eyebrows, wondering if she had any idea how bad that made him want to win. The more he leaned forward, the more she leaned back, making him want it all that much more. The glaring issue — that she was relationship material and he wasn't—seemed less important, becoming second to winning her by any means necessary. In Delta's books, if the ends justified the means...

Unfortunately, his thoughts were cut off as they were swarmed by a couple of the guys, including Warren, putting the conversation on hold. As Delta and Kendra were absorbed into a bigger group, clinking beers and slapping hands on backs, shot glasses full of tequila were thrust into their hands. The group enjoyed a few more—maybe several more—pints before Delta pushed away to find the restroom. He didn't like leaving Kendra with them, but he had to piss like a racehorse, and surely she'd stick around.

The excursion having taken longer than he would have liked, due to a small lineup, he found himself gazing left and right when he re-entered the bar, searching for her. Quickly, he realized that she wasn't there anymore.

Fuck.

Where the fuck did she go? Who else left the bar? It was well past sunset and getting late into the evening. That protective tension crept up his chest at not seeing Hunter anymore either.

"You okay?" Warren asked cautiously as Delta approached.

Delta ran his hands through his hair, trying to make sense of what had happened. Heat rushed up the back of his neck and sweat beaded on his forehead.

"The antimalaria drugs getting to you this time?" Warren nudged his friend, trying to keep it light.

"I just started them." Delta turned, looking out the patio where it connected to the beach. "The next rotation's going to be a bitch."

She has to be out there.

Without even so much as saying goodbye to his friend, Delta slipped outside. He quickly observed that she wasn't on the patio, either. Glowering side to side, he couldn't even see her on the stretch of beach. She was a grown-ass woman, but he didn't like it. His uncontrollable intensity sprang forth. In a flash, he whipped down the patio steps, finding his way onto the deserted beach.

Maybe it was just his lack of trust in people or his driving need to ensure her safety, but he told himself that he had to make sure she was okay, otherwise he wouldn't be able to sleep at night. His intentions were all altruistic. As he strode down the wide expanse of sand, trying to get eyes on any form resembling hers, he finally caught a glimpse of a woman slowly walking in the distance by the water — alone. That woman was definitely Kendra, based on the sway of her hips that he had memorized. Relieved to see her, he confirmed she was all right and not being stalked…by any other man.

"You shouldn't be out here on your own," Delta called out as he approached her, prepared to lecture.

Kendra spun, digging her heels in, twirling her blonde ponytail in her fingers as she watched him walk up to her. Something in her expression told him that she wasn't taking him seriously. He could almost feel her rolling her eyes, even in the dark.

"I think I'll be fine." She turned with a shrug, returning to walking down the beach.

He caught up quickly, his long, strong legs outpacing her. The glittery waves crashed against the sand beside them as they walked together, illuminated by the big white moon overhead.

"Why'd you leave?" he challenged.

"I needed a bit of air," she replied, nodding back to the bar, which was growing farther and farther away as they walked. "It can get a little intense, surrounded by so many of your type."

"My type?" he questioned, full well knowing the answer.

"I think you know what I mean."

"And I think you should listen to me when I say don't walk on the beach, alone, at nearly midnight. It's dark, it's deserted and there's a bar full of drunken guys who would love nothing more than —"

She cut in, stopping him. "Than what?" She dug her heels into the sand, folding her arms protectively like a shield over her chest.

He pivoted. "I don't need to tell you."

"And I don't need to be babysat. I'm a big girl."

Squaring himself to her, his tone changed. "You're stubborn as hell, aren't you?"

"So what if I am?"

"You should watch your back. Your boss is into you. I wouldn't trust him. He could be out here, waiting for his moment." Delta nodded around to the dark bushes lining the top of the beach.

"And what about you?" The accusation in her voice was clear.

He stood still, that hunter impulse driving his focus towards one thing only.

"You are used to people taking orders from you, huh?" she continued, holding her position. "You don't know Hunter. He's harmless…unlike *you*."

"Unlike *me*?" Delta stood back on his heels, staring her down. "Looks like you've got my type all figured out. Now, I know *your* type. You're the type that always goes it alone and never asks for help."

She fidgeted in the sand, unwilling to answer him, which was when he knew he'd got her. Even in the moonlight, he didn't miss the fire in her eyes — a fire she no doubt stoked to survive.

He continued, trying to get her to open up, "I bet it was a big deal for you that you accepted my help on the ropes today. You don't like being *rescued*, right?"

She gaped up at him, concession in her eyes. He'd hit the nail on the head. Why couldn't he have seen it earlier?

"I bet you never let anyone help you."

"I've managed on my own this far, haven't I?" She shrugged, nonchalant yet revealing all the same. She dropped her hands, fidgeting with the pockets on her jeans, averting her gaze.

She was too alluring, and Delta found himself edging in closer to her, drawn to the fact that he was the one who'd cracked her — no one else. The waves crashing in the background made the perfect backdrop for what was about to happen. Her scent filled the air between them — that rosy musk of sweetness. It was damn intoxicating. Maybe a little scared, she flashed her eyes back up to him, parting her lips in the obvious awareness that they'd lost the comfortable distance between them. With a look like that, he well and truly couldn't help himself. He knew he shouldn't do it, but he was unable to stop.

Losing control, he reached out, roughly gripping her hourglass waist, pulling her up and into him. Growing breathless, she yielded to his touch, giving in — showing him that she wanted it, wanted him.

"We're looking for different things," she whispered as he slowly dropped his head.

He hovered his mouth above hers. "Maybe."

"Don't kiss me unless you mean it," she pleaded, vulnerable. "Don't—"

He didn't let her finish her thought, closing the remaining gap between their mouths. He took her lips with his, kissing her well and thoroughly. At first, she pouted as if to refute him, but her gaze lowered, her eyelids growing heavy. She welcomed his tongue, and he tasted her for the first time, the flavor exactly as he imagined. Erotic, sensual, he started slow, but passion drove him to quicken the kiss, a sense of urgency lingering. Her flawless body sank into his and warmth permeated through her into his damn cold chest, which was starting to remember what it was like to be that near someone.

With every sensation, she softened a little more, until it felt like she was completely his to do with as he wished. Like he'd finally won his prize, he tightened his hold on her, drawing her flat against him, feeling her breathe as he let his tongue tango with hers. Her mouth was just as sweet as could be, both wet and delicious. It was becoming a little too clear that he couldn't get enough as he kissed her, adored her, consumed her—forgetting that what he knew would keep them apart.

"Delta, you're too much." She moaned, tilting her head back as he kissed down her neck, feeling her running her hands up his biceps, toward his chest.

"Matteo," he corrected, surprising himself, aroused as hell from her exploration. "My name's Matteo."

Raising his eyebrow, he grazed his teeth along her delicate neck, realizing that he'd never told anyone his real name except her. He wanted her like he'd never wanted a woman before and he was making it damn clear with his frenzied hunger.

To her intensifying breathing, he added, grinning, "My mother had to fight my entire Italian family to name me that and not Michael."

She groaned his real name in response, something he knew he'd never get enough of. Running his hands down her back, feeling her hot, tight ass through those damn jeans, his cock pulsed in need, like it was ready to explode. Goddamn, she was something. *They don't make girls like her anymore*, he thought, determined to feel every inch of her skin before the night was through. Logic had flown out of the window, along with any sense of care. He'd lost control—the only thing that mattered anymore was her body intertwined with his.

Chapter Sixteen

Present day

Delta flipped the invitation to his Medal of Honor ceremony back and forth in his bloodied fingers as he sat in the shadows on the couch in his living room, watching the street in front of his house. It was past midnight, but he couldn't sleep.

He couldn't blame the aching feeling in his fists for keeping him awake, despite how hard he'd pummeled Hunter at the bar. Hell, he should have done something a lot worse. Watching the sniveling coward wrap his arms around Kendra had burned so deeply, almost as much as seeing the hate on Kendra's face as she'd accused him of fucking around. Familiar tension coiled through Delta's body as he tried to push the thought away.

Why the fuck were they there?

Running through scenarios, letting his exhausted, hurting body sink into the couch that he never sat on, he wished for sleep. He'd been burning the candle at both ends for too long. Enviously, he watched his dog, Timber, curled up at his feet and snoring. Her warm body immobilized him.

I've been away too much lately, he thought, as he watched his good girl sleep. He wasn't taking care of her, let alone himself. He was lucky to have a good neighbor. Mrs. Romano, who was there for them both, like the mother he'd lost.

Delta closed his eyes, ordering sleep, unable to stop occasionally squinting to check out the quiet street, as if expecting someone to show up. What was he—an idiot? Kendra wasn't coming, he reminded himself. She'd seen enough. She'd had enough.

And, damn, he'd had enough too.

He'd let her slip through his fingers once again. Or, more accurately, pushed her away violently...with intent. What the hell was he supposed to do? They didn't belong together. It was something they both needed to end, though neither of them seemed to be able to. An unrelenting anger filled his body, directed more at himself than anything. Through his own selfishness, all he was doing was causing her to suffer. She made it all too damn clear, and she wasn't wrong. He wasn't right—at least, not right for her.

Piercing his thoughts, his cell pinged with a new message, and he lunged to grab it off the coffee table, like a junkie. *Is it her?* He was sorely disappointed to see that it was not. It was Warren.

Alive?

Barely. What's up?

Checking in on my asset — making sure you aren't dead.

Nice guy.

Who else is going to do it? That lady cop you've been seeing?

Are you fishing?

Can you blame me?

Delta clenched his jaw and flipped off his cell, not wanting to hear it anymore. Warren was the well-meaning big brother that Delta couldn't handle right now. So he sat in silence, feeling too much pain for his own tolerance. He needed a distraction.

Suddenly, out of the corner of his eye, he saw movement in his driveway on the other side of his truck. When he bolted upright, even Timber awoke with a start. The old service dog was no stranger to threat and stalked alongside Delta as they looked through the edge of his living room window. Nothing was out there.

Nothing that he could see.

Snapping into work mode, Delta stalked through his house — through the living room, into the kitchen at the back where he'd kept the light on. He flexed, feeling that icy heat in his veins, as he approached the side door off the kitchen, the one that led to the driveway.

He heard rustling outside the door. He was right. Someone was there. Deadly focused, he inhaled slowly, calming his racing heart. Instructing Timber to stay back, he flung the door open, establishing six-foot-three inches of threatening force in the doorframe.

An elderly Mrs. Romano stood there, shaking in an oversized wool coat with a frilly pajama dress flowing out from underneath. Her eyes widened in fright as she gazed up to Delta, who immediately calmed, jumping out onto his stoop to greet her.

"Mrs. Romano, what are you doing up so late?" he said apologetically. He couldn't contain his astonishment and reached out to stabilize her shaking frame.

As he held her arm, offering support, she regarded him with worried eyes.

"I'm so sorry to bother you, son. I saw your light on. I just—" she began, but didn't finish, gazing back at her house.

"Go on," Delta urged, dropping his voice to her level.

Tightening her coat, she continued, "I woke up and I heard a noise—like someone was in my house. All I could think of...was to come here."

Timber finally broke free from behind Delta and rushed forward to lick at Mrs. Romano's hands. The two of them were like old friends. As Mrs. Romano leaned over to pet the dog's long, silky coat, a smile broke across her face. Timber was the friend she needed.

"I'll go check your house," Delta said quickly, assessing her property. "I'll make sure no one was there."

Her voice cracked, sad and rattled. "I don't think there *was* anyone in my house."

"I don't mind."

Sunken, Mrs. Romano nodded, allowing Delta to quickly check. He didn't doubt that she was right. No one had been in her house. It wasn't the first time she'd gotten scared in the middle of the night since her husband had died. *It's hard for her being alone.*

And vulnerable.

After he had Mrs. Romano safely back at her house, he insisted she keep Timber for the night. His dog practically lived there half the time anyway and would be more than happy to get a homemade almond biscotti before bed. When the US Navy had retired Timber, no one could have ever expected the laser-focused service animal would be eating cookies on a frilly bedsheet with an elderly Italian lady.

As Delta got back home, he flicked off the lights, determined to find sleep. Falling down on the cool, dark sheets of his bed, he stared at the ceiling. The entire house was silent. His mind was anything but. Lying on his back, he was too damn awake.

He had one thing on his mind.

The memory of Kendra on that hotel bed, her back arching underneath him, pleading.

Closing his eyes, he felt a rush of unwanted emotion that he fought hard to keep under control. There was something so different about the way she'd felt, so much softer. Squishier, even, like she'd gained a few pounds. He fucking liked that—really liked that. He loved feeling those new curves. As he ruminated, he found himself shutting his eyes slowly. The last thought before he drifted was that one day, he had to tell Kendra the truth.

He fell into a semi-comatose state, like a drunken sailor without the booze, and that was exactly why it took him a little longer than usual to come to his senses when he heard a scratching noise emanating from down the hallway in his house—near the kitchen. Groggy as fuck, he took a second or two to snap back to reality. The scratching persisted, barely audible, so he jumped off his bed, rubbing his hands on his face to wake up. He reached to his side table, gulping water to help.

Listening, he crept out of his room — just enough to see all the way down the hallway into his kitchen, where the side door was situated. He realized that someone was breaking in. Through the door came a female frame. Then he saw it — a glint of blonde hair as she quietly shut the door, creeping low along the kitchen. *Well, look who came to play*, he thought as his heart raced.

Kendra hadn't stepped foot on his property since that one night she'd slept over...a year ago.

He slipped back into his bedroom, hiding back against the wall. Since his entire house was silent and dark, he had full advantage, not that he needed it. Behind his bedroom door, he waited and waited as he listened to her approach, hating all the shit he was feeling. Here she was, breaking in, which he was both giddy with anticipation and abjectly furious about.

She was good. He'd have to give her that. If he didn't know what he was doing, he may have been surprised as she crept around the corner, treading into his bedroom. She looked left and right, obviously there to assess. Looking at his bed and obviously realizing that he wasn't in it, an enraged grunt escaped her lips.

"I fucking knew it!" she spat, her hurt showing. "Deserter."

The accusation rushing his senses. He slammed the door and shoved her down on the bed. She yelped, struck her fists out and connected with his jaw, driving pain up his face. Damn, she hit hard. Feverish, he pinned her down, subduing her wild movements. With a sadistic grin, he stared down on her until she gave up, realizing she couldn't win. He was too strong, too big and far too determined.

"Knew what?" he demanded, enjoying how she writhed under his grasp.

"Fuck you."

He pushed down harder, driving more weight onto her wrists to get her attention and send a clear message.

"Why the fuck are you here?" Delta questioned.

"I think that much is damn clear."

Wincing in probable pain, she sucked at her teeth, but she stopped fighting back. He let up a bit but stayed firmly in control of her, waiting for her next move. But then he saw something bleed across her face that he didn't expect.

Hopelessness.

Stunned, he released her right away and edged back. That wasn't the Kendra he knew. As he was gazing down on her, she gradually caught her breath and rubbed her freed wrists. She tilted her chin up to him, fire in her eyes and angry as all hell.

"Who is she?"

"She calls herself Sky," he replied slowly, but Kendra cut in.

"Sky?" she snapped, pushing her agenda. "Are you fucking her?"

"No," he said, categorically.

It apparently wasn't good enough. Kendra sprung up on his bed, shooting a condemning look, unmistakable tears in her reddening eyes only enhancing the piercing marine blue of her irises.

"Why do you keep lying to me? Why can't you tell me the truth?"

"I told you from the beginning—" he started, but Kendra cut him off once again.

"What? That you are the fucking worst?" She jumped up and shoved his chest. "Why do you keep luring me in just to push me away? I *never* wanted this."

Never. The word hit him hard, and he felt a darkness come over him. How could she say *never* when she was right in front of him—in his room? She moved to leave, but he stepped in front of her.

"Let me go." She heaved at him again, but he caught her wrists, yanking her into him.

"Like hell."

"You used me," she cried out, staring into his dead eyes. "You've always just used me. I—"

His grip on her tightened so she'd stop, causing her to wince again. Incensed as all hell, he curled his lip, staring her down. Watching her hate him, he fell silent, unwilling to give her anything else. As the burning rage inside stilled him, the tension in her wrists subsided. She'd stopped fighting back...hopeless.

Her head dropped, her gaze downcast, giving him a view of her bright ponytail that was starting to look fucked up. Her shoulders were heaving, and Delta stared. He oscillated between painfully aware and just numb, like a light flickering on its last legs. As her body started shaking, he released his grip on her wrists, letting them fall back into her. She was crying.

But he'd fallen silent.

"You've never given a fuck what I wanted." She wept.

"When have you ever told me what you wanted?" he snarled, removed.

"Christ, what is the matter with you?"

On autopilot, he pulled her trembling body flat against his, hovering his mouth near her ear. Blinking rapidly, like he was trying to regain lucidity, he found his lips grazing her ear, and he took in the scent of her hair. Inhaling her brought him back, somewhere. His teeth found her ear again, tasting it—teasing it. It was the one thing he knew how to do.

There was something about Kendra that immediately made his cock ache, springing him into action even amid a bloody war. Near her, he could rely on feeling a strong, uncontrollable urge to kiss her senseless and fuck her until she screamed his name, until he could pretend she was his. Sex was easy, especially with her.

He dropped his head even lower, slowly kissing down the side of her face, angling it just right for him. In a barely audible sigh, she let three words slip that sounded like *please don't stop*. Good, because he didn't want to stop. He didn't want her to want it to stop.

"What was that?" he growled, demanding her deference, needing her to confess.

He kept on, using his best tactics against her, getting harder as she breathed the words again. They were maybe a little less coherent but exactly what he wanted to hear, not that he needed an official invitation. She let out a soft moan as he kept her jaw gripped with one hand, provoking her as he kissed up her face, back to her ear. Her responsiveness drove him wild, and he settled comfortably into control. With his other hand, he explored her, up and over her breasts until he got more of the reaction he craved, until he felt her back arch towards him in arousal. It was always about winning.

"You know why they started calling me Delta?"

"Why?" she breathed out, closing her eyes.

"They said I'm the difference between a dream and a nightmare." He recalled the words of his chief after his first grisly battle.

"Are you *my* nightmare?" Her voice cracked, resentful and bitter, throwing sand in his face.

He drew his head back, locking eyes with her. She didn't know the half of it. He wanted to tell her the truth. *There's something wrong with me.*

She inched out of his arms, taking a step back to the bed. He stalked her, stepping to where she stood. She sucked in a breath as she observed him transforming, fear crossing her face. He liked seeing her scared. Hunger overwhelming him, blood coursed through his body, with that same eerie icy heat. That side of him — that uncontrollable side — broke out of whatever thin veil of civility he had. She'd never harbored illusions that he was a nice guy anyway.

"I hate what you do to me," she ground out, igniting something in him that he couldn't explain. "I hate that I can't trust you."

"Do you hate me?"

She bit her lip, tears blinking out of her eyes, and whispered back, "Yes."

"Good," was all he could grunt out before plunging to take her mouth, startling her.

Shocked, she stiffened in his arms and half-heartedly pushed back, refusing him. But he wouldn't be denied, not with her standing in his room, right before his bed. Giving her one more damn good reason to hate him, he savagely kissed her, whether she liked it or not.

Her plump lips parted to welcome his tongue, proving to him that she didn't hate him at all, allowing him to taste the wetness inside her that he'd been fantasizing about all week. As he held her jaw, angling her mouth perfectly to receive him, she pulled at his shirt, finding her way to his core. She groaned as she felt up his abs, and he knew why. Maybe he was a cocky motherfucker, but he wasn't stupid, and he was happy to hear her adoration. He tore his shirt off, sending it to the corner of the room. Her subsequent gasp drove his cock to attention, standing high and alert.

He locked eyes with her and remained silent, but a terrible smile spanned his mouth. It was damn well for the best that she thought she hated him. It made things a lot easier. She had no idea what was coming. In that moment, all he wanted was to feel her skin underneath his, giving herself to him, telling him what he wanted to hear. Aggressive as fuck, he dove and took her mouth again, kissing to thrill and forever brand her as his. She'd never forget it.

He gripped her hair, intertwining and controlling, and she willingly received his tongue, exactly how he wanted.

"Are we doing this again?" Kendra whispered in between kissing.

"Is this what you want?"

"Yes."

She made quick work of dropping his jeans and boxers to the floor, letting him kick them off as he stood before her naked and raw. That little breath that came out of her mouth as she watched him in the moonlight was enough for him. He pumped the length of his manhood as he pushed her back onto the bed, ready to undress her and appreciate her exactly the same. The only thing more welcome than the fact that she was giving him a much-needed release was the fact that she was making him a little less numb in the process.

With no effort at all, he had her shirt and bra off, leaning her back down to rip away her jeans and panties. He gave no fucks, shredding lace in the process. Once she was stripped, he looked down in pleasure at his prize sitting before him on the edge of the bed—gorgeous and breathtaking. The way her hourglass figure curved out just right at her hip was something he needed to sink his teeth into—and he planned on it.

As she drew her hands up and down his cock, teasing him to no end, he watched her bouncing tits press together. That was the type of shit that would make him lose control. Not able to take it anymore, he drew his cock upward toward her lips, and she sucked in his throbbing cockhead enthusiastically, like he knew she would. She caressed and teased his shaft, threatening to make him come then and there, but he kept it together. He didn't want to disappoint her on their last night together.

It seemed they had different playbooks, because as he tried to pull away, she drew his cock deeper into her mouth, taking it to the back of her throat. His thick, engorged manhood was at its maximum size, choking her as she was determined to make him come, determined to win. He realized it was turning into a power game, a symbol of their whole dynamic.

She wanted him to come in her mouth.

And, damn, he wanted to.

But he was always in charge—and he always had to win.

Pulling out of her mouth, as hard as it was, he stared at the beauty before him. She was too fucking perfect.

"Turn around," he ordered, cold.

"No," she refuted, grabbing at his cock again.

He pulled even farther away, determined as hell.

"Come back," she pleaded, watching him reach into his side table.

And so he did — but with a rope in hand. She bit her lip — a sexy move that always sent him over the edge. He held on to his throbbing, aching cock, needing release from her. She sat in front of him, leaning in to take his manhood in her mouth again.

"I told you to turn around," he growled low and commanding as he leaned down, kissing her lips.

She stirred under his touch as he ran his finger up her wet pussy. She was fucking ready.

"Face down, ass up." In one motion, he tossed her onto the mattress. "You know the drill."

Just as quick, even though she was fighting him, he tied her hands behind her back, maybe a little too tightly, but he didn't want her to forget. Leaning over the bed, he had her feet touch the ground — and her ass met his pulsing cock.

"I'll make you trust me." He opened her legs with his hands, feeling the wet entrance to her pussy.

She moaned as he touched her, beyond aroused. *Good*, he thought — it was mutual. Pressing his cockhead against her throbbing opening, all he wanted to do was thrust up fast and hard and fuck the shit out of her. But he had to be patient. He had to wait.

"Start by making me not hate you," she implored, pressing her ass backward into him.

He felt a wicked smile spread as he held her hips still, teasing her opening with his cock. She was going to regret breaking in.

"You don't really hate me," he said, pushing his cock one inch into her.

Her writhing body told him she was in agony, needing his full length. Her moans confirmed it.

Sadistic, he held firm, continuing, "Tell me the truth."

Keeping his movement stilled, he let his thickened member fill her entry, toying with her. Panting, she seemingly needed release as much as he did.

"Say it, Kendra." He let his cock slip one more inch inside her — the perfect tease.

Finally, she cried out in torment, "I don't hate you. Quite the opposite."

Chapter Seventeen

"God!" Kendra prayed as she took the entire length of Delta's rock-hard cock inside her pussy.

It was too good to be right.

Her confession had unlocked his full appetite for her. He clutched her waist with one hand and her hips with the other, as he pumped his cock harder and harder into her. He rocked her like he was splitting her in half, and his cock was big enough to make her feel that way. He drove her toward orgasm in such a familiar way, pressure mounting within moments of him thrusting into her.

She bucked her hips as her pussy got wetter and wetter, held down by his powerful grip, totally at his mercy with her hands tied behind her back. Pain shot up her waist as his hold intensified, but she liked it. He wasn't being gentle, and she didn't want him to be. He was giving her bruises — she had no doubt — but a little part of her loved the idea of marks on her body to prove it had happened. She already knew there were some dark ones developing on her wrists from where he'd so tightly bound her.

"You can take a fucking cock." He groaned. "But that's not the only reason why I love you — "

He stopped mid-sentence, though her mind refused to register it.

Her whole consciousness was engulfed by the moment — and the things she shouldn't be doing. Her legs wide open and exposed, he filled every inch of her in ways she didn't know she could be. An orgasm mounted and suddenly it rushed up and down her body, sending her over the edge.

"God, I love your cock," she cried out at the height of it, a little muffled by the sheets against her face.

He growled in reply, gripping her hips so hard that she thought the skin would break. Harder and faster, he fucked her while her cum dripped down her legs, the aching in her pussy deepening.

"What else do you love?" he probed, pushing her tied wrists up until she shrieked.

It was a welcome distraction. She didn't want to answer, afraid of what she would say. The casual throwing around of the word *love* was stirring discomfort in her. She bit her lip, refusing to let anything out other than a moan. In her mind, he was still just a player who was going to play her — a man not to be trusted. And, unfortunately, a man she desperately needed every inch of.

Pumping his manhood into her, Delta seemed not to mind her lack of reply, perhaps chalking it up to the heat of the moment. He grunted instead about how much he loved feeling her climax. She'd never heard the man use the word 'love' — *ever* — let alone a handful of times in one setting. As he pumped into her, something emotional rose in her chest. *Maybe, just maybe.*

She could tell he was close to the edge, his cock beyond rock hard. And damn good—she was losing her mind. She wasn't sure how much more she could take. Her nipples scraped against the bed as he rocked her back and forth, driving in and out of her. She twisted as the intensity grew almost unbearable. Everything in her body was screaming.

He did something amazing to her.

Another wave of mind-blowing sensation rushed her pussy, her back arching as it passed. For some reason, Delta paused, seeming to just enjoy watching her come down from the high. He lunged forth, yanked her up and flipped her around to face him. Deftly, he untied her hands behind her back, tossing the now-unneeded rope aside. He thumped down on the bed, sitting for the first time. Drawing her down to straddle his lap, he promptly guided his throbbing erection back into her.

She stirred as he began to rock her back and forth again, almost unable to bear how intimate this new position was. It was a first time like this for them, and it awakened intense and unexplored feelings in her. Now, she was staring into his eyes—intense and passionate. With untied wrists, she explored his muscled shoulders and inked biceps, adoring each hard curve. Her touch seemed to be welcome, and that look in his eye, the hardness in his jaw, told her he was moments away from climax.

She wanted to take his seed inside her. She wanted every last drop. The thought of it turned her on, buckling her spine as she ground hard over him—

fucking his cock up into a pussy that had already been fucked hard enough.

"Matteo," she screamed out as things got too crazy.

He grinned in response, quickening his pace.

"It's only ever just been you," he confessed, his voice hoarse.

He reached up to her jaw, planting a wet, open kiss on her mouth, biting her lip as he pulled back. Then he just held her face, grimacing as he came damn hard, unloading inside her. Releasing all the tension in his body and face, he gasped as his eyes softened. He caressed her cheek and neither of them seemed inclined to move. Her mind was blank and her body was sated, if not paralyzed. Breathing heavily, he hugged her into him, kissing her cheek and forehead. She inhaled his scent—sweat and masculinity.

Finally, he collapsed, pulling her into his bed. As she fell into him, he kissed her again, perhaps more affectionate than ever before. Grinning at her through narrowing eyes, it was clear that he was run ragged.

She traced down his cheek toward his tattooed chest and outlined a deep scar under his collarbone. His body had been through a lot. She guessed most of it was from war. She had never really given a lot of thought to just how difficult it would be to live the life of a SEAL—LA to Iraq, dinners out to shoot-outs, here one day, gone the next.

"Am I going to wake up alone?" she whispered, noticing his breathing steady as he held her.

He let out a soft laugh, seemingly amused. "No."

"Really, don't leave." She touched the scar on his cheek again, caressing him. "Don't leave me again."

He drifted off as he nodded in agreement. "I won't. I promise, I won't."

With his eyes closed, she studied him. In his sleeping form, he was vulnerable, as vulnerable as she'd ever seen him. And there was something different about him, but she couldn't put her finger on it. Maybe it was the absence of his calculating eyes or his intimidating glare. She didn't know. It gave her the chance to see him for what he really was.

A man who made her feel.

As she closed her eyes, her mind too exhausted to push on, something inside her became aware of something different growing between them for the first time. She smiled as he dropped his hand down her body. Finding her arm, he curled his fingers around hers, holding her hand. All she could think of was their son and that maybe he'd feel his father holding him one day soon, too. The welcome fantasy of the three of them together relaxed her, allowing sleep to overtake her.

Chapter Eighteen

Kendra wasn't sure what time it was or how long it had been when she was startled awake by a body violently spasming beside her. Snapping open her eyes, alarmed, she sat up and reached out for Delta on the bed beside her, but quickly stopped herself as she observed him. He didn't seem lucid, and his body was tensed. He shivered while he grumbled something, sounding urgent.

She pulled back, trying not to freak out. It looked like he was having a night terror. She felt like she was invading his space, witnessing something he'd never want her to see. She flitted her eyes back and forth, watching him, hoping he'd stop — but he didn't. In fact, it just got worse. Delta grew louder, like he was shouting for something, but she couldn't figure it out. Unnerved, she felt powerless watching his body coil, like he was in real pain. And just as sudden as the terror had started, it stopped, his body becoming heavy and still in the bed, like nothing had ever happened.

Stunned, Kendra lay awake beside him, waiting for him to fall back into a more peaceful sleep. There was so much more to him than he'd ever tell her, and her mind wandered to the glove and the results she still sought. Whatever good feelings sex had given her were replaced by a strange anxiety that threatened to keep her awake for the rest of the night, thinking about her son and what the hell she was doing. Lucky for her, exhaustion finally won out once more, and she drifted into the lightest sleep, almost sleeping with one eye open, never knowing what would be next with him.

Not long enough later, Kendra woke to the sound of Delta stirring in bed beside her. She snapped her eyes open, thinking he was leaving her. As she came to her senses in the early rays of morning, he grinned at her and pulled her in close to him, planting a gentle kiss on her lips.

"Morning."

The dark circles under his eyes did not look like a man who'd caught up on sleep at all, and for the first time, she understood part of why that was. She squinted at the clock — *barely seven in the morning.* They needed more rest, but she wasn't sure she was going to get it, knowing she had to get back home sooner rather than later for reasons she wasn't prepared to tell him. Her nerves already surging under his gaze, he brushed her stray blonde hairs out of her face.

"Sleep well?" he asked, reaching down her back to massage her. He shook his head, showing his disbelief. "You look too damn good for someone who just woke up. Tell me your secrets."

She froze at his words but released as he laughed it off.

"Thanks," she replied, a shy little smile forming on her lips.

His casual nature softened her up as he kneaded the tension out of her body with the roughest, warmest hands she'd ever felt. The way he touched her was nothing short of erotic. She craned her neck as he massaged, his selfless hands working even harder, making her feel too amazing for that early in the morning.

He pulled her in close once again, kissing her. "I don't believe you are here. This must be a trick."

And as he held her, something in her mind questioned if maybe she'd overreacted about the girl at the bar. It wasn't like she had been upfront with what she'd held back from him.

Delta flipped to his side, stretching his arms above his head, and crawled out of bed, giving her a full view of his naked ass. It was an ass of gods. *Damn.* Sucking in breath, she lost it when he turned back to her, reaching up to smooth back his dark blond hair. His olive Italian skin was perfect in the morning sun, and he was a sculpted statue of muscle. The scars, gashes and bruises only added to his aesthetic of a warrior. But what struck her was that so many of them weren't healed and too fresh to make sense.

"What are you doing to yourself?" she quizzed as she took in the scars decorating him.

"That...we can talk about after coffee." He tapped the doorframe before making for the washroom across the hall.

"Matteo, I want to know everything," she reiterated, calling after him.

It irked her that he wasn't immediately upfront about it, but it was hard to be mad at a man who was showering her with adoration. It didn't take long for her to throw on his old T-shirt and follow the scent of coffee.

Once she had a steaming cup in hand, sitting on his soft gray couch, she started to realize that it was beginning to feel too much like a dream. Hugging the handmade cappuccino that he'd just made her, watching him in the kitchen, she inhaled the rising steam. *It smells amazing*, she thought, as she brought the fresh coffee to her lips. And it tasted even better. Surely a dream couldn't give her such sensations.

"This must be a real Italian coffee," Kendra commented as Delta waltzed back into the room, plunking himself down beside her, holding his own steaming cup.

"I learned from the best."

The two of them, side by side, her in his crumpled T-shirts was a picture she'd never thought she'd see. Falling into him, he grinned at her, like they were an old couple enjoying their usual routine. He squeezed her leg, toying with her inner thigh, causing her legs to part naturally in response, as if she hadn't been fucked enough yet.

"My dad was serious about espresso and making it right. He'd disown me if I ever bought one of those puck machines."

"You are a man of hidden talents," she offered, biting her lip as she shot him a look.

She enjoyed the grooves at the edges of his eyes when he smiled naturally. And he seemed more than relaxed after all that mind-blowing sex, even with the lack of sleep and the obvious nightmares. The laughter in his eyes warmed her heart, especially so seeing him there in the morning light in his own home. It was a side of Matteo Valente she'd never seen before. Affectionately, his hand ran across her thigh.

"You look good on my couch. I could get used to this."

"Me too."

Leaning back, he put his other arm around her, pulling her in. She breathed in slowly, knowing that that was her moment. There would never be a better time.

"Thanks," she whispered, barely audible.

"For what?"

"For saving me last night. Hunter's going to have a real nice black eye this morning—" she started, but he waved her off.

"It was nothing."

"It was something"—she turned to him—"to me."

"Anytime." He nodded, his tone serious.

She took in a deep breath, steering the conversation. "It's been a bit of a ride."

"It has been." He remained still, stoic.

"I'm a little stunned to be here, on your couch," she admitted, swirling the remaining coffee in the cup, "after everything."

"Honestly, I am, too."

She pursed her lips to speak, but pivoted and said something else, something lighter.

"We've got a lot to catch up on, I think." She nudged into him, watching his reaction.

He let his lip curl into a grin, but it didn't feel as natural. He remained silent, studying her, so she continued.

"Things are starting to feel different," she started, her voice getting pinched, "between us."

He shifted, his demeanor changing. His gaze slipped, turning his head to the kitchen.

"Delta."

"Yeah." He gazed back.

Everything she wanted to say rushed to the tip of her tongue, but she just held it there, watching him, needing him to ask her to say it. She paused, waiting. He watched her, saying nothing. She bit her lip again, not knowing how to start a serious conversation—a thing she truly struggled with, especially with him.

"What is it?" He sipped his coffee, cool but knowing.

Shaking her head slightly, she dismissed herself. "I can't—"

"Yes, you can."

She caught that same encouragement in his eyes that had been there once before. There was the look that made her feel like she could do anything—climb a rope obstacle, rappel off a tower. She had to tell him. She opened her mouth to begin, but it didn't matter. She was saved by a knock at the very side door that she'd broken into the night prior.

Pulling her in, Delta kissed her hair once more and stood, dropping his espresso cup on the kitchen island as he strode to the door. Kendra followed, a little behind, curious to learn more about him. She had so many presumptions and was finding it impossible to parse between what was real and what was the façade.

As Kendra crested the kitchen, she saw over his shoulder that an elderly lady stood on his stoop with a German Shepherd dog in tow. The dog promptly barked, excited, and jumped on Delta with happy sounds, as if telling him an entire story.

"Hey, girl," Delta replied to the canine, roughly petting the dog's fur as he bent over to hold her. "How was your sleepover?"

The elderly lady, in a matronly blouse and slacks, smiled as she looked behind Delta toward where Kendra stood. Suddenly, Kendra felt underdressed — and judged.

"And who is this?" the lady pried, which seemed to trigger the dog to come sniff Kendra's legs.

Delta looked backed to his stoop, beckoning the lady to come in. Then he glanced at where Kendra stood, a sly look on his face, and introduced her to Mrs. Romano.

"Mrs. Romano, my apologies — this is my friend, Kendra."

Kendra lunged forward to greet her more politely, but Mrs. Romano did not want to step through the doorframe, citing that she had too much gardening to do. The twinkling look in Mrs. Romano's eye told Kendra that she was pleased to see Kendra there and wanted to leave them alone. Her gray curls whisking over her shoulder in the breeze, she gave Kendra a welcoming nod.

As the door closed and Delta got some dog food out of the fridge to put in a dog bowl, he turned his head up to Kendra, grinning.

"And this very good girl is Timber."

Kendra chuckled as Timber dove headfirst into the bowl of food, ignoring her. She knew dogs well enough to know that nothing else mattered when food was laid out.

Delta moved toward Kendra, putting his arms around her as he locked her against the kitchen counter. She didn't miss that look in his eyes — the one she was coming to know well. He planted a kiss on her lips, soft and sensual, but just as quickly pulled away, leaving her literally breathless.

"Ready for a shower?" The grin on his lips made her quiver.

"I should get home—" she sighed, checking the clock.

"Live a little on the wild side." He shot her a sly wink, making her ache.

So, she nodded deferentially and watched the father of her baby disappear down the hall. In her heart, she knew she owed it to her son to give him everything she had. For the little extra time away from him, maybe there was a chance to give him a daddy.

Hearing the shower turn on, she followed Delta like he was a piper. He drew her in—in a way she could never explain. He'd left the door open for her, she realized, as she entered the steamy washroom. The dated fixtures gave a vintage feel, like they were in the 1950s, except for the large modern mirror hanging over his sink. It looked brand new. It was all very California.

A few feet from the sink, he cracked open the glass door to the shower, inviting her in with him. She took him up on it. His tall, wide frame was almost comically large in the powder-blue-tiled shower stall. Under the water, she rinsed her face, ridding herself of whatever small amounts of makeup were left over from the night at the bar, feeling his body right behind her, holding her.

"Would you rather have something average for a long time"—he ran his hand down her wet back toward her ass—"or something amazing for a short time?"

"I don't know." Her heart pounded with his words, and she found herself biting her lip as was her nervous habit.

He sprayed the hot water all over her body. With soap, he massaged her shoulders and neck, making her feel like a wet noodle in his grasp. Working his way down, reaching around her, and he didn't avoid her breasts and nipples, giving each the attention they deserved.

"What about you?" she moaned as he touched her.

"I don't have a choice. You do."

He ran his calloused hands even lower, along her abdomen and lower, until he finally hit her shaved mound. She couldn't contain herself as he did, opening her legs in an inviting way. His touch never ceased to blow her mind.

"I love this part." He groaned.

Slipping under her lower lips, he touched her pulsing clit, making her need him again. He knew how to draw the right circles around it, playing games with her body. He traced her slit to the opening of her pussy, which was so sore from getting fucked so damn well the previous night.

"Baby," she let out, experiencing intense pleasure.

He spun her to him and dropped his head, kissing her underneath the falling water as he thrusted his finger up inside her. He made a come-hither movement with it in her pussy, rubbing against the spot that drove her wild. She loved it when he took control – and he knew that. He drove up two and three fingers, making her gasp for air. He was so close to making her come again, just with his hands.

"You're too good at this."

"Tell me more," he growled, growing more aggressive with his movements.

As she opened her eyes, she took in the crazy look in his. With something likely up his sleeve, he slowly spun her before him. She didn't miss the now-bouncing erection standing at attention between them. *Just so damn hard.* He was aching, the same as her—and ready to fuck.

"Bend over and touch your toes," he demanded in a low growl, turning her once more in his arms.

She obeyed without argument, feeling light and pliable. Behind her, he teased her legs apart, finding her opening again, but he put his cock in her this time. She enjoyed how long and hard he got, filling her up just like the night before. The only difference was that this time, hot water splashed over their bodies as he fucked her like he was savoring the moment.

His hand on her ass, he traced her crack all the way. Slapping her wet ass like a savage, he groaned with every thrust he drilled into her. She gasped, falling forward as he hit the perfect spot with his thick manhood. She smacked her hands against the wet tile, and she tried to steady herself, getting lost in the hot steam.

"Is this what you wanted?" he grunted, panting.

"God, yes—"

"You can have it anytime."

"Fuck, I wish that were true," she groaned, loving his pulsing cock in her.

Gripping her ass as he drove himself in and out of her, he traced her crack again, the hot water cascading down between them.

"Me too," he grumbled.

His words, his hunger, the hot water, the passion of it all—Kendra was about to lose her goddamn mind. Grinding back into him as he fucked her, she realize that she needed more of him—everywhere. One of his thick fingers pushed into her rear hole, fingering her, pleasuring her, finding a spot inside that made her want to scream. He grunted, driving harder into both holes, pushing her against the tiled shower wall—demanding she take his full manhood in her already-aching pussy. She screamed out, the double penetration filling her in ways she'd never thought possible, giving her a rare electric orgasm.

As she climaxed, he came, groaning as his hot seed filled her then ran out and down the backs of her legs. He slowly released her body, retreating as he soaped her up all over again. Even though her hands were still against the wall, as if immobilized, she enjoyed the sensation of his hands running over her back and down her ass and legs with slippery, soapy bubbles. He treated her too good. *How can I hate him?*

Pulling her back against his chest, he held her to him, kissing her neck.

"You're damn amazing," he groaned, keeping her tight against him, like he never wanted to let her go.

She laughed. "No, I'm not."

"You are to me."

She sloughed it off. "If I really was, where would we be?"

"Don't be so hard on yourself." His voice dropped, and the reminder hit close to home. "My issues have nothing to do with you."

She parted her lips in surprise with the realization that he was starting to understand her too well.

Chapter Nineteen

In last night's clothes, Kendra leaned against the white granite kitchen countertop. Finishing the best damn omelet she'd ever had, she marveled at Delta crafting her a second coffee. *The man clearly knows what he's doing in the kitchen*, she thought, as he adjusted the dials of an expensive-looking machine to perfectly extract espresso from grounds. Simultaneously, he had the milk frothing, ready to pour into two beautiful cups, white and delicate with engraved flowers on the edges.

She could see his military training—focused, precise. He was as attentive and skillful in the kitchen as he was in making her body sing, something he seemed determined to do whenever he got his hands on her. Despite what he seemed to think, things were changing between them. She felt it, though she didn't yet know if that was for the better or worse, tepidly hoping for the first time that it could be the former.

Finally, Delta poured the frothed milk into her cup but not his—creating the perfect cappuccino for her and black espresso for himself, its own metaphor. As he handed it to her, she traced the flowers engraved on the cup, getting a closer look at the design. It didn't look like something she'd expect a man like him to own.

As if reading her thoughts, he explained without probing, "They were my mother's. My dad gave them to me when I bought my first house."

"This house?" she asked, which was met with a sly chuckle from him.

"No"—he shook his head, his thick hand practically gripping the entire cup as he sipped—"I've owned a handful of houses over the years, on either side of the country—near whatever base the Navy posted me to. Dad always taught me to put money in property."

"Where do your parents live?" she asked, eager to keep him talking about himself.

"DC," Delta started, adjusting his dark shirt over his fitted black jeans. "That's where I grew up—just with my dad. My mom passed away a long time ago."

"I'm so sorry. There's so much I don't know about you."

But Delta simply shrugged and turned away, the morning rays catching his face as he gazed out of the kitchen window. The room became filled with the sounds of Timber lapping up water in her dish. Kendra opened her mouth to speak but got lost in her coffee instead, unsure if cross-examination would be welcome.

Delta leaned back against the kitchen counter, putting down his cup and rubbing his unshaven chin. His expression turned more somber, and he looked over to her again, breaking the quiet.

"I don't want to get too serious —"

She flinched, her stomach dropping, fearing the worst.

He continued, "But we need to talk about Hunter."

Collecting herself, she realized she'd jumped too fast. He shot her a deadly gaze, getting on with it, and she briefly saw that other side of him — the one that gave her the wrong kind of chills.

Kendra acknowledged him, quizzing, "What do you think is going on?"

"I want to hear what you think."

Obviously assessing her, Delta let his tongue run across the bottom of his lip, clearly holding his cards tight.

"He's jealous," she conceded. "He's jealous of you."

"You have no idea how deep that rabbit hole goes," Delta warned, his tone dire. "What do you reckon is his endgame here?"

"Me," she replied, dropping her gaze to the dog.

"Could be."

She snapped her gaze back, locking onto him. The way he said that stirred her suspicion, as if he doubted that was all.

"What are you not telling me?" she demanded, that analytical side of her catching on.

He shot her a look — a very perceptive look. "There are things you don't understand."

"Like what?"

"Things."

"Are you going to tell me? Yes or no."

"No."

"What the fuck is this shit? Again?" Her eyes locked with his, and she had a sudden urge to scream at him.

Seemingly reading her, he crossed his arms, sending a similar message. She didn't mistake the fiery flush up his neck. A silent détente followed, awkward and stony.

Timber, satisfied with her hydration, tilted her nose up to Kendra while she licked at her whiskers. She trotted lazily over to Kendra's feet, sniffing. Kendra, stirring under Delta's gaze, leaned over to pet the canine's gorgeous fur. The dog was a big suck-up, and he and Kendra clicked right away. It was a welcomed distraction. Without ado, Timber let out a yawn and curled up into a ball on Kendra's feet, immobilizing her.

Delta glowered, rubbing his scruffy chin in thought, studying her.

"What?" Kendra snapped.

He shook his head, his forehead furrowed. "She doesn't like most people."

Then Delta narrowed his eyes on her, grazing his teeth over his bottom lip, like he was ready to sink them into her... again. Trying to be civil, Kendra ran her hands behind her along the countertop for support, knowing it was up to her to do the heavy lifting. She took in a deep breath and made one last attempt to get the conversation back on track.

"I don't want there to be any more secrets between us." She threw it out there.

"Neither do I."

"You've got things to tell me."

"So do you." He took a threatening step toward her, visibly intent. "Go ahead. Start talking."

Grasping at nothing, she shivered as he stalked even closer, dropping his hands on either side of the counter behind her, trapping her against the cold granite. His body holding strong, his face just inches from hers, he remained unapologetic. He lowered his head, almost brushing her lips, taunting her into submission. Time seemed to move more slowly as she fought herself.

"No more games, Delta," she held.

He grinned, uncaring, blowing a teasing line of air up her cheek, exciting and infuriating her. She pushed back against him, but he just pressed her down without effort, making her even angrier.

She cried out, "Christ in hell, please! Why don't you just fucking tell me what your goddamn dark secret is?"

His body flexed, tense as all hell, but he stood silent. Glaring. All those things he'd said, all those moments they'd shared cheapened, springing tears to her eyes. For all that progress, they seemed to have circled right back.

"Why do you have so many cuts and bruises?" she demanded, losing it. "Why do you parade around in a black hood and a mask? Why does it look like you never sleep? What is going on with you?"

He sucked in his breath. "That is none of your concern."

"You have no idea — That is absolutely my concern." She pointed at his chest.

"And why is that?"

She opened her mouth, but no words came out.

He growled, "Kendra, I told you —"

Then the room caught on fucking fire. Stiffening her spine, Kendra just snapped, shoving harder at his chest.

"You told me — what exactly?" She hated it but she couldn't stop. "You won't tell me *anything*!"

"What the fuck do you think this is? A sharing circle?" He grabbed at her hand, causing her to wince.

In a low growl, he moved the conversation on, "Now, I've seen enough shit. I'm handling things from now on. You are under my protection. You will stay here."

"What?" She pulled back, stunned. "Here?"

"Right here." He tapped the countertop behind her.

"Fuck, no."

She slid away from him and toward the door. But, swift as hell, Delta pounced, planting himself in the doorframe, snarling down on Kendra as she tried to get out.

"You can't leave" — he crossed his arms, emotionless — "until I say so."

"Get out of my way." She pushed to get around him, grabbing at the door handle, but he slammed his hand on the doorframe, trapping her in place once again.

That savage look crossed his face, startling and unnerving her as they locked eyes. Whatever darkness came across his face quickly turned menacing, and she saw the real Matteo Valente for the first time — the fighter, the warrior, in battle, ready to rock. She tried to push his arms aside, to free herself — but he wouldn't yield.

Nervously glancing around, she realized she didn't stand a chance.

"Is that all you can think to offer me? A cage?" she cried out.

Something in his face twisted as he snapped back, "Well, what the hell do you want?"

"Maybe more than just a one-night stand?" She cracked, tears falling from her eyes.

"It was good enough for you at the time," he roared, fierce and brash.

"No, it wasn't. And it will never be."

Never. That word ricocheted for a split second, and suddenly, she heard a snap, and realized that with a single-handed grip and a cruel look in his eye, he'd shattered the double-thick wood doorframe, sending wood fragments and splinters into the air. The door fell open, no longer held in place by anything.

"That's not possible," she breathed, panicking.

Then Delta lost all control. The man she knew vanished and a savage animal stood in his place, muscles tensing as he stared her down, hungry in the worst way. Something was happening to him right before her eyes. A deep, predatory growl escaped his throat as he dropped his head to take her mouth with his, but she dove to the side, terrified.

"Please, God—please, *no.*"

He let her go.

Gasping for air, Kendra bolted, lunging from the broken doorway, running out toward her car, which was parked on the road. Hyperventilating, she fumbled to get the car door open, then slammed it behind her as she started the engine. Still in disbelief, she couldn't process how his ferocious grip had snapped the doorframe clean in half. It just wasn't possible.

In the mirror, she could see Delta's hulking frame trailing down the driveway, his face cold and intent—staring at her.

"Please, please, please," she cried to herself as she nervously put her car into gear, pleading for something she wasn't ready to admit.

All she could think about was her baby, and what the hell he'd inherited from his father.

Chapter Twenty

"Are you paying for the monitoring service?" The technician wiped sweat from his brow as he stood from the front door, drill in hand.

"I am," Kendra replied, watching him connect the wires to her new security system. "Full monitoring with video."

He took his card out of his pocket, handing it to her. "This is the best system on the market. You won't have to worry about nothing. I'll get you registered."

She held his business card, feeling the hard edges. It was the first time in her life she'd felt the need to install a comprehensive security system in her home, and she'd lived in LA for a long time. She wasn't sure if it was Delta or Hunter that had changed that need, maybe both—but she had to protect herself.

And her family.

The distant sound of a baby crying flooded the house.

"I'm all done here. I'll let you get to that," the technician said, packing up his tools and moving to the front door.

Kendra nodded, seeing him out and locking the door behind him. She glanced up and down the street before shuttering her blinds.

She moved quickly toward the baby room, hearing the cries growing louder and louder as she approached. Pushing the door open, she proceeded to coo and assure the little guy that everything was okay. She was never going away again.

"Good afternoon, sweetheart," Kendra sang to Leo in his crib as she bent over to scoop him up.

Cradling him in her arms, she asked him how his nap had been and checked his diaper. He smiled back up to her with his darling little face. She shuffled backward until she found the rocking chair and plunked down. Rocking ever so gently, she kissed his soft forehead. God, he smelled so good.

"I love you more than anything," she whispered to him, hoping he understood.

Leo settled in her arms, staring back up to her in delight. As she rocked and rocked, she sang him nursery rhymes, making him smile. His rosy cheeks were enough for her to do that all day long. She was all he really knew, but one day, she was going to have to tell him. She had no idea what to tell herself, either.

One thing was for damn sure. She was never, ever going to have a relationship with Delta. She couldn't even process how that had ended, still stunned at what she'd seen. The only thing that still mattered was her son and doing everything she could to protect him.

She wasn't sure how long she sat there, holding Leo close, but eventually Sienna popped her head into the room, holding a warm bottle.

"Is someone hungry?" Sienna beamed at the baby, handing the bottle to Kendra.

"You should just relax. I've been putting too much on you." Kendra grinned up at her big sister, taking the bottle to feed the baby. Leo latched on immediately, hungrily drinking the milk.

"I told you. You are working, and I am not," Sienna reminded her, crossing her arms in the doorframe. "You've been looking so exhausted lately."

"Thanks," Kendra replied sardonically.

Sienna tilted her head. "*Emotionally* exhausted." She paused and walked into the room to start folding the baby blanket on the back of the rocking chair.

Kendra focused on Leo, feeling the warmth and support of her family all around her. Times like those, she didn't know what she'd do if she was well and truly alone.

"That's a pretty intense security system," Sienna probed. "You think that's really... necessary?"

Kendra bit her lip nervously, unsure how to reply. Yes, she thought it was necessary—but didn't want to scare her sister. She was holding Leo tight, but she didn't know if she could handle it if Sienna left.

"Is this about Delta?" Sienna continued. "He's making you think you need it?"

Kendra looked up, giving her sister a serious look. "Yes."

Sienna launched into it, venting, "That asshole. He's always trying to control you."

"It's not about him trying to control me," Kendra started, taking in a deep breath. "It's about what he can't control."

"Which is?" Sienna drew closer, waiting on her.

"Himself."

A little stunned, Sienna parted her lips as she absorbed Kendra's statement — darting her focus across her sister's face to better understand. Kendra pulled Leo in tighter as she repositioned him to start burping. Holding him against her shoulder, she methodically tapped his back.

"What do you mean?" Sienna finally responded.

"There's something inside Delta that he can't control, like a switch," Kendra said, rubbing circles on Leo's back. "I've seen it. It's not normal."

"Well, what about the lab results? His glove?"

Kendra rocked her baby, letting out a low breath, and looked back up at her sister. She regretfully explained, "Lily called me this morning about the results — the paperwork had just been couriered down from Bakersfield."

"And?" Sienna stepped forward.

"Someone stole the results."

"What do you mean?"

"They can't seem to figure it out. Bakersfield swears the paperwork was in the envelope when they sent it and the courier swears nothing happened. But when Lily opened it up, nothing was inside. The results were gone. Vanished."

"Oh my God." Sienna gripped the side of the changing table. "How is that possible?"

Kendra shook her head in equal disbelief.

"What are we going to do?" Sienna ran her hands up her face, clearly shocked.

"I don't know" — Kendra exhaled, beginning to feel desperate — "but this can't stop me. I need to find a way. I need to figure out what's in his DNA."

Leo burped, and with a wobbly head, slowly looked up at Kendra to smile.

Kendra kissed her son's forehead. "I have to do this for Leo. I have to find out if his father is a monster."

Chapter Twenty-One

"Where the hell have you been?" an angry feminine voice called out from the shadows as Delta ascended the fire ladder, cresting the rooftop of an old red brick building on the edge of the city.

"I'm here. That should be good enough." His voice shot over the ridge.

He adjusted his hood, making sure it concealed his head fully. Yanking down on the black fabric mask, he confirmed that it covered the skin on his throat. He was known on Willow Avenue, so he had to take all precautions he was able to remain unseen.

"Where the fuck is he?" He strode toward Sky's voice under the cold light of the full moon.

"I don't know what was so fucking important — but you left me on the lookout alone. I only have two eyes."

She pounced out of the shadow and held position, waiting for him. Looking down over the edge of the rooftop at the scientists' lab, she fidgeted with the steel blade hanging at her waist.

Delta glared around, calculating. "You didn't see anything?"

"He could have left from the side exit. I don't know. So, whatever delayed you, it better have been worth it."

"It was."

She crossed her arms before Delta, growing silent, staring at him – clearly pissed off. Their relationship had been hanging on a knife's edge lately, and now her eyes were electrified with wrath. He knew what it had come down to.

His cock twitched as he thought of Kendra and the reason why he'd been so late. He'd been following, watching her like a hawk, ever since she'd left him. He had run out of options. He had to do something. Sky didn't understand.

Finally, after a staring contest, she ground out, "If a body turns up tomorrow and we missed him..." But she trailed off. She stared over his shoulder with dark eyes, a deadly look crossing her face.

"Shit" – she took a step back – "he's here. He must have followed you." Her arms fell from her chest, grasping at her knife.

Delta spun to see a man at the top of the fire ladder on the edge of the rooftop. He flipped back to Sky, pushing her, and growled low and firm, "Get out of here. I'll handle this."

"No" – she shoved him back – "I can't leave you without backup."

He pushed her again, moving her toward the edge of the roof. "Go...now! You know what will happen if you don't."

His warning was ominous and potent. She wasn't battle-ready and had been left that way by the scientists. Finally, she conceded and jumped over the edge, climbing down the side of the aging building. He turned back around, striding across the roof to greet his enemy.

"Look— It's LA's Batman," Hunter called across the rooftop. "I knew it had to be you."

Delta didn't give a fuck. That made it easier.

He reached into the back of his jeans for his pistol, slowly cocking it and carrying it concealed by his side. His gloved hands held the metal, so comforting and familiar. The fresh predatory aggression of his approaching enemy validated everything Delta had believed.

"What the fuck are you doing here?" Hunter stopped in the middle of the rooftop, his own pistol in his hand.

"I should ask the same, but I already know the answer." Delta snarled, a rage rising inside him— thinking about everything the man had done. "I know what you've been up to."

Hunter smirked, as if it was all a joke.

"Having fun with the scientists, huh?" Delta grilled, raising his pistol, steadily aiming it at Hunter's forehead across the expanse. "How much do they pay you for getting rid of the evidence?"

"Fuck you."

"So, how far into your doxycycline cycle are you? Two weeks? Three?" Delta quizzed, trying to gauge how bad it was. "Once they finish with you, ever worry they'll kill you off, too?"

Hunter let out a low laugh, but Delta knew it was a stunt. His head was twitching—the question clearly irking him.

Mission-focused, Delta turned to his true purpose.

"Stay away from Kendra," Delta growled, "or you'll be a dead man."

"You came all this way just to waste your breath?" Hunter roared back, that ferocious look on his face. "I'm doing this — all this — for her. She'll understand."

"Yeah — how's that?"

"She needs a real man" — Hunter lunged halfway across the roof, stopping short of Delta — "and that's going to be me. The scientists have a solution for everything."

"You're fucking delusional." Delta expanded his back, flexing. It was damn clear that Hunter was desperate.

Hunter sneered, looking down at Delta's gun. Delta held strong, ready to go. With both he and Hunter carrying, it was a question of who was going to shoot first. Delta wasn't going to hesitate. He couldn't have another monster walking the streets.

Then Hunter spoke words that Delta hated because he knew how true they'd been.

"You are nothing but poison. You torture her, winding her around your finger until she gets so twisted up that she chokes."

"Are you pretending to care?" Delta spat, finding himself beginning to circle the man on the rooftop, looking for the best angle to slay him. "She doesn't want you."

The comment only enraged an obviously already-triggered Hunter, who released a loud rumble from his mouth, but neither he nor Hunter could move any closer with pistols out and aimed at each other. It was a stand-off.

Hunter bellowed, "Mark my words — when this is over, she'll be with me."

Delta stopped dead in his tracks, staring Hunter down. He should have known it would have led to this. The idea of Hunter's possessive hands getting around

Kendra's neck flashed before Delta's eyes and drove him to insanity. That eerie icy-hot feeling filled his veins and he just saw red.

Out of control, Delta's jaw tensed, his shoulders and arms fired and he lunged forward, seizing Hunter by the neck. Hunter's pistol clattered to the ground as he fought back, clawing at Delta's wrists, breaking the exposed skin between Delta's glove and sleeve.

"What the f —?" Hunter yelped, but Delta's choking grip lifted him off the ground.

Overpowering him easily, Delta held the man up and close to his own face, his menacing tone issuing a threat not to be ignored. A cool trickle of blood down ran down his wrist where Hunter had dug his nails into him.

"You can't hurt me, and I won't let you hurt her." Delta's voice was dark and earthy — demanding attention and obedience.

Hunter coughed out, grasping at his neck, "I know what's in your blood. I know what they did to you —" But his words stopped quickly, as did his airflow.

The sleeves of his sweater falling down his arms exposed Delta's icy-hot veins pulsing furiously as he held Hunter's throat, suffocating the man. A woman's voice called to him in the background, telling him he had to let go.

But Delta's own fury had taken over his awareness, far worse than any doxycycline-induced hallucination. He was determined and enraged, and hell would have to freeze the fuck over before he would let anyone hurt Kendra. That eerie feeling had consumed his whole body, to the point that he couldn't stop himself anymore.

Hunter, not getting in any more air, was turning shades of blue. He was dying.

And that was when Delta realized he'd lost control. There was always that *thing* inside him that he couldn't handle when pushed too far.

All he could hear was a woman's voice screaming to stop. *"Please, God – please, no."*

Delta shook out of it. She'd brought him back to his senses. He released his grip on Hunter, blinking rapidly as he realized what the hell he was about to do. Hunter crashed to the ground, sucking in air, trying to breathe.

"Stay the fuck away from her," Delta snarled, reaching down to break apart his opponent's loose pistol.

Moving backward, scattering pieces of the gun across the rooftop, Delta turned to launch himself over the edge and down the fire ladder. As his feet hit the cracked pavement in the alley, a sharp breeze gusted to his right. He let out a long breath when he realized it was just Sky.

"Is he dead?" she demanded, her eyes wide.

Delta shot back, "No. You were screaming at me to stop."

"No one was screaming, Delta," Sky said. "There's no one else around."

Delta rubbed his face, perplexed. "A woman was screaming. She was telling me to stop. It had to be you."

"It was her."

He leaned back against the cracked red brick wall, rubbing his hands over his face underneath his mask. Sky was right.

She continued, lashing hard, "Get her out of your head. Do you still even give a fuck about the mission?"

"Do you doubt that?" He pushed off the wall, staring her down.

She planted her hands on her hips, unmovable. "Maybe I should just call the cops."

"No" — he lunged toward her — "I told you. Hunter's a cop. We have to deal with this our way."

"Our way — or *your* way?"

He crossed his arms, unwilling to respond.

Sky puffed, drawing in breath, seemingly trying to steady her heartrate like he'd taught her. Hell, he was the only one who'd tried. She'd always be an unfinished product — too wild for the military, too broken for further experimentation.

After a few seconds, she conceded, gazing back up at Delta, switching tactics. He gazed down at the lithe brunette as she put her hand on his chest affectionately...his apprentice.

"Look, Delta. Ever since she came back on the scene, you've been distracted," she began, running her hand down to his waist. "I miss the *old* you — the cool, collected and focused man."

Her words hit him hard as he searched her up and down. It was clear what she wanted.

"Focused on us. Focused on what we are doing." She flashed a pleading look at him, hopeful and honest.

"I have to protect her. I have no choice." He took a step back from Sky, watching her pace after him.

"What about us? What about what you promised?"

"I promised nothing except to teach you," he clarified — which was damn true.

She gasped, lunging at him.

Holding her wrists, heaving her back, he snarled down on her, "I told you, Sky — I *can't*. And you know why."

Chapter Twenty-Two

A call came through Kendra's cell phone, linking to the car console as she sped up Southern California's arid, hilly terrain, lit by the low afternoon sun.

"Hello?" Kendra answered, seeing Lily's name on display.

"Kendra — I need to get back to the lab," Lily began. "We've got a backload of cases now."

"Look, Lily," Kendra started, taking a turn onto an isolated road. "I still want you to stay away. I don't want you to get caught alone with Hunter right now."

"Have you reported him yet?" Lily probed.

"I'm working on it," Kendra replied, her destination coming into sight. "I have some questions that need answers first."

"All right, fine," Lily exhaled, frustrated. "There's another thing."

"What?" Her grip tightened on the wheel, about to turn into the gate. "What is it?"

"I took another look, re-examined the doxycycline traces in the victims' plasma again. There was something else that I saw. Whatever pills those guys were taking, they weren't just antimalarial."

"What do you mean?"

"I can't totally conclude, but they all have distinct markers of recently having a virus." Lily let out a long breath, seeming to try to make sense of it. "It really looks like a lab-manufactured virus, benign but purposeful. I saw this exact thing at the Harvard lab."

"It was infused in the antimalarial drugs?" Kendra pulled her car into the gravel drive of a military base, which was non-descript and unobtrusive. "Like, a live organism, housed in the drug?"

Lily continued, "That's what it looks like. I just can't figure out why."

Kendra pulled her car up to the massive gate concealing the interior of the secretive Navy SEAL training facility down the Southern California coast. Her destination.

"I might be able to ask someone," she started to explain to Lily. "I received a call from someone in the military, someone who is offering to help me, if I can help him."

"Oh? Is he hot?" Lily quizzed. "You know I'm single, Kendra. Don't hold back."

"You don't need military guys, Lily — especially not SEALs." Kendra let out a short laugh. "Stay away from the lab and stay safe. I'll call you later."

As she ended the call, she realized that it was much later in the day than she'd hoped. *Driving anywhere in Southern California takes forever*, Kendra scoffed as she glanced at the time, irritated. Guilt crept up as she realized yet again that she was leaving Leo for longer than she'd like. Sienna was as dedicated as a caregiver could be, but Kendra wanted to be with her son every minute of the day.

"This is the last time," Kendra grumbled to herself, promising that she just needed to find out that one bit of information — and she'd be done. She owed it to Leo to find it out.

As she waited, her car idling in front of the gate, she tried to not fidget. Straightening her pencil skirt, she cranked her rear-view mirror down to check her lip balm. Nervous, exasperated, she had no idea how the plan was going to go.

The gated SEAL base loomed before her, unfriendly and exclusive. She knew what it looked like inside. She'd been there before. That was where she'd met Delta. That helped — because she was about to do something really risky, something she'd only do if she were desperate.

She was going into the lion's den.

After what felt like too long, a guard that looked like he was Naval enlisted walked out of the gate and lazily sidled up to her car — as if they didn't get many visitors. She rolled down her window as he approached, ready to drop her tin on him.

"Good evening, ma'am" — the guard leaned in, not removing his sunglasses as he inspected her and the inside of her car — "how can I help?"

She drew her badge up, catching his gaze. As slick as possible, she kept her story circumspect.

"I have a meeting. It won't take long."

The guard raised his eyebrow, not convinced. "A meeting — with whom?"

She opened her mouth, but before she could answer, a man she just barely recognized peered around a doorway in the fence and called off the guard. It was Chief Warren Cameron, one of Delta's closest friends. His reddish hair was glistening under the hot Southern California sun. She hadn't seen him since the day she'd met Delta—right here on the compound. He raised his arm, waving at her, instructing her to drive through.

As the guard stood back, the gate opened slowly, which gave Kendra the necessary time to wipe the distress off her face. Nodding at the guard and trying to remain calm, she drove into the compound, not missing a beat. Something eerie crawled up her spine as she entered, but she couldn't put her finger on it.

Military guys were still milling about as she parked her car next to the main building—metal and stone, as nondescript as one might expect for an off-the-grid facility. A few guys shot her questioning glances as she stepped out of her car, wondering what the hell she was about to learn.

Warren marched up to her from the gate. As he got closer, she observed his bright blue eyes that sharpened as his tall form came to stand firmly in front of her.

"It's been a while," he said, his face dead serious, "Kendra."

"Thanks for calling me." Kendra bit her lip, trying not to look as anxious as she fiddled with her bag. "I have to admit that I was surprised to hear from you."

"I was surprised that it came to this as well," Warren said slowly, never taking his eyes off her. His intense, assessing gaze reminded her of one other SEAL she knew.

"You said you have something to show me?" she asked, trying to understand what Warren was playing at.

He paused, narrowing his eyes on her.

"My understanding is that you've been seeing Delta again since our last rotation back. Is that accurate?"

"It's been a little off and on." Kendra nodded quickly, shifting in her heels. "More off than on."

Warren gave her an understanding look—pensive and reflective. There was obvious concern in his eyes.

"He trusts you," he stated, desert wind blowing sandy dirt up into their faces.

She tilted her head, a little surprised. "Why do you think that is?"

"He doesn't fuck around. If he's been with you, he trusts you," Warren pressed. "That means I can, too."

Her lips parted. She was taken aback. That was antithetic to everything she'd come to believe.

Warren continued, "Does he seem different to you since he's been back?"

"Yes," she breathed, barely in a whisper.

He leaned in, lowering his voice, "If you could help him, would you?"

"Yes," she replied without hesitation.

"Me too. Come with me," Warren said, turning on his heel and marching intently toward the compound's main doors.

Kendra had no idea what awaited her, but she didn't want to fall behind. Her heels grinding into the packed dirt underneath her, she stumbled toward the doors. He ushered her into the building, swiping his access card off his utility belt, bypassing any security protocols to get her in. Kendra followed, surprised. He struck her as a man who lived and died by the rules.

Down a long, shadowy hallway, even darker in the setting sun, he stopped halfway and turned back to her. He closed the distance between them, leaving only a foot of space. Leaning down, in a hushed, nearly inaudible voice, the Special Warfare Operator spoke.

"You are a scientist?"

"I don't know if I deserve that title." She tilted her head, perplexed. "I'm just a shelved cop who likes to play in the lab. Why?"

Looking troubled, Warren continued, "There's something that's been going on behind my back, something I've just been made aware of. He's not going to like that I've brought you here, but I've run out of options."

"Okay." She bit her lip, hesitant. "I'm not sure what I can do."

"I need a scientist right now—one I can trust."

Before she could ask what the fuck he was talking about, the chief had already turned and marched toward a door, which he flung open and ushered her through. As Kendra crested the entrance to the room, she realized she was entering a room filled with…SEALs. They were leaning into a long conference table, watching her as she stepped in. Her heels clicked on the floor, the only sound echoing in the room. The whole thing was almost like an out-of-body experience, and she almost stopped breathing as she avoided the gazes of the intense men.

He motioned for her to sit at an empty spot near the front.

"She was never here," he shot down the table, a clear threat in his tone. "What happens in this room stays in this room. Any questions?"

No one challenged him, telling Kendra that Warren had the most authority.

Kendra immediately sat, continuing to look away from the table. The tone in the space was cold. She had been undercover enough times to know how to play on the fly—but this was different. She was sharing a table with fifteen trained killers.

Heat rose up her neck as the chief began speaking again. He moved to stand at the smartboard near the front, where a presentation was waiting. She sat with her hands in her lap, taking no notes, making no noise.

Something about the tension in the room told her there was a big problem.

"We've all worked our asses off to be here," Warren started, standing firmly at the top of the table. "We've all tried every fucking program to make us stronger, fitter...*better* operators." He paused, looking around at heads nodding, and continued, "And that's why I have to share this with you."

Warren leaned over to the laptop on the desk, clicked a button and straightened up again to point to the images that had flashed across the presentation screen. She realized that it was a photocopy of a partially shredded lab report, signed by someone styled as a doctor. He flipped through sequences of RNA, getting to the Cas9 protein. Her mouth dropped open when she got what they were talking about.

"We find ourselves in a new era," Warren thundered down the table, "one where scientists are trying to enhance our biological abilities. They're trying to give us heightened advantage at the apex of battle. Power, focus, aggression—a thousand times more potent and a thousand times more dangerous. Yes, it's the plot to a bad sci-fi movie, but this is really happening."

Warren's line of sight lingered on one or two of the younger-looking SEALs, before turning back to the smartboard.

Kendra parted her lips, her brain running at a thousand miles per minute. She analyzed the data on the screen. *This is the missing piece of the puzzle.*

"They are using the virus to edit genes," she muttered to herself in disbelief. "I didn't think we were there yet."

Warren spun to her. "This makes sense to you?"

She stood, nearly trembling, analyzing the RNA sequence. She hadn't stepped foot in the Harvard lab, but Lily had told her about what they'd accomplished there. They'd figured out how to edit genes, triggering the edits via lab-made viruses, ingested by pill.

"The doxycycline... I didn't think it was possible." She shook her head in complete disbelief. "It wasn't just for malaria. It was to trigger the edits."

Warren nodded at her, continuing to explain to the group, "A few of my men were approached under false pretenses, pretending this experimentation was approved and good to go. These scientists are desperate for test dummies — in the form of living, breathing operators. They want you."

All the guys at the table grew quiet, and the air became heavy.

A guy sitting across from Kendra looked around in disbelief and questioned, "Is the Navy behind these tests?"

"Not a fucking chance," Warren replied, firm. "The Navy has no idea that this...this is what *they* are doing behind their back."

"Who are *they*?" Another fierce SEAL chimed in, spinning a bullet in his scarred fingers.

Warren put his hands down on the table, looking down at the guy then at his men.

"The scientists. Research and Development Group. But don't bother looking them up because you won't find anything. They are ghosts. They work in secret, to create and sell products to the military. Their latest product is trying to edit us, trying to build the best of the best."

"How did you get this?" The same SEAL nodded to the signed report on screen, detailing the tests.

"Delta," Warren replied. "He's put himself at great risk to stop this insanity."

Kendra remained still, trying to absorb it all. Her fears rose, proving that she'd been right all along. The victims' blood had all had traces of this, but she'd never have believed that this was what it was. It was too outlandish. But she had to believe it because she'd seen it with her own eyes. She'd seen those enhanced abilities just as described – potent and dangerous – in one man.

"Can you help?" Warren turned to her.

"What do you want from me?"

"An antidote. A reversal."

She stood firm and stared Warren down before looking at the kilodalton protein structure again. *Genetic editing.* She doubted even Lily or the Harvard lab knew how to reverse it.

"What did they do to him?"

"You'll have to ask him." He let out a low breath, averting his gaze.

With a curt nod, he rapped his knuckles on the table, indicating the meeting was concluded. He huddled over the table, flipping through papers and answering questions one-on-one. As the others stood from the table, pushing back their chairs, Kendra turned on her heel and moved out. She needed to process. She needed space.

Walking down the hall, back toward the entrance, she kept looking over her shoulder. She was absolutely incensed that Delta had never told her the truth – a truth that big. They'd clearly changed him in ways she'd never imagined. If this all held true for him, it meant that he'd literally edited his genome, his very being. The vision of his menacing frame, aggressive and powerful – and the scars on his body, the mask he wore at night – flushed into her mind. He had been changed, permanently. And now he couldn't control it.

As every man in the hall slowly drifted away, she was left alone with her fury. The hall grew quiet, and the setting sun cast a startling tone to the already-worrying atmosphere. Her heels clicked as she fell a few steps backward, sucking in air. Kendra took a deep breath, her mind spinning. She had to get out of there.

Stepping out of the front entrance, the last rays of the setting sun fell on her, the only light left in the facility. The high walls surrounding the compound cast long, dark shadows everywhere else. Not far away, her car was slowly becoming consumed by a darkness that unnerved her. That same eerie feeling she'd felt coming in was with her as she started moving to her car. She needed to get the hell out.

Her heels once again dug into the packed dirt as she moved to find her car, questioning everything she'd just learned. A familiar wave of anger hit her harder this time, and she bit her lip, feeling tears springing. It was all too much. Finally, as she found herself in the shadows beside her car, she looked back one final time at the building.

What the fucking hell am I going to do?

Then, she saw it —

Or *him*, to be specific.

Delta's unmistakable muscular form exited the side of the building, slipping off in the opposite direction — toward the motor pool, well in the shadows. He strode across the motor pool toward a desert-sand-colored HMMWV — or Humvee — parked off to the side.

He's here?

She grew hot, enraged, as she stared at a man she recognized but barely knew. Whatever was screaming in the back of her mind faded into the distance. All she felt was pure, unadulterated anger.

Chapter Twenty-Three

He was losing control. He could feel it, Delta admitted it to himself as he walked through the shadows of the motor pool toward the HMMWV. His arms surged with aggression, ready to fight, ready to rip heads off. The constant need to escalate and the need for violence rose within him, and it was unescapable.

Because he'd been triggered.

He'd seen Kendra enter that boardroom. He had been down the hall — in the shadows, prepping for his next steps.

Now she knows.

Warren had overstepped. That wasn't what the plan had been. They'd agreed he'd warn the guys, but Warren had left out the last little detail — that he'd called in Kendra, too. Delta had made it clear that it was something he was going to handle in his own way. Betrayal ran up his throat, his walls closing in. There was no turning back now.

She'd never look at him the same.

Reaching behind into his waistband, he pulled out the nine-mil pistol he kept there, ready to cock it. Tonight was the night. Delta was going to deal with his problems once and for all. The scientists were getting a wakeup call. No one was going to have the same fate as him. He was going to do it his way—no cops, no records, just fucking pain.

Something snapped in his brain, a changing chemistry he could feel, accompanied by a deep, burning anger he couldn't get rid of. He felt a tangible loss. The price he'd paid was too high for anyone else. No more soldiers were going to die, not on his watch.

Grinding his teeth together, he whipped down the rear hatch of the HMMWV, exposing the long bed. He placed the pistol on the empty bed. It was time to kit up for the night, in the darkness, silently and alone. He had no one left. Throwing on a tactical belt, and plated armor across his chest, he adjusted the Velcro straps.

Then he heard it—or *felt* it, would be more precise. Kendra's presence. An icy heat pumped through his muscles, engorging them. His fighter instinct heightened, and he was in full switch mode—ready to go.

Spinning quietly in the long shadow of the lowering sun, he observed her slinking into the motor pool, her eyes locked on him. He should have known she would come find him. She was persistent. Her stealthy form struck him, challenged him, and he clenched his jaw. Watching her, he leaned against the HMMWV, crossing his arms. He had to get rid of her before he did something he didn't want to do.

It was the wrong fucking time.

"Get the fuck out of here," he thundered as she approached, closing the distance between them. Only one thing flashed across his mind.

Silently, she kept walking toward him, stopping only feet away. He sensed the burning anger. The hatred. It was real that time, and it was exactly what he feared. She had learned his secret. She knew what he was. She *hated* him for it.

"Leave," he rejected her, and spun to march around the HMMWV, sending a clear message.

It was all he could do, he realized, as he tightened his arms over his chest. She darted behind him, her own gait much smaller than his large cadence, breaching the distance he needed.

"You should have told me!" she barked.

"And you shouldn't have fucking come here... behind my goddamn back."

Halting at the driver's door of the HMMWV, he twisted, fuming, realizing she was right fucking there — a foot behind him, within arm's reach.

Goddamn, she was furiously sexy. His cock twitched and his mind raced, screaming at him to stop. He took in her clever, angry eyes. She'd finally put it all together — and that put her in jeopardy.

Breathing down hot fire on her, he seethed, "You betrayed me."

"What choice did I have?" Her voice cracked as she lit into him. "Hell, you don't even know how fucked up you even *are*, do you?"

"I'm fucked up. That's all that matters." His body formed a hard wall — unmovable, untouchable.

That familiar impulse hit him, and his ability to resist was slipping. He needed to fuck her. He needed her to get the fuck away.

She broke, outraged. "Why did you do it? Why did you let them test it on you?"

"*Why?*" He snapped and his muscles flexed. He was already livid. "Because I wanted to be better."

"And are you...? Are you really better now?" she cried out, obviously needing no answer. "Look what has happened to you. Look what you've become!"

As her voice crept higher, more enraged with each word, he tensed. The muscles in his arms contracted, like their own beast, and he found himself gripping the mirror on the side of HMMWV, grasping harder at whatever humanity he had left.

"I can't control it," he warned. "I never could."

She inhaled, sharp. "These scientists... They are going to kill you for this, aren't they?"

"They are trying to."

"Matteo—"

He searched her—and he felt her pain—her deep and insurmountable pain that he'd caused and was continuing to cause. It only drove him further over the edge, out of control. He shook his head, pushing her away. Rejecting her.

It was all he could do.

"I am *not* doing this." He pushed her away before twisting to leave.

"You never could, could you?"

Silent, he turned back, locking eyes. She was damn right. *Too* right.

Her beautiful blue eyes batted out a tear, her face twisting in agony. He felt her aching. It was in him too. He regretted so much. He wanted to nod in understanding, but his twitching jaw wouldn't bow down. He couldn't let her in, not even an inch. It was too fucking dangerous.

He was ready to fucking explode.

"Why weren't you just honest with me?" she demanded, pointing her finger accusatorily at his chest. "Why did you keep lying to me?"

"You've been lying to me too."

He jutted out his jaw and cocked his head, looking down at her like all he saw was meat. And damn, she always made him fucking hungry. His chest heaving and his shoulders flexing, he trailed her body with his gaze. He was about to do something they'd both regret.

Scorching fire and glacial ice were mixing together, and the eerie sensations darted up his limbs, deep in his blood, as he felt his predatory scowl land on her luscious lips. His jaw slowly dropped, his eyes twitching, everything inside him ready to crack.

The wildfire she lit only fueled spite in his heart. A cruelty that he hated, but needed, reared its ugly head. Darkness fell over him. He felt it. There was no turning back.

"Please—" she panted, widening her eyes in fear as she realized what was happening.

"Tell me your fucking secret," he growled.

"I don't know what you want me to say."

"What the fuck happened while I was deployed?"

"You don't deserve to—" she started snapping back, but froze, watching him.

It was too late.

He sensed panic racing through her body, and she tried to lunge backward. He seized her arm roughly with one hand, and with the other, he intertwined his fist in her hair. Tears burst from her eyes, and she gasped as he yanked her into him. Velcro and stiff corners of his pocket flaps crackled as they scratched against her, the only sounds other than her cries.

"Please..." she implored, tensing in his rough hold, her body immobilized. "All I've ever wanted was your honesty. Couldn't you just have given me that?"

The words crashed through him. His actions in direct contradiction to his words, he spun her hard, slamming her against the metal side of the HMMWV.

He wasn't nice. He wasn't gentle. Her body was up against his, and she winced as something sharp in his gear pressed into her hip—*the pointed corner of my riggers' belt.*

"I just wanted you to confide in me," she cried. "To treat me like I was something more than a one-night stand. I just wanted you to *want* me."

As he gripped her, his needy cock began to throb, filling and tightening the crotch of his pants. He had few words, few emotions—just bitter intensity. Her fear-filled eyes still locked on him, he found his lips hovering low over her neck while he inhaled her feminine scent.

Before he could decide yes or no, she shoved at him, trying to flee, provoking his uncontrollable ire. When she was unsuccessful in her attempt, an exasperated sound escaped her mouth that only drove him wilder. She should know just how competitive he could be.

To teach her one final lesson, the lesson she seemed to desperately need, he dropped his mouth on her neck, taking and tasting the sweet skin. Biting and kissing up her delicate neck, he enjoyed her writhing body in his grasp. Letting out a rogue moan, she twisted in his locked arms, tilting her head back as he worked, giving him a better angle to rough up her throat. She didn't stop fighting him, though, not for one second.

It was a damn good thing that he loved it when she fought back.

They both knew exactly where it was going.

Electricity practically crackling between his lips and her neck and excitement pulsed through her body. He snarled, biting into her flesh, branding her as his, just the way she liked. He felt her heart thundering as he worked his way up her neck, the magnetism between them shifting them to a familiar place.

Her lip trembled as he worked, her hands slamming harder in desperation against his unmovable frame. She was fighting him as much as she was fighting herself, he could tell. He refused to drop his arms and make it easier for her. He needed her to hate him – to stay the fuck away. She was better off without him.

"I've always been a monster," he growled as he kissed his way up to her lips.

"You don't have to be," she disputed.

"I do."

A flash storm rolled in over the arid landscape and the air pressure dropped. It almost never rained in Southern California, and even less so in the desert hills.

"I'm going to give you a choice," he countered, making his terms damn clear. "Stay and you get fucked – hard – right here, against this truck. Or leave and get the fuck out of my life."

Her body stilled, and her gaze fell on him one last time. It was that moment that he saw deeply into her – deeper than he ever had. He grew sober, more conscious than he'd been in a long time. The storm was beginning to crack overhead, and it struck him that it was going to be the last time he'd ever see those sapphire eyes.

Then she slipped out of his arms, stepping away from him. Away from his body, out of arm's reach, a confession poured out of her mouth – an unexpected, explosive confession.

"You want to know what happened last year? I found out I was pregnant. I tried to tell you – but you left."

His jaw dropped as he were trying to find the right words to respond.

She continued, "But you already know, don't you?"

"I –"

He was too late. There was no more pretending.

"Stay out of my life," she threatened, livid. "You'll *never* meet your son."

Never.

Angry as he was, something inside him collapsed, watching her march away from him. He fell numb, unable to even flinch, as she grew smaller and smaller in the distance, finding her way out.

His cock ached, pulsed, needed relief. His mind pounded like he hadn't slept in months. He couldn't process any of what had happened, was happening. For the first time in a long time, dark clouds overhead opened, and Delta felt the cold, harsh rain of the desert dripping down the side of his face.

Chapter Twenty-Four

One year before

"I didn't expect this from you," Kendra moaned as Delta kissed up her neck.

The way he held her as he laid her down on his bed validated everything she was coming to think about this new mystery man.

"What didn't you expect?" he said, slowly lifting her shirt, brushing his lips down her throat, chest and abdomen.

"I expected a guy like you would just as soon have me in his truck." She gasped as he licked a line down her tight stomach, feeling ripples of excitement permeate through her core. "Let alone go through all the effort of bringing me to his home."

Slowly, he undressed her as she drank in her new reality. He'd driven her from the bar to his place, barely able to keep his hands off her during the ride. It had been the same for her. Everything was coming down to that moment. It was the first time she was letting herself have what she — and also Delta--really wanted.

As he unbuttoned her fly, stripping off her jeans, he kissed slower and more intently around her thighs and the lacy panties she'd donned, driving her insane with arousal. He was teasing her — and teasing her well.

"I thought you'd look good on my bed," he replied, grinning up to her. "And I was right."

Then his rough, warm hands found their way down her smooth legs, massaging and making her feel so damn good. He slid his tongue up her thigh toward her panties, tugging at the side of the thin cotton garment. He wasn't wasting time.

"You've just surprised me," she exhaled as he made her curl.

She moaned as he slid a few fingers underneath the edge, touching her hairless mound, teasing her throbbing lips. It was clear to Kendra that he was pouring every ounce of energy into pleasing her, doing what it took to make her feel amazing.

"Did you think I was just looking for a quick fuck?" he growled onto her pussy as he ripped her panties down her thighs.

She bit her lip, unwilling to answer that, weaving her hands in his thick hair as he licked her clit slowly. The way he worked her — he was testing her. He was trying to read her body, react to how she liked it. Damn, he was an attentive lover.

"You're not the type of woman I'd want a quick fuck with." He grinned as he ate her out a little harder, finding her sweet spot.

He slid his fingers up her thighs, massaging her lips and teasing the opening of her core.

"Then what would you want?" She exhaled through spasms as he drew waves of pleasure out of her pussy. God, he was so damn good at that.

"I want *you*."

As he slid his tongue up and down her clit, circling and massaging — he entered her pussy with his fingers, finding little spots of pleasure that she didn't know existed. He groaned heavily about how fucking good she tasted, how fucking hot she was, encouraging her to come all over his face. Whatever trepidation she had about letting someone she'd just met go down on her was quickly thrown out of the window.

And he'd been making her feel good all day — from the rappel tower to the bar — and now in his bed. The romance of meeting some amazing SEAL that wanted her, and only her, drove her to the most intense orgasm she'd had in…she didn't know how long. *How can this be happening to me?*

With her fingers in his hair, holding his head, she came hard. He held her down as he clearly enjoyed giving her so much pleasure.

"Fuck, now I really want you," he groaned as he lapped up her orgasm, running his fingers through the wetness that dripped out of her core.

She slowly sat up, biting her lip and watching the fully dressed man kneeling before her. She could get used to that. She never wanted it to end.

"So, have me," she whispered, beaming up at him, sinking farther back into his dark sheets.

That was all she needed to say. His pants and shirt flew off in seconds, and he moved on top of her. When she rested her head back onto his soft pillow, he kissed down her neck again, finding her breasts as she twisted and moaned underneath him while he worshipped every inch of her body. Kendra enjoyed the hardness of his cock in between her legs, still caged by his boxers. She reached down, pushing at his waistband, eager to see all of him.

He grabbed her hand, holding her still. He traced her up and down.

"We don't have to go all the way," he said, his hand shaking slightly. "I know you're more... a traditional kind of girl."

She beamed, running her hands up his core, which was all cut and rippling with muscle. Even hearing him say that blew her mind. The whole day, the whole evening — it had just romanced her to a point that she was willing to do something she never did. Maybe he was worth breaking rules for.

"I never do this," she whispered, pushing her hand through his and toying with his waistband again, tugging it down.

His pulsing cock was just inches from bursting out. She ached to see it, feel it — needed to be as close with him as possible.

"I believe in love and marriage... and the old-fashioned way of things."

"Okay," he said, as he planked over her, showing pure strength by effortlessly hovering his body as he waited.

"I'm not the type to do things casually."

"I know."

"Is this real?" She bit her lip. She was beginning to let herself believe that the fairy tale could be possible...with him. She continued, "Is this going to be a real thing?"

He let his face drop to hers, inches from her mouth, his eyes serious and studying.

"It's never felt this real before. There's something about you—" But he trailed off, dropping his mouth onto her lips, kissing her once again.

Kendra closed her eyes, feeling Delta's tongue playfully enter her mouth, tasting her. Caring. Loving. Teasing.

She moaned under his body as she helped him slip off his boxers, feeling his engorged member bounce between her thighs. As he kissed her deeper, faster, he pulled up her knees, positioning his pelvis just right. Then his cock was throbbing at her opening, testing her, feeling her wetness. She knew how bad he wanted her. And her arousal was out of control, the chemistry in her brain exploding with passion, driving her to feel like she was in heaven.

"Are you sure?" he asked again, in between kissing and rubbing his cock at the entrance of her pussy.

She kissed him once more and whispered onto his lips, "Yes."

Immediately, he pushed up, moving his thick manhood into her, driving a pleasure so deep that she nearly lost her mind.

Everything about his actions—the way he cared, the way he tried, the way he checked in—assured her that it was okay to fall so hard for him, to feel every good feeling she was having. He was no regular guy—and she'd finally found someone special. As he rocked his dick into her, he held her so firmly, and she just *knew* that it wasn't a one-night stand. It had to be just the beginning of her fairy tale.

Chapter Twenty-Five

Present day

Delta ran his scabbed hands along the cold metal of his Harley as he adjusted the tension, lying on his garage floor. The vintage motorcycle was a cruel mistress — beautiful, but she loved to hurt him. Every time he found himself gutting her, massaging her back to life, she would find a new way to demand his energy — only ever just to break his heart in the end, leaving him shipwrecked.

Shipwrecked... That was how he felt now.

As he worked the wrench, making needed tunings to the Harley, he let his mind wander to a different time — when he had been in Syria, making needed adjustments to his kit. His assault rifle out, in his hands, he purged the stock ammo, replacing it with the bullets he preferred. The guys laughed at him, like it shouldn't make a difference. But it made a difference to him.

It's cold in the desert at night, he reflected silently to himself as he sank deeper into the stone walls of the compound. He was isolated in his position — deeper in enemy territory than any of his men. He was reconnaissance, in the compound first to determine positioning and threat. He wasn't supposed to be alone, but he was the only one who'd made it in.

Carrick was stuck outside. Waiting for his sign.

"We're going to pull the chute." The chief's voice came into Delta's earpiece, a radio signal from their temp base miles and miles away in the mountains.

Warren was not a risk taker. He played by the rules to keep his men alive. Delta put his hand to his earpiece, pressing his mic closer to his mouth so he could whisper.

"No, I've got this," Delta reassured.

"It's too risky. You're the only one in," Warren reminded him.

"There's an American hostage in there." Delta's whisper cracked, his emotions running high. "I can't leave him."

"Fall back. That's an order," Warren commanded. "This is a risk we can't take. I can't lose you guys."

"Turn around, buddy. There are too many." Carrick's voice crackled into Delta's earpiece, joining the conversation.

"They can't hurt me," Delta growled into his mic as he was assessing the wide expanse of the Syrian compound before him using his night-vision goggles.

From his tiny corner, under complete darkness, he observed many enemy combatants around the compound with assault rifles just like his. They were heavily armed and on watch.

Why wouldn't they be? They'd just demanded millions of dollars in ransom from the American government in exchange for a journalist they'd kidnapped weeks before. Delta knew his President would not negotiate with terrorists—and that the hostage's life depended on Delta's next steps.

There wouldn't be another chance.

Delta knew that for damn sure.

"Acknowledge your order," Warren demanded, requiring Delta's obedience.

Delta shook his head, lifting his night vision goggles up so his eyes could adjust to the dark. He always fought better with less tech...less gear. And it wasn't just Delta's skill anymore. There was something else about Delta that made him stronger, better, faster. The chief still didn't know the extent of Delta's enhancement and the price he'd paid. He could risk things that Carrick couldn't.

Delta knew where the hostage was being held—right ahead in the main building, first floor. The damn guy was almost within reach.

"I'll fall back once I have him," Delta confirmed into his earpiece to the sounds of Warren's arguing.

"Fuck. I'm coming in with you," Carrick said.

"Like hell," Delta replied.

Dropping his earpiece out, Delta spoke the final words into the mic. "Get medevac prepped—and give me ten minutes."

Ten minutes turned out to be an overestimation.

With a bayonet firm on the end of his rifle, Delta stealthily stalked the compound, readying himself to attack. Once he broke his cover, he would be up against dozens of men. There was little chance he would survive, but if he did it right, he could save a hostage.

Counting down in his head as he watched one of the enemies getting closer, he found himself thinking about the decisions he'd made—and realizing that there really was no going back.

As the enemy got closer, Delta slashed out with his knife, killing the men easily. He sprinted to the compound wall and killed another...and another. Finally, he got to the compound door—slammed on it furiously. As the door opened backward, gunfire rained out of the dark hall, hitting Delta in the armor and slicing the skin on his legs. He pushed forward into the darkness without a care for his life, using his instinct to stab the gunman, but just as he pulled the blade out, he felt the man's arms flail one last time, and a hot laceration slashed up the side of his face. It didn't matter. Delt gritted his teeth and pushed on.

He stormed the room where the hostage was being held, feeling hot liquid flowing down his cheek.

"Who are you?" the hostage cried out in the dark, hope and fear in his voice.

Delta leaned in to slice the man's bonds, heaving him up and assuring him, "I'm here to bring you home."

"Jesus." The hostage literally started crying. "Thank you. How the hell did you get in here?"

Delta ushered him forward, keeping his eyes on all angles. Now was going to be the hardest part—getting the man out. Thankfully, Delta realized, he was no longer alone.

Warren's voice came over the perimeter, on the other side of the metal door on the stone wall. Within seconds, he burst through the door, kicking it down with his remarkable strength. Delta moved to pass the hostage to the chief.

"Get him out of here," Delta snapped, and shot at an enemy on the top of the roof who was taking shots at Warren. "We'll cover you."

Warren nodded, hoisting the hostage up and returning him to safety. Warren remained, standing beside Delta and shooting at the remaining enemies.

"We're not going to be able to get the fuck out of here!" Warren yelled, obviously realizing how many enemies were crawling onto the roof to shoot at them.

Warren and Delta were the only two left holding the cover. If they ran, they would be shot in the back immediately. Delta noticed to his right a way to climb to the top of the wall. From that point, he would have half-cover of the stone, and it would be at a good height to return fire on the enemy. He was a crack shot. He could do it.

"Run… I'll cover you," Delta demanded, ordering his best friend.

"No, I'm not leaving you. You'll die," Warren spat out, shooting at the roof — suppression fire.

"Trust me," Delta bellowed as he sprayed bullets at the roof. Dying was no longer a concern of his.

Warren let out a laugh that sounded less than amused, but he seemed to realize Delta's seriousness. Delta felt the absence of Warren's body behind him as the SEAL fled the compound, returning to safety. Immediately, Delta let out a spray of suppression fire to allow Warren cover and moved to climb up the stone wall, attracting the attention of the enemies.

Delta's sheer strength allowed him to push upward quickly, gaining footing on the top of the wall. He stood fiercely, looking the combatants in the eye across the expanse. Then he did what he was trained to do — what he'd signed up to do.

With calculated precision, focus and intensity, he shot mercilessly until every last enemy was dead. Breathing heavily, his eyes widening over the dark scene, he finally put his earpiece back in.

"Brother," Warren's concerned voice was growling into Delta's earpiece. "Brother, you there?"

"Present and accounted for," Delta replied, hearing an immediate sigh of relief on the other end. "Enemy neutralized."

"Fuck, man — that's not even human."

"I know," Delta replied, his voice cold and distant.

"Damn — you're going to get the Medal of Honor for this, you know?" Warren said finally, a tone of disbelief in his voice. "You just saved an American hostage single-handedly."

And that was when Delta's stomach dropped, and he felt something for the first time that he didn't want to feel. He didn't want anyone to know. *What I did was impossible.*

Delta's mind came back to the present and he touched the scar running up the side of his face, thinking about Kendra again and when she'd held her hand there. Every time a thought came up, he stifled it, trying to think about something else, trying to think about why being with her would never work. She wanted things that he could not give her — and he'd finally come to terms with that. He had to end it.

And now, he had to end it for their kid.

A part of him had known it all along. He'd been watching her, protecting her, and one day he'd seen her walking with a stroller outside her house. He'd known exactly what it was, but he'd stuffed it so far down into his steel vault that he'd denied it. He'd lied to himself.

He'd pretended he didn't know. He'd pretended it wasn't his.

Because it made it easier.

"What the hell was I supposed to do?" Delta rumbled to himself, thinking of Kendra, chucking a wrench backward on the concrete with his final adjustment.

"I don't know" — a deep-voiced man stepped into the garage — "but you could have told me what was going on with you."

Delta's eyes snapped up, observing his chief halting on the edge of the concrete, his arms tight across his chest. They stared each other down for a second before Delta rose to his feet and squared himself to Warren.

"Get the fuck out of here," Delta spat at the man he'd served too many tours to count with — the man who'd betrayed him.

"You've been hiding." Warren's accusation was clear, and he was standing tall behind it. "You've been running from the truth."

Delta stiffened, ready to fight. "That wasn't your fucking truth to tell, was it? I told you I was going to tell her — on my terms, in my own way."

Warren cocked his head, as if wondering whether Delta was serious. Colleagues, friends — the two of them weren't afraid to have it out.

Delta's expression grew ice cold as his chief stared him down. He said nothing else, his muscles contracting with the urge to punch.

"You've got orders to rotate out at the end of this week, after your ceremony." Warren pushed the conversation forward. "You are still planning on going, right?"

"I don't care," Delta dismissed, grabbing a rag off his workbench and turning his attention to cleaning up his Harley.

"Well, she came to the base because she cares, for some fucking reason," Warren argued, approaching the Harley to get into Delta's space. "Why didn't you just fucking tell her?"

Delta refused to reply, grumbling cutting profanities under his breath.

"She cares so fucking much. She'd do anything for you. That much is clear. But you're such a goddamn asshole that all you do is push her away."

"I was trying to protect her," Delta roared back, snapping fiercely at his friend. The thought of his son rang through his mind.

I had to protect them both.

From me.

"The way I saw her leave yesterday, it doesn't look like she gets that," Warren challenged, hitting on what Delta knew to be true.

"You know what? Stay the fuck out of my affairs." Delta spun.

Like brothers, they fought when they needed to — and Delta had no qualms with fighting him now. Eye to eye, Delta and his chief exhaled the need for violence.

"You've got this weird thing going on, man," Warren scoffed. "You don't have to be so fucking alone. We can help you, buddy. She can help you."

"No, she can't — unless she's trying to get herself killed."

Delta snarled and threw his rag to the side, back at his workbench. He hated it — but the choice had already been made for him.

"You're not as bad as you think you are." Warren held strong.

Delta let out a vicious laugh.

"I've changed. See it?"—he dropped onto his bike, gripping the steel—"I can't be with her, let alone my goddamn son."

"Your...son?"

Delta stopped, reaching for the ignition, turning on the roaring engine. "Forget it. She's better off without me. They are both better off without me. There's only one place I belong now."

"All I hear is you saying that *you* are better off without them," Warren countered.

Delta spat out, "So what if I am? All I've ever done is use her."

"No."

Delta turned, his face dead serious, "I did. I used her. And I fucking knew what I was doing the *entire* time."

Warren's mouth opened, but then he tightened his lips, silence growing between them. He stepped back, staring down the SEAL under his command. There was a code, and Delta was breaking it.

He couldn't pretend anymore. He was a monster, and there was no changing it. He couldn't control it. It controlled him. And that meant he was only good for one damn thing. He was nothing more than a product...a weapon.

And he would *never* have her again, even though the memory of her caused places in his body to ache.

Delta shook his head, trying to forget, revving the engine.

"Where the fuck are you going?" Warren challenged.

"The base," Delta retorted, like the cold-hearted asset he was. "I'm deploying in a few days. Did you forget?"

Peeling off, Delta settled into that comfortable numbness he enjoyed. Ripping down the coastal highway, ocean wind against his skin, he was reminded of another time. Something reminded him of her — and something forced him to realize that it was no longer just his cock that ached, but his heart.

And that was exactly why he had to get back to being a SEAL — and being in control of something.

Chapter Twenty-Six

Her hair catching an evening breeze off the nearby Pacific Ocean, Kendra rocked Leo's stroller back and forth while sitting on the park bench near her house. It was a cool day — by Malibu standards. She had her son all wrapped up in a cozy micro-fleece as he comfortably napped in his cocoon, perhaps more out of a need to bubble-wrap him than anything.

It was truly a beautiful sunset, another gem to be enjoyed in the oceanside community. Southern California never ceased to disappoint. The only thing was that Kendra didn't feel alive enough to enjoy it, or anything. A lump had grown in her throat, rooting there and unrelenting.

Singing a gentle song, which was carried through the breeze, she gazed upon her baby boy. He was everything to her. The only bitterness she tasted when she looked at him was that he was never going to know his father. He was never going to *have* a father. Obviously, at this point, she couldn't allow it. The things she'd learned about Delta, the things he'd never told her... She didn't really know which was the worst part anymore. All she knew was that he was a goddamn monster, confirmed.

It wasn't fair to Leo—and it wasn't fair to her. She found it unbelievable that she would be in that situation, and it was the worst feeling for Kendra. She'd mixed her genetics with his, creating the most beautiful human she'd ever seen. But whatever subconscious fantasies she'd once held about the three of them being a family... Well, they had all turned out to be unbearable. She was never going to see him again.

What was done was done—and nothing was ever going to change. Tears rushed to her eyes just admitting that to herself, admitting that it was all over. Accepting that had become much harder than she'd ever thought. That missing ring on her finger had once seemed so damn important, but now she realized that was the least of her concerns. The health of her son had become the most important thing in her mind in light of recent developments.

As she rocked Leo back and forth in his stroller, soothing him during his sleep, she sensed a shadow growing in her mind. Things weren't right. Things weren't going to be okay. She was at the foot of a very ominous mountain. That shadow, it seemed, popped out of her mind and into the park, nearing her right side.

When she glanced over her shoulder, every muscle in her body froze. A familiar lithe brunette strode toward her across the long green grass of the well-manicured park. It was the same woman who had been in the bar with Delta. Kendra jumped up immediately, ready to bolt, when the woman raised her hands in a gesture of peace. Stopping a safe distance from her, the brunette offered her a conciliatory smile, a little more wild than civil.

"Kendra—right? I just want to talk to you. I'm not here to cause trouble."

"Right." Kendra hesitated. She positioned herself in front of the stroller, protecting Leo.

"I'm Sky."

Distrusting, her blood pumping, Kendra gazed left and right—but she stayed put, taking a deep breath, seeing how well populated the park was. If at any point the woman made a move, Kendra wasn't alone.

"How can I help you?" Kendra asked, watching suspiciously.

"Look... I've been working on something with Delta, and he keeps telling me not to call the cops. He's got trust issues. But you're a cop, right?"

"I am."

"I need you," Sky explained, taking a piece of paper out of her pocket and placing it on the edge of the park bench.

"What's that?"

"It's an address," Sky told her. "Meet me there tonight."

"I don't understand," Kendra replied, confused. "Why me?"

"He said not to call the cops," Sky replied, a promising look in her eyes. "But he didn't say not to call his girlfriend."

Kendra gave the woman a look, in no uncertain terms, that screamed 'don't be ridiculous'. 'Girlfriend' couldn't be further from the truth. Seeming to get the message, Sky gulped, shifting uneasily in the park grass.

"He trusts you."

"So why would I go behind his back?" Kendra bit her lip, knowing she had already done just that.

"I'm trying to help him." Sky's voice rose, ire flashing in her eyes. "You know sometimes he can't help himself."

Kendra took a step back, pushing the stroller with her. Sky raised her hands again.

"Look, just meet me there." Sky stepped back, watching Kendra's reaction carefully. "You'll get answers. Answers you need to know."

Her focus drifted back to the stroller where Leo slept. Kendra leaned in, blocking her gaze, protectively covering the stroller.

"Why should I believe you?" Kendra twisted, looking over the park for the nearest person she could call to for help.

"Because they can fix him. They have the data you need."

Kendra snapped her gaze back, widening her eyes at Sky. "No—"

"Yes," Sky pushed. "A way to make him normal again. You'll find it there."

Kendra opened her mouth to refuse but was distracted by a fussing Leo. When she looked up, the woman was walking away again through the busy park. Kendra watched her leave, conflicted. She reached into her stroller, picking up Leo, cradling him with love. She gently kissed his face—his soft, squishy baby cheeks.

As soon as the woman left the area, Kendra reached over and picked up the paper on the bench. Stuffing it into her pocket, she marched her stroller in the opposite direction, toward her house. As she went whipping by sauntering evening ramblers, an eagerness and urgency rose in her. She had an address. Potential next steps. Stifling flashing red warnings, she grew more determined and more inside her own head.

Tenacious as she could be, it was an opportunity she couldn't shelve. She didn't know if she should do it, but she couldn't deny the pull she felt. Would she forever regret not going? What if it could help her son?

What if it could fix Delta?

When she returned to her home and explained her cocked-up plan to Sienna, it was not well received. Their disconnect grew as they stood face-to-face in the hallway of Kendra's bungalow.

"This is not your responsibility. Why do you think you should be doing this—let alone doing this by yourself?" Sienna was livid, her tenor rising to levels Kendra never heard.

Kendra held her ground, digging her heels in.

"I owe this to Leo. I have to find out."

"You owe it to Leo to stay safe. This isn't safe. If it's so important, why don't we ask someone to help you?" Sienna stood up to Kendra, straightening her spine.

That only made Kendra more entrenched, as she fought back through a tight jaw.

"I have to do this."

"You think you have to do everything, but you don't," Sienna continued. "You can be so stubborn, Kendra. And one day, it's going to be a very big problem for you."

The warning was clear—but Kendra snubbed it.

Shaking her head, she countered, "This is the only way I see."

"That's exactly the problem, isn't it? You only see your way," Sienna cried out, turning to walk away.

Over her shoulder, she snapped back, "Just call Delta. He should get that information. Not you."

"I can't call him," Kendra grumbled behind her.

Sienna stopped dead in her tracks, her groan echoing through the hall. "I understand your lack of faith in this man, but he's the fucking Navy SEAL, not you."

Kendra opened her mouth but closed it quickly. What was she supposed to say to that? As Sienna marched down the rest of the hall, leaving Kendra in her wake, she found herself gazing at the front door, torn between the fantasy she'd always have and the reality she didn't want. The sun finally dipping beneath the horizon drowned her in shadows, lonelier than ever.

Chapter Twenty-Seven

"You have arrived at your destination," the app announced, "Twenty-five Willow Avenue."

At the address given to her by Sky, Kendra braked her car in front of a non-descript five-story red brick building on the edge of the city. *Here I am*, she thought as she parked and looked for signage advertising what the building housed. She saw nothing. And no one.

Where the fuck is this chick?

The sunset dragged low on the horizon, and it was the last vestige of warmth Kendra felt. Leaving Leo once again, a coldness had overtaken her chest, complementing the frosty little lump wedged in her throat. She felt like she'd left a piece of herself behind, and along with it a piece of her sanity.

Let's just get this over with.

As she turned her car off, her neck and jaw tensed. Something sinful rushed over her — immediate guilt. Taking a deep breath, she prepared herself to just get the information Sky was dangling then get home.

Her cell phone pinged as she approached the aging front doors of the building. It was Lily.

If you can wait, I'll come with you.

Kendra responded as she strode into the unwelcoming, deserted building lobby.

There's no time left for waiting. I need answers – now.

But the message didn't send as her cell service dropped as soon as she was a few feet inside. A weird feeling crept over her, like she was being watched – and not just by the security cameras.

Nearly giving her a heart attack, Sky jumped out of the shadows, making a 'silence' motion with her finger to her lips. Pulling herself together, Kendra nodded, understanding as Sky motioned to the elevator, signaling the number 'five' with her fingers.

Okay...

Kendra watched as the sly brunette disappeared again and wondered if she was covering her. *Or not?* Determined to keep it snappy, Kendra hit the button to call the elevator, hearing clanking noises inside the shaft that didn't instill confidence. As the door creaked open, revealing a mirrored cab inside, Kendra hesitated. But she didn't have a choice. Sky planted her hands on her back, shoving her inside the elevator.

The door closed swiftly as Kendra tumbled in, grasping at the cab walls. *What the hell?* She looked around frantically, feeling the motion of being cranked up, floor by floor. In a split second, she realized she was getting into something that was not as it had been advertised. Claustrophobia kicked in, but not nearly as

242

pronounced as the fear of what was going to happen next.

Stopping at the fifth floor, the doors shakily opened, revealing a high-security entrance that was much more modern and expensive-looking than anything else she'd seen in the building. Out of the elevator, she tepidly paced through wide-open security doors into the shadows beyond. No one was at the guard post — that she saw.

Down a long dim hallway on that top floor, everything was still. Silent. She slowly crept forward, listening for anything. Wasn't Sky supposed to be there? She felt a chill but saw no windows. The hallway was barren, with nothing but vinyl flooring and occasional secure doors lining the walls.

Halfway along, she peered through an open door, spotting a lab inside. It looked a bit like her lab, except bigger and more expensive.

Then she saw him.

A youthful man with thick raven hair, possibly in his thirties, was bent over a microscope at the lab bench. Adjusting dials, he made notes on a pad, seemingly entrenched in his work.

"Come in," he said, his gaze remaining downcast.

"Who…me?"

"Yes, of course. I thought you wanted to see this." He scribbled away, seeming to record his observations.

She stepped through the doorframe but stopped short of the lab bench. It was long, white and bare — except for his station, which was peppered with samples and notes. There was something about him that made her not want to get too close, something that felt off.

"I told them you'd never come," he mused as he looked through his microscope. "But you've gone and proved me wrong."

Kendra inched back, realization dawning. The scientists. *It's a trap.*

He continued, his gaze still averted. "Genetic editing... You did know it was possible, didn't you?"

"I just didn't think we were there yet," she replied from several yards away, ready to bolt.

"CRISPR changed everything," he sighed, reeling her in. "You should keep up with your journals. Any scientist worth her salt would make a point to keep up, at least in my time."

In his time?

Curiosity overtook her sense. Kendra tilted her head, analyzing the seemingly youthful man in front of her. The speed at which he worked and the method he employed triggered her suspicion.

"How old are you?"

"Ninety — I was damn near on my deathbed before we figured it out," he laughed, his eyes on the microscope. "All we had to do was find a way to tell my cells to behave like younger cells, and voila, here I am. I haven't felt this good in about, well — in about sixty years, right?"

She couldn't believe what she was hearing, but she didn't doubt it was the truth. The cutting edge of science was beyond imagination at points. She was seeing what was next.

He pulled back from the microscope again, jotting in his pad. It was so bizarre — the whole conversation, he had never once looked at her.

"I could give you eternal youth, you know." He grinned downward as he carried on with his work.

"Is that what you did to him?" Her tone grew angry, inescapably so.

"No, he didn't want that."

She found herself striding forward, glaring down on the man's notes. She recognized the structure of the virus, the live organism, found in the victims' plasma. Lab-made, just like Lily had thought.

Lab-edited, just like Delta.

Kendra snapped, "So what did he want?"

The scientist grinned again, wicked and pleased. "He wanted to be the best — toughest, fastest, strongest. He wanted to be fearless. A highly competitive subject, dominant in his field. He always needs to triumph, that one. Worked for me, since I wanted to succeed, too."

Irritated, Kendra sucked in air, knowing that was exactly what he was like. She pressed, "Tell me how to reverse it."

"Ha — well, there's always a way, but I don't think he wants that." He tossed aside his pad, fiddling for another sample.

"Of course he does. He can't control it."

"He can't — but we can."

"How?"

"A kill-switch." The scientist's gaze finally shot up to her, revealing his blood-red irises.

Kendra gasped, stumbling back from the bench as the scientist's red eyes followed her. Clearly amused at her horror, he collected his samples, spinning away from the bench and striding to the back of the lab.

I have to get out of here.

She jumped back across the doorframe, into the hallway, but then it happened. She heard smashing and crashing in the distance, and a man yelling at the top of his lungs. Anger and hatred permeated the space. The lab door slid shut, locking in front of her, trapping her in the hall. She fumbled, her shoes squeaking on the vinyl flooring, hitting the concrete wall behind her.

Her mind screaming, Kendra struggled to breathe. She was in danger. And Leo? Her son. Why the hell had she come here? Her own obsession with doing everything on her own had driven her into danger.

Then she heard heavy footsteps coming down the hallway, further validating her realization. She immediately dove to the side into a large, unlocked storage room and hid behind a rolling cabinet. Her heart pounding, she heard a man talking loudly in the halls. Was he talking to her or himself? She couldn't quite make out what he was saying.

Sucking in breath, her heart pumping, she hovered her fingers over her phone. She couldn't make a call — her signal was still gone. *What the hell am I supposed to do?*

Sweat beaded on her chest. *Shit, shit, shit.* The worst was happening. *Why did I come here?* It was all a goddamn mistake. Such a mistake. Going it alone wasn't the answer, was never going to be the answer. She had to think of her son. He couldn't grow up without a mother. How could she be so careless?

She should have listened to her sister, listened to anyone. *Listened to Delta?* She cringed at the truth in that question. They'd been warning her all along — and she'd proved them right. She had to do everything alone. She refused to be rescued.

The madman's yelling echoed through the lab's long hallway — and she could hear him breaking down doors at the end of the hall.

Kendra ran her fingers over her face, realizing the hard truth. She had to stay alive for more than just herself now. She had a son. She had responsibilities. And if someone was a danger to her, they were a danger to her child as well. Her mindset shifted in a split second with the sudden realization. She'd been so used to taking herself for granted that she'd forgotten how it affected the people she loved the most.

I need help.

"I shouldn't have come alone. I can't do this by myself anymore," she panted to herself as she felt a tear rolling down her cheek. "I just can't."

More smashing glass came from down the hallway, signaling a man who had lost all control.

"Fuck." She pressed her fingers to her lips, thinking about Leo's face.

One thing she never admitted to herself was how much he looked like his father. His beautiful olive skin, golden hair and dark eyes, like a Northern Italian. His face even looked like his father's, something she never breathed out loud.

But she'd always known.

Trembling ran up her arms and thighs as she ran her fingers over her phone. A rogue single bar of cell service appeared. Kendra jumped. She had to make a decision.

The deep, dark, much-avoided truth was that Delta was the only man she knew, without a shadow of a doubt, who would show up to save her. And he would absolutely fucking destroy whoever laid a finger on her.

She bit her lip and dialed his number, waiting for her cell to connect.

But the call dropped, and her signal went cold.

Chapter Twenty-Eight

"Come out," the man's angry voice called for her, echoing in the hallway. "I'm not going to hurt you."

Terrified, Kendra slid down the side of the cabinet, feeling things escalating fast. Her heart beat out of her throat, cortisol rising through her sinuses. She was so goddamn vulnerable, she thought, as her eyes darted back and forth for an exit.

Kendra felt tears springing to her eyes. The call to Delta still hadn't gone through. She stuffed away her phone, debating what the fuck to do. Run and hide deeper in the lab? Could she make it unseen, unheard through the back and get into the parking lot? All she knew was to stay hidden — stay out of sight. Her mind analyzed the options, immediately struck by fear. She would never be able to make it.

Not by herself.

Peering around the cabinet where she was hiding, she got a quick glimpse through the partially open storage room door, seeing into the hallway again, assessing.

Then she saw him — the angry man.

It wasn't the scientist. That wasn't who was freaking out, smashing things and yelling after her.

It was Hunter.

What in God's name is he *doing here?*

From her vantage point, Hunter stood in the hall, glaring back and forth, searching. His face was beet red, along with his bulging neck, sitting on top of a body in a pure fighting stance. Whatever he'd done, his transformation was complete. She gripped her bag tighter as she realized he was carrying a semi-automatic assault rifle. As heavy as it probably was, it swung in his arm like it weighed nothing.

"Why are you hiding from me?" Hunter's angry voice echoed throughout the hall. "I know you are here. They told me you came."

His neck started twitching, sending his head in a bizarre cocking motion. Before she knew what was happening, a deep, rage-filled bellow came out of his mouth and blood trickled from his lip like he'd bitten himself. She sucked in air, whipping back behind the cabinet, gripping her tote bag like a life raft. She again chastised herself for being so reckless, for coming there.

Then gunshots rang out from the lobby, telling Kendra everything she needed to know. It was all going downhill quickly.

She dug her cream-colored flats into the vinyl flooring under her feet as she crouched lower, trying to breathe. She mentally visualized the emergency exit down the hallway, flexing to prepare to run. She could get to the side of the building — and run to the main street, call the cops.

She stood and looked around the cabinet yet again, readying herself. Hunter was moving into a different lab, clearly searching for her. It was a matter of time before he came into the storage room. She could run in the opposite direction—and make it out. But just as she started to stand, an eerie silence filled the building that made her catch her breath and stumble backward for balance.

Sinking against the cabinet, she darted her focus left and right, but she didn't dare move a muscle or peek out. Heavy footsteps were all that she heard—the sound of hard leather boots hitting the flooring—and they were getting closer to her. Her heart rising in her chest, through her throat, she shot her terrified eyes to the left as he crested the corner—a crazed Hunter with bloodshot eyes and a face that screamed murder.

Clenching his jaw, standing several inches taller than her, he reached forward and grabbed her by the neck of her halter, pulling her toward him. Shaking, grasping at his boulder-hard hands, she tried to wrench him off her.

"Let me go," she pleaded as she tried to escape, but his grasp only tightened and he turned, bringing her with him.

"Nah, we need you. Isn't that what Sky told you?" he said, pushing her forward as he made his way through the building, heading toward the lab.

"What?" Kendra coughed.

He laughed. "Come on. We are all sick of Delta's shit. It's time to join the team."

His thick boots crunched broken glass on the ground that had fallen victim to his anger, and he stuck his rifle in her back as he moved her along, forcing her to go where he wanted.

"Let me go," she cried out again, her voice cracking in fear as every victim's face flashed across her mind.

She was about to become a victim.

"I'm getting tired of playing second fiddle to that asshole," he spat, foaming at the mouth, clearly out of control and beyond enraged. "It's time you see me for who I really am. I'm the guy who wins, not him."

All she felt was his rifle jabbing into her back, and his grunting for her to keep moving or he'd kill her. She tripped over a chair leg in front of her, falling onto the table beside it. The man's bear paw landed on her shoulder, peeling her back up—forcing her to look into his hateful eyes.

Should I try to fight him, grab the gun? Or should I bolt and test my luck?

Veins visibly pulsed hot blood up his throat and jaw, showcasing muscles that looked jacked up. Quickly, his attitude snapped, showing her that she was onto something—the man was *on* something.

"So, you came to fix your boyfriend?" He snarled. "Yeah, we'd like to fucking fix him up, too."

"I just want to go," Kendra shouted.

"They kept asking me how to get him back in here. I told them all we had to do was get you." He laughed, revealing a neck too thick to be natural. "Get her, and he'll come. That's what I said."

"What—"

He lunged forward, grabbing her throat and lifting her off the ground. Suffocating, all she could see was the rage in his eyes—and the pleasure he was taking from hurting her.

"Hell, it worked when I drove you off the road. It worked at the bar. And now—I bet it's going to work right now."

It has all been a trap.

But Kendra couldn't breathe anymore. She was suffocating. Everything came crashing before her eyes—her son, Delta, her sister... Blackness crept into her vision.

Just as she felt her throat about to collapse, a man in full black with a black mask covering his face crashed into the hallway, leaping at Hunter. But it was a masked man she'd seen many times before.

Delta? the last lucid part of her mind questioned, trying to connect what she was seeing. *Is it really Delta?*

The man in black sent his rock-hard fist into her assailant's face, impacting faster and harder than anyone could have expected. Upon contact, Hunter's grip on Kendra's throat opened, dropping her from his grasp. She sucked in air as fast as she could and heard Hunter's assault rifle clatter to the ground. As she fell, she couldn't find the ground safely and collapsed backward, whacking the back of her head on the corner of one of the glass cabinets in the hallway. Immediately, things got fuzzy, and blood began trickling down the back of her neck.

Hunter stumbled to the side of the hall, leaning against the wall to collect himself. Delta stood tall, menacing. There was no doubt what he was prepared to do.

Lying on the ground, Kendra watched the battle unfold through dizziness and a pounding head. It was then she knew that she'd hit her head too hard to get up and walk away.

She was at Delta's mercy.

She just had to have faith.

Chapter Twenty-Nine

Delta squared himself to Hunter, fighting over Kendra's slumped body that was bleeding out on the ground. Hunter's metamorphosis was clearly complete. He'd finally altered his genes just enough to entrench the results. Delta knew exactly what that was.

It was damn lucky that he'd geo-fenced Kendra's car, because he would have never gotten there in time otherwise. With his son in the picture, he couldn't deny his heightened protective instinct—his heightened need to fucking kill any man who hurt either of them.

He stared down Hunter, feeling violence course through his veins. Icy chills rans up his rippling biceps, which were tightening and flexing. Focused, he was about to *slaughter*. That other instinct he had—the one built for missions in hellholes—was at the forefront. He had transformed into the side of him that was a ruthless warrior, ready to do whatever was necessary.

Keeping his eyes on the crazed man in front of him, Delta was prepared to fight. The assault rifle was on the ground, to the side, and Delta's pistol was in his waistband.

"I was hoping you'd come, too," Hunter snarled, touching a mass of blood pouring out of his brow from a fresh gash that would no doubt need sutures.

But Delta wished he'd hit him harder. Hunter was stronger, more powerful than ever before. He had been preparing for that moment. Delta silently stalked him, circling—flexed and fearful for the first time. He didn't know what was going to happen. He just knew that he couldn't lose her.

"Time's up." Hunter jumped forward. "You've been out to pasture for too long."

"So, kill me—like you killed the others?" Delta blew up, striking Hunter square in the jaw.

Hunter spat out blood, his shoulders heaving, and he lunged again.

"It's time to end this—right here, right now. Say goodbye to her."

"You fucking wish." Delta defended himself, thrusting Hunter backward.

But Hunter twisted and caught Delta, hitting him hard in the shoulder. It was the same shoulder where Delta already had a gash, and he cringed in pain. Hunter then dashed closer to Kendra, looking down on her still body. Blood trickled from the back of her head and her eyes were glazed over. She was losing it.

"You think you can win? You have no idea how strong I've become. They've made me a better version of you. And now…it's time to fix you. Permanently." Hunter's gaze dropped to Kendra's position, revealing everything.

Delta broke, seeing Hunter too damn close to her. It was a tactical misstep, but he had no choice. He had to get the sick fuck away from Kendra. So, he rushed forth, exposing himself while slamming Hunter into the wall. But Hunter fought back viciously, swinging his arms and making contact with Delta's ribs. A trained SEAL, he absorbed the pain, but he had been hit harder than it had likely seemed. As Hunter kept coughing up blood, an enraged Delta growled into his face.

"I've done things you only wish you could have done. You'll never see what I've seen, done what I've done. You'll never be me."

Delta thrust forward again, trying to finish Hunter, but instead he received a massive punch to his ribs again, sending him backward against the wall. Delta panted to the side, trying to catch his breath. Hunter stood tall, his self-satisfied eyes flashing to Kendra, and he flexed to attack Delta again.

The mere sight of Hunter looking at Kendra filled Delta with a burning hate he couldn't even describe. With clenched teeth and a loud roar, Delta thundered off the wall to rip Hunter to shreds. His passion and fury caused him to overlook his vulnerability, letting Hunter once again connect with his jaw, sending Delta to the side, the taste of blood in his mouth.

He was losing.

Hunter grinned, bloodied but still strong, and called out in threat. "There's only one way for this to end. There's only room for one of us."

And that was when Delta realized that he had to regain control. He had to cool down. Whatever was pulsing through his veins, he had to override it. Breathing in deep, Delta repositioned himself, focusing only on his opponent. He had to let everything else go—his fears, his desires, everything.

He had to gain control.

Hunter smirked, probably from seeing the blood on the side of Delta's face.

"So, you think you deserve her more than I do?" Hunter gnashed his teeth as he lunged forward again.

"Hell yeah," Delta replied, cold and precise, grabbing Hunter and quickly spinning him around. He dropkicked Hunter, purposefully impacting his spine and collapsing him to the ground in agony.

"How can this— I *am* you," Hunter growled on the floor, exasperated, choking on his blood.

"No," Delta said as he reached down to grab the assault rifle. "You can *never* be me."

The monster within roared to finish Hunter off, kill him—but Delta paused for a split second. Kendra's body was bloody and unresponsive on the ground. She needed him.

So, using the assault rifle, Delta sent a hard smack to the back of Hunter's head, rendering him unconscious. Using the rifle's strap, he threw it over his shoulder so it hung behind him. *There's no question now who's the better man.*

"This isn't over," he growled. "You'll pay for what you've done."

Delta then jumped forward, lifting Kendra into his arms and promptly carrying her to the fire escape balcony. She blinked quickly at him, and he saw she was almost blacking out. He had to get her help. Holding the back of her head, he leaped out of the broken exit, down the fire escape and away from the building. He carried her under the shadow of night, down the alleyway, toward a distant parking lot.

Setting her down on a large decorative rock, he held her trembling body close. He assessed that she wasn't totally out—but she wasn't lucid either. He brushed her hair from her face, bringing her head under his jaw, holding her against his chest, inhaling her scent. *God, she always smells so good.*

After kissing her hair, he slipped his hand up the back of her head, feeling her wound. It had stopped bleeding. That was good. It meant she probably didn't need sutures.

"I have to take you to the hospital," he exhaled onto her, checking her pulse and feeling her breathing. *Both normal.*

She stirred as he said it, mumbling back a very clear, "No—*please.*"

"Kendra, this is serious," he said, but her regaining consciousness was reassuring him. She was doing better than he thought.

"No—no hospital."

He ran his fingers down her hair, wondering what was with her fear of the doctor, wondering what he'd missed when she'd delivered their son. He closed his eyes, thinking about her being a mom, thinking about the son he hadn't met. He'd saved her. He'd rescued her. He'd fucking pulled it off. And now she'd be going back home to their son. Something rushed up his chest as he felt, for the first time, worthy of holding her in his arms.

And maybe a little more worthy of being seen as a hero.

She stirred in his arms, tilting up her chin, looking at him through glazed eyes. Pouting her pink lips, she furrowed her forehead. He knew he was going to have a lot more explaining to do—eventually. The wind off the ocean climbed the hill, catching her hair. He fished his cell phone out of his pocket, readying to make one of the most important calls he'd ever make.

"You're bringing me out of the dark," he whispered down on her, knowing his day of reckoning had come.

He slowly dialed the number, holding the phone to his ear. She pressed her eyes shut, but before she sunk into his chest, he swore he saw a little smile on her lips.

"9-1-1 emergency," a voice came through the other side of the line. "Police, fire, ambulance?"

"Police," he answered.

Chapter Thirty

Sometime before the sun rose, Kendra woke up nearly naked in bed, wearing nothing more than a thin black tank top and matching black panties. *How the hell did I get here?* Frantic, she reached up and held her throat, feeling the bruising from where that psycho had gripped her, threatening to choke her out at the lab.

But, then...she calmed herself down. She was okay. She was safe. She was home.

And...*I'm alone.*

Her house was silent.

In the shadows of her bedroom, she touched the back of her head. Surprisingly, she felt a lot better than she'd thought she would. No headache and no blood was a good sign. Some scabbing on the back of her skull seemed to be all that was left of her injury. Delta had really saved her that time, though she didn't fully remember how. Things had gotten really fuzzy after she'd hit her head, and she only had scraps of memories.

Reaching to her bedside table, she grabbed her phone to check her notifications. Lily had texted her. Someone had called the cops. It had been all over the news. Hunter had been arrested to answer to it all—the murders, the tests. The scientists were going to get a lot of questions. But, despite the fact that the cases were solved, she still felt a weight on her. As she finished reading the messages Lily had sent her, Kendra noted that there was one thing absent from her notifications...

There was no word from the one person she really needed to hear from.

He wasn't there. He'd left without a word. *Par for the course.*

She turned in bed, hugging her blanket tight. All she could think about was the past few weeks. Delta...? Well, he'd crushed her heart, again. Her eyelids grew heavy, and she realized just how run-down she was. She'd been chasing a ghost. And with him, she'd always be chasing.

It was laughable that she thought she'd learned her lesson with him. They'd been down that road before. He'd once been all charm, all temptation. She'd given in, given herself to him. It hadn't ended well. But here she was with her eyes closed, curled into her bed, thinking about how it felt when he'd held her—when he'd saved her.

It all pointed back to something that she desperately wanted to disappear. She wanted to bleach her memories and forget him—forget that he'd ever made her feel that way, forget how crazy she was about him and the real reason why she'd never been with anyone since she'd met him. No one could compare.

"Matteo," Kendra whispered to herself, pressing her eyes shut, "what have you done to me?"

It was a question she was finally ready to answer. The smack to her head had made her ten times more honest with herself, and she was unable to repress it anymore. He had her number in such a way. She had it so bad. The sweet memories she had replayed like a black and white movie, lulled her into a light sleep.

Slowly falling, she dreamed she was with him, lying in his bed.

He rescued me.

The hazy, sensual dream promised her things. Beside her, in between his sheets, his dark eyes melted her armor as he caressed his rough hand up her arm. He whispered the things she'd always wanted to hear. He'd shown up. He'd proven to her that she wouldn't be crazy to have faith in him.

Even in the sleepy fantasy, she felt his touch as though it were real. Goosebumps ran up her body and her eyes rolled back. God, it was crazy how much she still wanted him. It was all so fucked up. Her pussy started aching just at the sight of his mouth hovering over hers. She was reminded how amazing it was to taste him, to feel the bristle of his unshaven jaw against her chin.

She fantasized about him slipping his strong hand down the sheets, finding her throbbing clit between her wet lower lips. Gently touching herself and drawing circles around her wetness, she let the sinful dream wash over her, pretending he was right there on top of her.

He kissed her like the first kiss—on the beach. It made her feverish. Pressure and pleasure drew to the tip of her clit, threatening to burst. She was already getting so close to the edge and having the memory of him all around her was intoxicating. She never wanted to wake up. She wanted that dream to go on forever, feeling so damn aroused.

"*Matteo*," she moaned as he intensified the kiss.

She bit her lip, arching her back and grinding into the sheets. God, he made her so hot. So needy. All she could do was relish every raunchy night of sex they'd had. The memory of his thick cock when he'd fucked her was the one she needed to let out a deeper moan. She opened her legs wider and felt him drive his fingers inside her hot, aching core. She needed it. She needed *him*. It wasn't the first time she'd dreamed of him — and wouldn't be the last. Secretly, she knew she'd fantasize about him forever.

She let out a wilder cry, the feeling of his touch so real, conjured by the need to feel close to a man who wasn't there and was never going to be. She was gasping for breath when she felt an orgasm coming, and just as she released, she was startled awake by a loud noise.

Eyes flashing open, she realized it was the noise of her bedroom door crashing open with a real-live *Delta* standing in the frame, a deeply concerned look on his face. In the early morning rays, his disheveled head crooked left and right, clearly ready to fight someone. Then he focused on her, seeming to realize what was happening and why she'd let out a cry.

Unable to contain her dreamy orgasm, she came right in front of him, showcasing pushed-aside panties and a very wet, aching pussy.

"Shit," Delta grunted, pacing back yet unable to look away.

"What are you doing here?" Kendra cried out, snapping up into a seated position and grabbing the sheets to cover herself.

But before she could say anything else, he'd already disappeared down the hall of her home. Jumping up out of bed, she threw on her white satin robe that was cut at the top of the thigh. Tying it up, she ran after him, shouting his name intertwined with profanities.

"I *will* shoot you!" she threatened as she turned the corner into her sunny kitchen, where he leaned against the granite bar, staring her down.

"You've said that before," he said and took a step toward her, seeming to analyze her for symptoms. "You've got to work on your follow-through."

His slick, over-confident words burned her, pulling a disgruntled noise out of her mouth as she stared him down. The entire house was quiet, telling her that Sienna was out on her usual early morning walk with Leo. *God bless her.*

"Why the hell are you in my house?" Kendra demanded, guarding herself once again. "Did you break in? Do the rules not apply to you?"

Grinning, he crossed his arms, barely inches from her, in his classic form of intimidation—like her questions were nothing but a joke to him.

"I stayed," he countered, "to keep an eye on you."

She bit her lip, sneering, "Do I need babysitting?"

His grin widened to reveal his perfect teeth.

"No, but you hit your head hard enough last night, and you full stop refused to go to the hospital. So, I got to play doctor. Don't you remember?"

"Not entirely," she confessed.

"That's too bad. You loved being examined," he growled, irritating her to no end.

Beholding his stupidly charming face, reliving how tough it was to deny him, only made her want to scream and break things. She couldn't go through it all again.

"You have to go." She folded her arms, mirroring him, and nodded to the front door down the hall. She had to get him out before Leo came home. That was a first meeting she wasn't ready for.

"We need to talk."

"I'm not getting on that rollercoaster anymore." Desperation mounted as she spoke. "*Please*."

"You know I love it when you beg."

He brought his thick hand forward and snatched hers — the hand she happened to touch herself with during that damn hot dream, the one that had felt her wetness, bringing her orgasm out at the thought of his lips. Clearly, he hadn't forgotten what he'd seen.

As he held her hand tightly, he never allowed his focus to leave her eyes while he brought it to his mouth and took her fingers between his lips, sucking off the remnants of her cum. She flinched as he did it, watching him enjoy her taste. The way he stared into her eyes caused a flush to rise up her throat. She desperately needed him to kiss her again.

To *take* her again.

"The only thing I love more than you begging is you admitting you were wrong."

"*I* was wrong?" She balked but knew the truth — she *had* been wrong about a lot of things.

"Don't be a brat," he growled at her, narrowing his eyes, obviously knowing her game.

He ran his tongue over his bottom lip as he let his eyes drop down to her white robe, clearly coveting her. She tensed, unwilling to accept his attention. It wasn't safe to do so.

"From what I remember, there were people out to kill you." She tightened her belt and clenched her teeth, sending him a clear message. "They might just thank me if I do it first."

"Please, do it."

She bit her lip, letting out a frustrated noise. Looking between the door and his muscular frame, she worked through ways to push him out. Only then did she catch her reflection in the mirror hanging on the wall across the kitchen. Her blonde locks were everywhere, and her face and neck were still swollen from the night before...from where she'd been attacked. She shook her head, closing her eyes, willing the memory to go away.

"You don't have to worry about Hunter anymore," he cut into her thoughts. "He's fucked now."

"And what about Sky?"

"She broke the code"—his face darkened—"so I dealt with her."

"The code?"

"SEAL code. Yeah, she was once on my team—a supporter in the shadows. She got roped into the same bullshit as me. I did everything I could to set her on the right path, use that power for good, but here we are."

Delta paused, as if reading her mind. He looked her up and down with exaggerated slowness, so damn cool and collected. In that moment, Kendra stopped shifting on her feet. In the reflection of his dark eyes, she recognized her own stubbornness, her own guardedness.

Even though he was there, standing in front of her. He'd *stayed*.

"I just don't understand." Her voice grew smaller as she looked up at his great height.

"What don't you understand?"

"You," she said, her mind buzzing. "And why you are still here."

He didn't reply, simply assessing her in silence. It suddenly felt hotter in her house, and she found herself fanning open the top of her robe an inch or two for air.

When he was good and ready, he conceded, "I dropped my glove on purpose, you know."

"On purpose?" she questioned. "But you took it back? And you were so angry when Warren told me?"

He nodded. "Part of me needed you to know the truth — and the other part of me hated that."

She was stunned at his confession, hearing unadulterated honesty pouring from his mouth for the first time. *Who is this man?*

"I've been so angry for a long time, but something lifted when I accepted that you really knew and there was no turning back," he admitted, stunning her even further. "I don't want secrets between us anymore."

The change in his tone struck her, making her tilt her head as she studied him.

"Then, what do you want?"

"I want to meet my son," he responded, a thickness in his voice. "Now."

She fell back a step, catching herself against the wall behind her, a little scared and very stunned at the direction the conversation was going. He followed, his once-brown eyes now nearly black — driven and full of purpose. This was a moment she'd worried about.

"Why now?" she asked.

"I need to protect you, Kendra. I need to protect both of you — and I'll do whatever you want, if you let me stay."

He pressed his hand against the wall beside her, leaning down mere inches from her face. A darkness crossed his face as he pushed his body against hers. The heat coming off his strong, wide chest filled her senses — that same delicious scent she'd gotten used to. Goosebumps flushed up her back as he stared down at her, locking on her, refusing to budge. He was saying things she'd never thought she'd hear him say.

"There's something different about you," she breathed out, the realization dawning.

"I'm trying to change."

"Why?"

"Because, I've realized" — he trailed his gaze up and down her lips — "realized that I'm in love with you."

Chapter Thirty-One

Delta understood that his words had sucked the life from her. Hell, they'd had the same effect on him.

She parted her lips as she breathed out what little air probably was in her lungs. Looming over her, trapping her against the wall, he grew more intense, more serious. He'd just admitted the painful truth to her. He was in love with her, not that he knew what to do with that information. He dropped his head like he was ready to take her mouth, the only thing he knew how to do.

"You've always meant something to me," he said.

He reached his hand to the back of her head, angling her just right. As she bit her lip below him, he could feel her anxiety. It was going to be her life — their life. He tilted her chin up to him, feeling ready as hell to do a lot more than just kiss her.

"I still have to deploy. I still have to leave," he explained. "I'll be on a plane at the end of this week."

"You're leaving...so soon?" she asked, tensing. "For how long?"

"Eight months."

She froze. He wasted no time running his hands down her frame, warming her.

He assured, "But I'll come back."

He watched her as she bit her lip, deep in thought. She was clearly on the fulcrum of a decision — to let him in or not. And damn, he wanted her to let him in. He wanted it more than anything.

"I'll come back to you, if you want me to."

She flitted her gaze back and forth, likely thinking through things. His heart pounded through his throat as he waited for her to say something — *anything*.

"Kendra," he prompted, unable to wait. "Say something."

"I love you, too." She blinked, tears filling her eyes.

His chest felt light and airy as he closed the gap between them. Her words moved him, and he discovered something inside he hadn't known was there. His feelings were for her were beyond those words.

"I just— I can't quit you," she whispered just as he lowered his mouth onto hers.

As he kissed her, tasting her lips, a moan rose up her throat. He slipped a hand upward to gently feel her neck, knowing it was still sore from where she'd been attacked. He caressed her delicate skin all the way up to her chin and cheek, playfully darting his tongue into her mouth to dance with hers. Her mouth was supple and willing under him, and he set the pace for how he wanted to kiss her — slow yet passionate.

She whispered onto his lips, "And there may be an antidote, if I can just figure out how to reverse-engineer your edits—"

He pushed his fingers up her lips, telling her to stop.

"You are my antidote. You help me control it." As he confessed, a warmth radiated through him like no other.

Feeling a little less hopeless for the first time in a long while, he wrapped his arms around her, pulling her up and into him as he deepened his kiss, his cock hardening with the prospect of exploring her yet again—and again and again. He grew more and more excited as he told himself that finally, she was all his. He could have her all to himself.

He had never been good at sharing.

He ran his thick paw up her thigh as he hiked up her leg, knowing exactly what he was going to do next. Her robe slipped open and he felt every inch of her hip and waist. Underneath her tank top, he caressed her incredibly soft skin to her breasts. Playfully working it, he twisted and pinched her nipple as they made out more heavily, him drawing those hot sounds he fucking loved out of her mouth.

He dropped his hand down her abdomen to search for the matching slickness between her legs, something he loved to taste. She grew breathless as he found the top of her silky shaved mound, tracing a line down her wet slit and pushing down her panties.

"I'll never get enough of you."

It seemed to drive her crazy as he grazed his teeth down from her ears to her throat, but he made sure not to put too much pressure on her injured neck. Once she healed, there'd be a time for roughness and teaching her more lessons. He loved it as she slipped her hands under his dark shirt, feeling his flexing abdomen, whispering things about how hot he was. Taking it in, he slid his fingers all the way down, opening her, circling around her clit and feeling her arousal. Her pussy grew noticeably wetter and hotter with his touch, even more so when he pushed two fingers inside, searching for the spot that made her scream — his primary goal.

Determined, he gripped her waist with his other hand, feeling softness.

Aroused as hell, he grunted, "I love this new mommy-body you have."

She tilted her head back, moaning in pleasure, and smiled at him — pure and sweet. God, it was too fucking much. He could feel her getting closer and closer, her back arching in that way he loved, grinding her pussy as he fucked her with his hand.

"I wish I'd been there," he let out as she ran her hands down to his belt and fly, unzipping and releasing his hard, caged cock. He was ready to explode.

"You're here now" — she pumped him up and down, playing with the pre-cum that adorned his thick head — "right where you belong."

"Hell yeah," he groaned, kissing her again, harder and faster.

"I don't want you to leave again," she panted as he brought her closer.

"Me neither," he said, pushing himself inside her. "Especially not now."

He picked her up, positioning her just right, and slid her body down the length of his cock. Holding her between the wall and him, he bit her lip again before kissing her again deeply. She moaned as he pumped into her, fucking her with a promise. Her mouth parted as he did and betrayed the deep rush that he was giving her. She dug her fingers into his shoulders as he increased the rhythm, watching her wither in ecstasy. He could see the heat rushing up her neck — and he felt it too. It wasn't hard to get off when they were together.

"Fuck, Matteo — I love you so much." The words burst out of her mouth. "I've only ever wanted to be with you. Just you."

As she said it, he groaned in a mix of pleasure and agony, his climax bursting from his cock into her. Holding her tight in his arms, he kissed her hair a thousand times, swearing that never again would they fall apart as he lowered her to the floor.

"No matter how far away I go, how long I'm gone" — he exhaled slowly into her hair — "I'll always be with you. I'll always come back to you."

She gazed up at him, stood on her tiptoes and planted a loving kiss on his lips, but was interrupted.

Down the hall, the front door cracked open, breaking their attention. A tall, blonde woman who looked a little like Kendra sauntered in with a stroller, before halting dead in her tracks.

"What the fuck is this?" the woman belted out, livid.

She didn't seem thrilled to see him at all, her gaze dripping in suspicion. Yet he didn't return her scrutiny. He couldn't take his focus off the stroller.

"Shit," Kendra grumbled as she gripped his biceps. "Delta, meet my sister — Sienna."

Protective for sinful reasons, he didn't release her, gripping her tight like a hard-won prize.

"What the fuck are you doing here?" Sienna called across the hallway.

Staying silent, he shot her an unimpressed glare. But he reminded himself to keep cool. Now was not the time to pick battles... especially not with sisters.

Sienna flashed to Kendra. "Are you hurt? Did he hurt you?"

"No—he saved me."

"Saved you—from what exactly?"

"It's a long story," Kendra said, a little grin pulling at her lips at she gazed back up at Delta, who was still holding on to her tightly.

Then Delta heard it—the soft cooing sounds of a baby coming from the stroller. Kendra moved toward her scowling sister, scooping the baby out and having a brief exchange of hurried whispers. As she turned to him, he really saw for the first time for what she had become.

She's a mommy.

He strode forward, looking down on the baby as Kendra held him up.

"This is Leo," she explained, beaming. "It's about time he met his daddy."

Some strange reflex overtaking him, Delta extended his arms and took the baby, as tender as he could. As he brought the little guy against his chest, his son smiled up at him. It was the cutest smile he'd ever seen on the tiniest human.

Holy fuck—he looks like me.

"He's...pretty rad." Delta glanced up at Kendra.

She was crying—but not in a sad way. She was smiling as tears streamed down her face.

He teased, "Can we keep him? Please, Mommy?"

"Jesus," Sienna groaned in the background, crossing her arms in disapproval. "Where'd you find this piece of work?"

Delta brought his son up to his face, pressing his lips to his son's soft forehead. *Damn, he smells so good.* Then an inexplicable drop of clear liquid dripped down the baby's cheek. *What the fuck?* Wiping it off with the blanket, Delta looked up for a leak on the ceiling. But then his gaze drifted to the mirror in the front hall, and he saw something odd. And that was when he sensed it...running down his cheek.

He was crying.

For the first time in God knew how long.

"See? You're human after all." Kendra nudged him with a self-satisfied grin.

"Well, I guess so."

She lunged at him, wrapping her arms around his thick body and their son in the middle. The three of them breathed out, finally together. Leo let out a squeaky giggle as he grabbed onto his daddy's overgrown scruff with his baby fingers.

"Oh boy," he shot back at Kendra, shaking his head, "how fucking sorry I am for missing this."

"Yeah, I'm sorry for not telling you," Kendra got out through a cracking voice. "I shouldn't have tried to do this alone...to do everything alone."

"Together from now on?"

She grinned, kissing Leo's soft head. "Yes, Daddy."

He grazed his teeth on his lower lip as he watched her, unable to keep it in.

"Good—I've always wanted to get with a hot mommy."

Sienna lunged forward, her hands outstretched. "But he's a monster. He even said it himself. He can't be trusted to be a father, let alone your man!"

Kendra bit her lip, looking back up to Delta.

He turned to Sienna, holding strong. "Last night I learned something. When it comes to the people I love, my protective instincts override my...*other* instincts."

And from the corner of his eye, he didn't miss the wide grin growing across Kendra's face.

Chapter Thirty-Two

Kendra scooped up the bright green baby maraca that had fallen by Leo's car seat as they were escorted to a ceremony that she never thought she'd be attending—not in a million years, especially not one that she was almost late for.

Squeezing her baby's hand, she peered out of the rear window of the luxurious black car that had been sent to get them at the DC airport. They were pulling up to their destination. She smoothed out her black pencil skit—a part of the business suit she'd agonized over. *What does one wear to a Medal of Honor ceremony at which the President himself will be presiding?*

She tried to press out one final wrinkle in her skirt using her hand, a leftover from a long, delayed flight. That time around, the flight from LA to DC had seemed longer than usual because that was the first time she'd been flying with a baby snuggled up in her lap. Delta had flown ahead.

She'd seen him less than she liked as he prepped for deployment. But she reminded herself that he was committed to the Navy — to their country. And whether he liked it or not, he was a hero to her.

As a side gate to the White House opened, they pulled through the many security checks. Already, the chill of DC was getting to her, though she couldn't be sure the goosebumps weren't just nerves. The winter weather was frigid, a far cry from LA at that time of year. She pulled her woolen jacket tighter. She breathed in slowly, calming her worries, reminding herself of Delta's words as she straightened Leo's socks and boots.

The car finally reached a set of doors leading into the White House. There were plenty of people around — no one she knew or recognized. As the driver got out of the car, assistants came up to open the door for her and help her remove Leo from his car seat. She opted to hold him in her arms, allowing one assistant to keep the folding stroller on call should she need it. For now, Kendra felt like she needed the security blanket of her son against her chest as she was ushered into a grand hallway.

"Ms. Kendra Larose," an assistant introduced her to security staff, "the girlfriend of the Medal of Honor recipient."

As a lanyard was placed around her neck, the assistant leaned in with a clipboard in hand, taking a note.

"Your son — I didn't get his name?"

"Leo."

"Mr. Leo — ?"

Kendra squeezed him tighter, nodding.

"Leo Valente."

The assistant scribbled it down and shuffled to the side.

Kendra took in a breath, realizing it had been the first time she'd said his full name to anyone else. It was beautiful and rich and rolled off the tongue.

She heard the assistant introducing them to other officials — as Ms. Larose and Master Valente. She bit her lip, wishing they had the same last name. Not only that, but she wished she wasn't just there as 'his girlfriend'. She shook her head, telling herself to calm down. They were together, and that was a start. She was damn proud to be with him, but she was traditional, and it seemed he was anything but.

With their introduction, staff seemed to part like the sea, letting her and Leo move through the hall toward what sounded like a busy conference room where Delta was waiting for her.

She was officially freaking out.

After the longest walk of her life, doors were opened for her, ushering her into the rear of a big room where many spectators sat. The ceremony looked like it was about to begin. The loud hum of talking allowed her to slip in unseen. As her black heels padded softly on the dark red carpet, she found herself along the back wall and looked at the assistant to her side.

"I'd like to stand at the back in case my son gets fussy," Kendra suggested, though the truth was that she just didn't want to be front and center.

She didn't want a spotlight on her.

"Anything you'd like, miss," the assistant agreed, placing Kendra in a quiet, inconspicuous spot.

As she stood at the back of the room, her son in her arms, she wanted to melt into the many flags beside her that were lining the walls. She bounced her baby more out of habit than need, trying to stay low-key. There were enough people in attendance that she didn't think it would be an issue if she and Leo just stayed quiet.

Finally, the ceremony started, announcing the President himself to issue the award. The President strode out onto the podium, brushing back his graying hair as he looked out over the crowd. His power and confidence were remarkable, sending chills up her spine as she waited to see Delta for the first time in days.

"We are here to honor a man for unbelievable courage, unimaginable fortitude in the face of certain death," the President began charismatically, looking out over the sea of people watching.

He continued, "It's my honor to introduce Special Warfare Operator Matteo Valente, known as Delta."

Then a tall, poised man marched out onto the stage in a white Naval uniform to the sound of applause. He appeared so clean-cut and formal that she didn't recognize him at first. But then she sucked in her breath.

It was him.

He looked like… He looked like a *king*.

Like many times before, she shivered as she drank him in, observing how the military uniform made him into a different man, his jacket decorated with all sorts of medals and honors. And here they were, awarding him another one. The ultimate one.

She felt like screaming.

As she was squeezing Leo tight, tears sprang to her eyes.

She was so goddamn proud.

Beaming, the President waved his hands over the podium, getting into his speech.

"It's my honor to award SO Valente the Medal of Honor today for conspicuous gallantry. In Operation Medusa, he singlehandedly rescued an American hostage from behind enemy lines, putting his own life in jeopardy. And I cannot exaggerate this, people... SO Valente defied all odds when he stormed the enemy compound. His survival and success are a testament to his unwavering bravery, resolve and skill. A real hero. Congratulations." The President turned and nodded to him.

Delta stood at attention, staring straight ahead, as a military man would be expected to do. Kendra could only guess how hard it was for him to be standing there, hearing people applaud him for being a hero. She found herself grinning, grazing her lips on Leo's head.

The President moved behind Delta, removing the Medal of Honor from an assistant's hands and placing it over his neck.

As the medal was awarded, Delta remained unemotional, stoic, his gaze moving upward and locking on Kendra. Through it all, he found her. He saw her. He didn't let up.

A powerful feeling flushed over her. He was sharing that moment with her. He wanted her to be a part of it. The sheer emotion drove her to tremble.

And Leo sensed it, as he started stirring and fussing. As Delta turned to shake the President's hand, she popped Leo up on her shoulder and slipped out into the decadent hallway, excusing herself to assistants who helped her find her way to a quiet nook. Cradling the baby in her arms, she stood in a ray of sunlight that was beaming in through a window in the private space.

The warmth settled on her, and she had a reality check. It had all been such a blur, but here she was. A week ago, she'd never have believed it. Looking down on their son, she smiled as she observed how much he looked like Delta. Especially the little smile on his face—it was so much like his daddy's. That fact was new to her. She'd only just started letting herself see it.

But she'd really known it all along, just like she'd known that he had never been a monster. He could be wicked—but never malevolent.

Suddenly, her phone pinged, and with one hand she fumbled for it in her tote while holding Leo in the other hand. It was Lily.

I opened an unmarked envelope this morning—with the results from that glove. Jesus, you are not going to believe this.

Kendra read and re-read the text message several times.

For something she would have jumped at just days ago, now she was holding back. There was a voice inside her head whispering things she didn't expect. Holding her phone, she rocked Leo, grazing her lips on him, listening to herself, listening to how she felt.

Delta had shown another side of him. He'd shown her that he could control himself. He could control *it*.

She started typing out a message to Lily, carefully reading it several times before sending. Was that really what she wanted? She sucked in a quick breath and hit send.

Shred it.

As she watched the message get delivered, she saw everything she'd been obsessing over rinse away. She didn't need it anymore.

Tucking her phone back in her tote, she poured all her love into her son, knowing that things were going to be different.

"Hey." Delta came up behind her.

She turned around, looking up to Delta as he strode toward her, light catching off the gold buttons and medals adorning his white uniform. The way his uniform hung on his fit, muscular body was something like a dream.

"Congratulations." She grinned as he stepped closer, putting his arm around her back and looking down at Leo.

He leaned in and kissed her slowly, whispering how much he loved her. When he drew back, his dark gaze quickly assessed what she'd been trying to hold back — a sadness in her eyes.

"What's wrong?" he quizzed.

She shook her head, not wanting to ruin the moment or his day.

He pulled her closer to him and placed his other arm around Leo. Breathing down into her hair, he said, "It's because I'm leaving today, isn't it?"

"Yes," she whispered.

"It's not going to be easy for us. I'm gone a lot and my job is dangerous." He kissed her hair.

She grazed her lip with her teeth, guilty that she would put it on him. She was truly so damn proud of him. It was a day for celebration, not pain.

Then he tilted her chin up to look at him, his focus drifting back and forth between her and Leo.

"Kendra, I was running from all this. I thought you guys were better off without me."

He fumbled in his pocket and brought out a small royal blue velvet box. She watched him absently turn the box in his fingers and glance out of the window.

He looked back at her, confiding, "I wasn't going to show up to this ceremony. I didn't want this medal."

"But you deserve it," she replied in a soft voice, confused.

"Do I?" He shook his head, at first in disbelief, but then he said, "Maybe I do. I don't know. Things have changed. *I'm* changing."

"Why?"

"Because of you. You gave me a reason."

He locked his dark eyes onto hers, melting her. He grinned and popped open the box to show her a gorgeous, way-too-expensive sapphire ring surrounded by diamonds laid over a white-gold band.

"When I rotate back, I want to marry you," he stated, watching her carefully. "I want us to be a family."

She gasped and he scooped up Leo from her arms, holding him against his shoulder with one arm. They were so at ease with one another, so natural, that no one would have believed that father and son had really only just met. Seeing them together, bonding and connected, filled her heart in ways she'd never felt.

With the other arm, a determined Delta held the box in front of her, waiting for her reaction.

"I'm not promising it will be easy and I'm not promising that I'll be perfect," he added. "But I'm promising to love you, and I'm promising to *try*."

She flitted her focus between the ring and his gorgeous face, her chest feeling full, her head feeling light.

"What do you say, little guy?" Delta asked their son. "Should Mommy and Daddy get married?"

Kendra didn't know if it was fate or coincidence, but Leo let out a big smile as he started sucking on one of the gold buttons on Delta's uniform. She reached forward to the box, removing the ring and slipping it on, seeing how it sparkled on her hand. It was heavy and beautiful — and made her want to cry. He'd done all that for *her*.

She just felt speechless, taking him in as she gazed back up. Just the way he looked down on her, the sunshine catching his golden face, their son pressed against his white uniform — it was all too enchanting. A part of her wondered if she was about to wake up from another dream — a remarkable, unbelievable dream.

"So, what do you say?" Delta demanded again in his low, seductive voice. "Mrs. Kendra Valente?"

The way it dripped off his lips gave her chills. She bit her lip in her usual way, her eyelashes flickering up to him.

"Yes, Daddy."

Then he dropped his head and kissed her, showing her just how much he loved and wanted her.

Want to see more from this author? Here's a taster for you to enjoy!

Unbreakable Heroes: Under Fire
Zoe Normandie

Coming Spring 2022

Excerpt

"No, I am already cleaning three houses." Alisa Kelly ran her golden-brown fingers around the edges of the note that was handed to her by her manager. Analyzing the property details, she shook her head upon hearing her manager's challenge.

"You don't want an extra hundred bucks a month, then?" Maria asked. "This will be a regular client."

"I don't have time for more work."

"This client is rarely home. He's usually away for work, so you won't have to deal with people."

Maria, a middle-aged lady with dyed eggplant-colored hair, leaned back in her white office chair, something twinkling in her eye. She waited for Alisa's next move.

Alisa frowned, tossing her long black hair behind her shoulder.

Maybe it wasn't so bad. *Three-bedroom home in a gated community. No kids. No pets.* She grazed her teeth over her bottom lip, thinking. She *did* need the money, but she needed time for her studies as well. Skipping out wasn't an option, even for a few hours, not if she wanted to get licensed the following month.

"Look… Try it out once, and if you can't manage, I'll give the job to someone else, okay?" Maria said as she shuffled papers on her desk. It was her typical signal that the meeting was concluded.

Alisa peaked her eyebrow. The cost of her exams flashed before her eyes. Those things weren't cheap, and the last thing she wanted to do was put her hand out to beg for money. She was almost at the finish line.

"Fine." Alisa pushed herself up and out of her chair, stuffing Maria's note with the address into her purse.

She'd have to find a way to make it work, which was what she'd been doing for the past four years anyway. Buried in a textbook most of the time, all she'd done was study, work and study some more.

Maria shot her a self-satisfied smile, grinning like the cat that ate the canary. It was the look she gave when she was up to something. Running a property management company, Maria was the sharp-as-hell businesswoman and motherly figure—always watching out for Alisa like she was her daughter. Damn right, Alisa had endless respect for Maria's business acumen and, frankly, her sheer nerve—the type that Alisa hoped to grow over the years.

"One last thing"—Maria reached behind her desk and pulled up a used shopping bag—"the client is expecting our services this morning."

"This morning? Like, right *now*?"

"Like, *right* now. I promised him."

"No"—Alisa waved her hands, unwilling to bend—"I didn't wear clothes to clean in. This was supposed to be my study day."

"We work around the client's schedules, my dear. You know that." Maria tossed the bag at her, a devilish glare in her eyes.

Catching the squishy bag, which clearly had clothing inside, Alisa knew without a doubt that Maria had a game plan. And when Maria was conniving, it wasn't good. The matron stiffened her spine, shooting Alisa the 'don't defy me' expression.

"*God*, fine. You owe me," Alisa said.

It sure as hell wasn't how she'd wanted the day to go—but jobs were scarce, let alone ones that were flexible enough to work around her demanding schedule. So, Alisa did what she had to do. Tucking the bag under her arm, she spun and strode toward the office's door.

"Enjoy," Maria said.

The matron's self-satisfied chuckle forced Alisa turn back, perplexed. Maria then offered a wink, validating all Alisa's concerns.

"Let's get this over with," Alisa grumbled to herself as she exited.

She took a deep breath and pushed out of the small building toward the parking lot. She had to get the job done fast if she had any designs on studying how voxel pixels were made to be proportional to the sum of the attenuation coefficients.

The drive across the city toward the Bixby Hill gated golf community could have been a lot faster if Alisa hadn't been slowed down by at least ten car accidents on the way. It was unbelievable how slow LA traffic could be, even considering it was just past morning rush hour. Signing in at the golf community's security post as the house cleaner, Alisa silently huffed that she didn't have time to change at a coffee shop along the way. Side-eyeing the lumpy bag of clothes provided by

Maria as she drove into the beautifully manicured neighborhood, Alisa regretfully accepted that she was going to have to change at the house.

That wasn't something she liked to do. God only knew the type of people who lived there.

Her clunky silver economy car — too old to be nice, too new to be vintage — brought her to the address provided, making a strange new noise that drove an embarrassed flush up Alisa's cheeks. The car was beginning to whine like a dying rhinoceros. She groaned quietly to herself, wishing her entrance could sound a little less conspicuous — a little less helpless. She shouldn't have ignored that check engine light for so long.

She parked in the driveway next to an expensive-looking navy blue pickup truck, turning her car's engine off as quick as possible before the damn thing blew. She grew a little more anxious as she drank in the beautiful stonework and natural wood finishes on the outside the sizable home she was approaching. *Who the hell is the client?*

With her bag of mystery clothes in one hand and her wide black purse in the other, she walked up the three stone steps toward the front door. That was always the hardest moment — meeting the client.

Her hand trembling, she outstretched it to ring the doorbell, but oddly, the door flung open before she got there. She shuffled back, drinking in the mouth-watering physique filling the frame of the wide doorway — the type of male specimen she'd only seen in movies.

"You the cleaner?" The man smoothed back his vibrant auburn hair, leaning into the frame.

Tall and intimidating, he was adorned by rippling muscle, broad shoulders and a big chest. Clearly impatient, he narrowed his gorgeous crystal blue eyes on her, waiting for her reply.

She stuttered out nothing, shifting foot to foot, eventually choking out real words.

"Uh, uh…yes."

He opened the door fully, beckoning her inside with exposed tattooed arms, which appeared tanned and weathered from a lot of time outdoors. As she fumbled behind him, she inhaled that noticeable smell of a new home alongside distinct traces of leather and pine. His house smelled…*amazing*. The man paced into the hall, shooting her a quick side glance.

"I'm Warren," he said, crossing his arms and looking her up and down from his great height…assessing, judging. His face was stone cold, if not strong and perfectly aligned.

"A-Alisa."

She tried to smile but felt stiff. That was par for the course for her.

Wasting no time, he nodded to a closet on the side of the hall. "Everything you need should be in there."

"Oh, okay," Alisa murmured. Holding the bag of clothes so tight, like a safety blanket, she warily eyed the most perfect-looking man she'd ever seen.

He peaked his eyebrow, clearly trying to draw a conclusion, like was she human or was she an alien?

Alien, for sure.

Alisa cast her eyes down, the only way she could return to the task at hand. *The job*. She needed to get at it and change her clothes. She refused to clean in the only jeans she owned that actually were decent enough to wear in public. She bit her lip, flashing her gaze back up him. Should she ask to use the washroom?

"Need anything else?" he asked, as if sensing her unease. The way he studied her was sharp and quick.

Under his gaze, she felt a tension coiling inside her, a pressure — but was sure it was one-sided.

"C-could I use the washroom?" Alisa squeaked, following up with a mumbled "please."

"Of course."

Warren shot her a sly grin, widening his mouth, showcasing a row of white teeth. He motioned to another door in the hallway beside him. Relieved, she started heading in that direction, moving a little closer to him as she did.

"Help yourself. I'll try to stay out of your hair…" but as he spoke, his words trailed.

She halted, just a foot in front of him.

His gaze drifted from her long black hair, falling loosely over her shoulders, to her waist — kept trim from being overworked, underpaid. The unexpected twist in their interaction — from awkward to heated — nearly sent Alisa backward. She felt dazed.

But she composed herself, thankfully, and scurried into the washroom.

Only once the door was shut behind her did she let out a breath that apparently she'd been holding for far too long. *This guy… He isn't the type I'd anticipated running into*, she thought as she yanked the lumpy clothing out of the bag. She tore off her jeans and tried to figure out what exactly Maria had sent her with. There was something that looked like a white T-shirt, but then she realized it wasn't. It was a pair of bright white shorts. *Shorts?*

Looking in the long bathroom mirror, Alisa held them against her semi-nude golden-brown body. Sure, it was a hot LA summer, but the stretchy shorts looked like they'd barely cover anything. Panic seared up her throat. *Holy hell. What is Maria up to?* Alisa again dug into the bag and found that there was also a stringy white tank top. It looked like someone's hot yoga outfit—not an outfit that lent itself to modesty.

Immediately, Alisa flipped out her cell and texted Maria, sending her a pic of the outfit.

Are you setting me up?

Shit — I gave you the wrong bag. That's my yoga bag!

Maria… OMG.

I'm so sorry, girl. I've got the other bag here. I'll drive it to you.

That will take an hour. I can't just wait here for that long!

He's not going to bite…really.

Please. How well do you know this guy?

Well enough… Give him a chance.

"You okay in there?" Warren grunted from the hall.
"*Fuck, fuck, fuck.*" Alisa chewed to herself, widening her dark eyes into the mirror.
"Hello?"
"Yes, sir. I'm good," she called back and realized her fate was sealed.
It's too late to run.
So, she did the only thing she could do. She sucked it up and buckled in. *This is what life has come to*, she grumbled as she threw on the ridiculously skimpy hot yoga shorts and matching tank top and stuffed her jeans and shirt into the shopping bag. She looked like she should be serving drinks at one of LA's hottest bars,

much to the appreciation of a sea of men, something totally foreign to her. She'd killed off that sexy, fun side of herself long ago, her intense ambition driving her to focus on only one thing—her growing collection of textbooks.

The words *no, no, no* running wild through her mind, she tried to breathe, pulling back her hair into a high ponytail that kissed her back and browned shoulders. Alisa shook her head, contemplating herself in the mirror. She nervously toyed with the long, thin gold chain around her neck—falling low, down the line of her cleavage. The ring on the end of the chain seared into her breasts.

I shouldn't be doing this.

Hoisting the bag over her shoulder, she put on a fake confident smile and pushed her way back out into the hallway, only to release it when she realized that Mr. Perfect wasn't waiting there for her. *Thank God.* She let her mouth drop into a neutral hyphen, absently flinging the bag holding her jeans onto her purse and went searching for that damn cleaning closet.

It was time to get to work and pretend that no part of her was secretly enjoying sharing air with that absolutely terrifyingly perfect man.

About the Author

I'm a mom with three sweet young daughters. I have three jobs - mom, author, and analyst. Years ago, I grew up in a military family, went to a military university, worked alongside the military as an intel analyst, and my husband is (surprise!) a veteran. I've tried to write for anyone who wants to feel what it's like to be with someone from that world - with all the good and the bad.

My heroes are grounded in reality, and are inspired by guys I know in the special forces. Guys who've been in combat, tasted war, and fought for what they believed in. They are really heroes, but raw and rough and broken in their own ways.

My heroines similarly come from the best parts of the women I know, and the challenges we all face. The relationships that they fall into have familiar characteristics for many, myself included. These heroines represent all of us, with our good and our bad laid bare.

In my stories, I illustrate, romanticize, and celebrate the harsh realities of duty, service, and sacrifice.

Zoe loves to hear from readers. You can find her contact information, website details and author profile page at https://www.totallybound.com

Home of Erotic Romance

Sign up for our newsletter and find out about all our romance book releases, eBook sales and promotions, sneak peeks and FREE romance books!

www.ingramcontent.com/pod-product-compliance
Lightning Source LLC
Chambersburg PA
CBHW020600260626
47157CB00003B/792